BRENDA JACKSON

is a die "heart" romantic who married her childhood sweetheart and still proudly wears the "going steady" ring he gave her when she was fifteen. Because Brenda has always believed in the power of love, her stories always have happy endings. In her real-life love story, Brenda and her husband of thirty-six years, Gerald, live in Jacksonville, Florida, and have two sons.

A *New York Times* bestselling author of more than seventy-five novels, Brenda is a recent retiree who worked thirty-seven years in management at a major insurance company. She divides her time between family, writing and traveling with Gerald. You may write Brenda at P.O. Box 28267, Jacksonville, Florida 32226, by email at WriterBJackson@aol.com, or visit her website at www.brendajackson.net.

New York Times and USA TODAY Bestselling Author

Brenda Jackson

Strictly Confidential Attraction

———————

Taking Care of Business

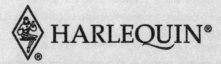

HARLEQUIN®

TORONTO • NEW YORK • LONDON
AMSTERDAM • PARIS • SYDNEY • HAMBURG
STOCKHOLM • ATHENS • TOKYO • MILAN • MADRID
PRAGUE • WARSAW • BUDAPEST • AUCKLAND

Recycling programs
for this product may
not exist in your area.

ISBN-13: 978-0-373-68811-1

STRICTLY CONFIDENTIAL ATTRACTION &
TAKING CARE OF BUSINESS

Copyright © 2010 by Harlequin Books S.A.

The publisher acknowledges the copyright holder of the individual works as follows:

STRICTLY CONFIDENTIAL ATTRACTION
Copyright © 2005 by Harlequin Books S.A.

TAKING CARE OF BUSINESS
Copyright © 2006 by Harlequin Books S.A.

This edition published by arrangement with Harlequin Books S.A.

For questions and comments about the quality of this book please contact us at Customer_eCare@Harlequin.ca.

www.eHarlequin.com

Printed in U.S.A.

CONTENTS

To my husband and best friend, Gerald Jackson, Sr.
To the members of the Brenda Jackson Book Club.
This one is for you.
And thanks to my Heavenly Father
who gave me the gift to write.

STRICTLY CONFIDENTIAL ATTRACTION

Prologue

From the diary of Jessamine Golden
September 12, 1910

Dear Diary,
Brad and I had another picnic on the lake today and there, beneath the branches of the willow tree, he told me that he loved me. His words stole my breath and everything around us got silent with such a profound statement from him. Then he gave me a heart-shaped pendant that was etched with two intertwining roses. Engraved on the back were our initials and he said his gift would always be a symbol of the love we share.

His words and gift brought tears to my eyes and when I told him how much I loved him, he pulled me into his arms and held me like he never wanted to let me go. And he kissed me in that special way of his that makes me want to be with him always and give up my quest for vengeance.

But I can't.

The circumstances as they are, I know what we are sharing can't last forever, although I want it to, more than anything. But I have to be honest with myself and with him. Brad is a man of duty, honor bound to do the right thing, and I have made a vow of revenge which goes against everything the man that I love stands for.

Oh, diary, my life is filled with so much turmoil. The woman in me longs for Brad's kisses, his touch and the way he makes me feel. That part of me wants to take what he offered me today—a love greater than any I have ever known that will last for all eternity.

However, I can't forget what I must do before my father can truly rest in peace.

I had vowed not to give my heart to any man before I settled a score, but it is too late. I feel the loving heat of the pendant as it rests between my breasts while I pen this entry. Brad Webster has my heart and I am deeply torn between love and duty.

Chapter 1

"I need you, Alli."

Alison Lind's breath caught and she looked up from the papers in her hand and met the intense hazel eyes of Mark Hartman, convinced she had misheard his words.

Her heart flipped automatically whenever he did more than give her a casual glance. His teakwood-brown complexion held features that were rugged, sexy, mesmerizing. Broad-shouldered with a muscular build, he stood tall at a height of six foot one, and whenever he spoke in his deep, husky voice, her pulse raced.

She had secretly loved her handsome boss ever since he had returned to Royal, Texas, two years ago to open his self-defense studio and she had been hired as his secretary. Recently, he had changed her job title to administrative assistant, and the only time he'd ever indicated that he needed her was when he summoned her to his office to confirm an appointment or to discuss some other urgent business matter.

Inhaling in a deep breath, she held his gaze and asked in a hesitant voice, "You need me?"

"Yes," he said, coming around to sit on the edge of his desk. "Desperately."

How I wish, she thought staring at him, trying to keep the heat of desire from showing in her face; and trying even harder not to notice the way his jeans stretched tight across firm, muscular thighs. There was no doubt in her mind a miscommunication was taking place and he hadn't meant the words the way she hoped. In all honesty, there was no reason her insides should be feeling all giddy and she wished she could stop that warmth from intensifying between her legs. Too bad the attraction was one-sided. The majority of the time, Mark acted as if he didn't know she was alive. To him, she was his ever-efficient administrative assistant and nothing more.

Alli took another deep breath and asked, "You need me for what purpose?"

"Erika."

She raised an eyebrow. "You need me for Erika? I don't understand." Erika was Mark's eleven-month-old niece. He had become her legal guardian three months ago when his only brother and sister-in-law were killed in a car accident. Thoughts of the little girl sent a soft feeling through Alli. Erika was such a darling little girl and captured the hearts of all those who came in contact with her.

Alli watched as Mark blew out a breath before answering her. "I'm at the end of my rope and I don't know what to do or where to turn. As you know I've been having babysitting issues ever since Mrs. Tucker left to take care of her elderly parents in Florida. It may be months before she returns, if ever. So far I haven't been able to hire a dependable, not to mention competent, sitter. Yesterday was the last straw when I dropped by the ranch unexpectedly to find Erika's caregiver too absorbed in her soap opera to notice that Erika had crawled away and was outside on the patio, just a few feet from the pool. I told the woman a hundred times to always keep the door to the patio closed but she had forgotten. Yesterday wasn't the first time it's slipped her memory."

Alli shuddered. She didn't want to think about what might have happened had Erika tumbled into the pool, but looking at Mark, it was evident that he had thought about it. "You let the woman go." It was a statement and not a question. She couldn't imagine anyone being that careless where a child was concerned.

"Yes, immediately."

Alli nodded. "Who's keeping Erika today?"

"Christine. She's been kind enough to be Erika's backup sitter. Lately I've been using her more than I had intended. Now that she and Jake are engaged I'm sure she has more to do with her time than watch Erika for me."

Alli had to agree. Christine Travers was one of her closest friends in Royal and had become engaged to Jacob Thorne a couple of months ago. Christine had mentioned that she had taken care of Erika a few times and that she had enjoyed doing so. Alli knew all about Christine's busy schedule, especially since Jake was running for mayor and Christine was his campaign manager.

Alli met Mark's gaze. "You still haven't told me what specifically you need me for." For a moment he stayed silent as he studied her and Alli felt the increase of her pulse as the seconds ticked by.

"I know it's a lot to ask, but you're the only person I know I can truly depend on. I've watched you with Erika before when I've brought her into the studio. Not only that, I've seen you with other kids when the mothers come by for their classes and assume we have babysitting service. You're a natural, Alli. Kids take to you and you are the most responsible person I know."

Alli shrugged. His words weren't exactly the accolades she wanted to hear from the man she loved, but something was better than nothing. Besides, he was right. Her ability to care for children came naturally. She had grown up in a household with her mother and her baby sister Kara, who was seven years younger. Her father had abandoned his wife and daughters when Alison was twelve and never looked back. To make ends meet, Alli's mother had worked two jobs, leaving Alison to take care of Kara the majority of the time. When her mother had died right before Alli's seventeenth birthday, Alli had become Kara's sole caretaker. She couldn't help but smile knowing that Kara was doing wonderfully now in her second year of college at Texas Southern University in Houston.

"I'm asking you to be Erika's nanny."

Mark's words cut into Alison's thoughts and she blinked and looked at him, hoping she had heard wrong. "Excuse me?"

Mark met her gaze. Held it. "I need you to be Erika's nanny, which means you'll have to move in with me at the ranch and—"

"Whoa, wait a minute," Alli said, coming to her feet. "There's no way I can do that. Have you forgotten that I work every day? I'm your assistant. I'm needed here and—"

Mark held up a hand, cutting her off. "Erika and I need you at the ranch with us even more, Alli. You're the only person I can depend on. The only person I can trust to take care of her. Knowing what could have happened yesterday took a good twenty years off my life. If anything had happened to her…"

Alli swallowed the lump in her throat. She was seeing a side of Mark she had never seen before, a vulnerable side. It was clearly evident that Erika had wiggled her way into her uncle's heart. When his brother and sister-in-law had been killed so unexpectedly, Mark hadn't been prepared to become a parent at twenty-eight, yet he was doing so and was trying to take care of Erika as best he could. But still there were obstacles in the way of what Mark was asking her to do and she decided to point them out to him.

"I'm majoring in computer engineering and attending college two nights a week—Tuesdays and Thursdays."

"I'll make sure I'm at home those nights so that won't be a problem."

Fat chance, Alison thought. He was asking her to move in with him at the ranch, which was a major problem. She was in love with him for Pete's sake. How could she handle being in such close proximity to him? Working with him at the self-defense studio was bad enough; but she wasn't sure she would survive sharing living quarters with him. Although she knew from the one time she had dropped off papers for him to sign that the Hartman Ranch was a huge place, the idea that they would be living under the same roof was unsettling.

"What about my work here?" she decided to ask.

"I'll go through an employment agency and find a temporary replacement. I'm willing to pay you double what you are making here."

Alison's eyes widened. "Double?"

"You heard me right. As Erika's nanny I'll pay you double. I need you just that much and as far as I'm concerned what you'll be doing is invaluable. You can't put a price on peace of mind."

Alison sat back down. *Double?* She breathed in deeply. As his administrative assistant she was getting paid what she thought was a very good salary, but she could certainly use the extra money for Kara's tuition. Kara had gotten a scholarship but that hadn't been enough to cover all the expenses. Alison had gone into her savings the last two semesters and if an emergency was to come up any time soon, she definitely would be in a tight spot. What Mark was offering would put more than a boost in her savings.

"And there will be a bonus."

Alison glanced up and met Mark's gaze. Once again his words had grabbed her attention. "A bonus?"

"Yes. One thousand dollars up-front just for agreeing to what I'm offering."

Stunned, Alison went speechless for a moment. *One thousand dollars?* That was money she could use to put down on another car. She was still driving the one she had bought right out of high school seven years ago, and lately it had been giving her problems. Just last week she had broken down while coming from class. Luckily, someone had stopped to help her, although the man had given her the creeps most of the time he'd been doing so.

She breathed in deeply. Mark was making his proposal hard to resist. And that in itself was the key word. *Resist.* For two years she had had to resist him, refusing to give into temptation and sharing her feelings. Instead she had fought her attraction and fully intended to continue to do so. She knew the last thing she needed was to place herself in a position where her heart could be broken if she assumed too much. But still, what he said was true. He and Erika needed her and there was no way she could not help him out. And she couldn't overlook the fact that he was helping her out financially as well.

"This will be a temporary arrangement, right?" Alison asked, feeling the need to have that point clarified.

"Yes. I'm hoping Mrs. Tucker is coming back to Royal in another month or so."

"And if she doesn't?"

"Then I'll run another ad in the paper and pray the results are better. There has to be someone in Royal who's responsible enough to keep Erika every day."

Alison nodded. "Will it really be necessary for me to move in with you and Erika at the ranch? I can stay at my place and drive to your—"

"No, I prefer for you to be there at the ranch with us. I may have business to take care of at night."

Alison nodded again. She was fully aware that he was a member of the Texas Cattleman's Club. Membership in the state's most exclusive club was restricted to wealthy ranchers, prestigious businessmen and oil tycoons. She'd heard that the members would often get together a few nights a week to play cards, share drinks and discuss business. But most of the good people of Royal knew that wasn't all they did. There were those who claimed through the generations, the club members had accepted the responsibility for the town's security and over the years had put their lives on the line for justice and peace. The only thing Alli did know for certain was that the club did great things for the community in the way of fund-raisers like the annual Cattleman's Ball, where the proceeds went to various charities.

Christine had talked Alison into attending Royal's Anniversary Ball that had occurred several weeks ago, and she had to admit that she had enjoyed herself…at least until Mark had arrived. Once he had walked into the room, she had found herself constantly watching him, as every other unattached woman had done. And as usual, he hadn't noticed her.

"So will you do it?"

Anytime and anyplace with you, she wanted to say. She hated her wanton thoughts, but when it came to Mark Hartman, they just wouldn't go away. She sighed deeply and did what she always did whenever her thoughts toppled onto the side of fantasy instead of reality, which was to scold herself inwardly and get back on track. Mark didn't have a single clue about how she felt about him and she intended to keep it that way.

"Alli? Will you help me out?"

She met his gaze and almost drowned in the plea she saw in his eyes. He did need her, or at least, thought he did. And although it wasn't in the way she wanted, it would have to do.

She stood and smiled. "Yes, Mark, I will help you out with Erika."

Half an hour later, Mark released a deep breath when Alli walked out of the room, closing the door behind herself. Both elated and frustrated, he moved away from his desk to walk over to the window. The plans had been finalized. He had contacted a reputable temp agency who would be sending someone in the morning. Alli was to train the person and by tomorrow evening she would be ready to move in with him and Erika, which was both a curse as well as a blessing.

From the first moment that Jake had told Mark about Alli and how efficient she would be as his secretary, he had been eager to interview her for the position. When he had seen her, he had gone almost speechless and had immediately known things wouldn't work out because of the sudden attraction he felt toward her. But he had needed a good secretary and everyone in town claimed she would be the best. Although she was a private person, most people knew her from working as a secretary for the Royal school system.

He had hired her on the spot, presenting her with a higher salary than she had been receiving. That was one move he hadn't regretted making. She had been the efficient, if shy, Alison Lind during the early months and had been instrumental in helping to get his studio off the ground. She had done the marketing, promotion, advertising, accounting...just about everything, freeing him to do what he did best, which was teaching the art of self-defense, primarily to women.

To him it was important that all women knew how to protect themselves. He doubted he would ever forgive himself for not being around when his wife had been attacked and killed while leaving the shopping mall late one night. As part of the marine's special forces, he had been away on a mission in the Middle East at the time. He knew he could not bring Patrice back, but maybe what he was doing would help other women who found themselves in a similar situation.

His thoughts shifted back to Alli. During the two years that they had worked together, he had tried like hell not to notice her, not to be attracted to her, not to want her. And for a while he thought he had gotten his pretended nonchalance down to an art form. But then all it would take was for him to walk out of his office and catch her unaware of being watched, as she filed away some document on a high shelf. He'd notice what a gorgeous pair of legs she had, or admire her small waist, pert and firm breasts and curvy thighs, and his nonchalance would be history.

And now she had agreed to move in with him.

His blood heated at the thought, but he quickly cooled it down. Whether Alli worked for him here at Hartman's Self-Defense Studio or at his home as Erika's nanny, their relationship would remain a business one. A serious relationship with any woman was the last thing he wanted or deserved. He had not been there to protect Patrice and, as a result, a part of him felt he couldn't be trusted to keep women safe. No woman needed a man who wasn't trustworthy, so living the rest of his life alone was something he accepted.

Well, he wasn't actually alone, he thought as a smile touched his lips. A few months ago he had been living the life of a carefree bachelor and hadn't been prepared for eight-month-old Erika Danielle Hartman. The first question that had come to his mind was what in the hell was he supposed to do with a kid? But soon the answers had come. He was to do just what his brother Matthew and his wife Candice had known Mark would do. He would provide not only a home for their daughter, but also he would make sure she received every good thing life had to offer, which was something he definitely could afford to do since, during his grandparents' time, oil had been discovered on their property, making the Hartmans instant millionaires.

He glanced at his watch when he heard the sound of the phone. He was expecting a call from Jake. His friend certainly had his plate full with the mayoral campaign while being an active member of the Texas Cattleman's Club, especially now when there were a number of strange things happening in Royal.

Mark reached his desk and quickly picked up the phone. Alli had already left for the day. "Yes?"

"Mark, this is Jake. There will be a meeting at the club tomorrow night at eight. Think you can make it?"

"Yes, I'll be there."

"What about Erika? Do you need Chrissie to watch her for you?"

"No, Alli has agreed to be Erika's nanny until Mrs. Tucker returns or until I can find someone dependable."

"Alli?"

"Yes."

"She's going to be both your assistant and Erika's nanny?"

Mark smiled, knowing Jake was confused. "No. I'm getting someone from a temp agency to handle the assistant duties for a while. Alli will be Erika's full-time nanny."

"Well, hell, Mark, how did you talk her into something like that?"

Mark sat in his desk chair as he thought about Jake's question. "I simply told her that Erika and I needed her." After a short pause he then said, "I also told her I would double what she was making here and I even threw in a bonus of a thousand dollars."

"Whew, you sound like a desperate man."

"When it comes to Erika's well-being, I am."

"Are you sure that you're only thinking about Erika. I can clearly recall your reaction to seeing Alli that night at the Anniversary Ball."

Mark leaned back in his chair. It was at times like this that he wished Jake had a short memory. He couldn't help but remember how speechless he had gotten when he had seen Alli the night Jake was referring to. She had looked nothing like his efficient, shy assistant. She had taken out the knot that she usually wore in her hair and the thick, silky strands had flowed around her shoulders. And that dress…wow! Seeing her in that dress would be forged in his mind as a delectable memory. On any other woman it would have been a simple black dress, but on Alison Lind there hadn't been anything simple about it. He had found himself drinking an entire glass of wine before realizing he had done so while staring at her.

"Okay, so I found her attractive that night. What of it?" he finally asked.

Jake chuckled and then said, "Nothing of it. I'll see you at the meeting tomorrow night. I understand that we have a lot to discuss. Logan heard from Nita Windcroft again today."

Mark rubbed a hand down his face. "She still thinks the Devlins are behind the mischief going on at her place?"

"Yes, and of course the Devlins are still claiming they know nothing about anything."

Mark shook his head. Having grown up in Royal, he knew that Windcrofts and Devlins had been feuding for years. He couldn't help but wonder if perhaps Nita was blowing things out of proportion, given her temper and her obvious dislike of the Devlins. "And what about Jonathan's death? Any new leads?"

It had been discovered a few months ago that instead of dying of a heart attack, Jonathan Devlin had been murdered with a lethal injection of potassium chloride. Sheriff Gavin O'Neal, who was also a member of the Texas Cattleman's Club, was leading the investigation into Jonathan's mysterious death.

"If there are any, Gavin will bring us up to speed. See you tomorrow."

After returning the telephone to its cradle, Mark stood and walked back to the window and stared out. Getting out of the marines after Patrice's death, he had decided to return to Royal to escape the memories. Within a short period of time he had become a member of the Texas Cattleman's Club, a front for members who worked together covertly on secret missions to save innocent lives.

Investigating Jonathan Devlin's death, as well as the incidents Nita Windcroft claimed were happening at her horse ranch, were keeping them busy. Then on top of everything else, there were still the mysteries surrounding the vandalism of the Edgar Halifax display and the map that had been stolen from the Royal Museum.

The latter bothered him more than anything because he had been assigned to keep an eye on the map while it was on the podium. However, he, like everyone else, had gotten distracted when a chandelier fell, nearly killing Melissa Mason, a television reporter, who'd been filming a scene that included the map. During that quick moment of chaos when fellow Cattleman Logan Voss had rushed across the room to save the woman he loved, thwarting an accident that could have been fatal, the map had vanished off the podium. Mark and his fellow club members were determined to get it back. The thief had been caught on film, but it turned out to be just a blurred image of a woman.

And speaking of images… The faces of two females filled his mind. The first was a beautiful little girl who was under his protection and the other was a stunningly attractive woman who could get under his skin if he wasn't careful.

Chapter 2

As Alli passed the huge wooden marker of the Hartman Ranch, she couldn't help but ask herself for the umpteenth time whether or not she was doing the right thing. That question was temporarily forgotten when Mark's home loomed into view. It was massive as well as beautiful and she easily could place her modest house inside of it three or four times over.

She recalled the only other time she had been to this ranch and how in awe she had been. She remembered hearing around town how his grandparents had struck oil on the property and, as a result, the Hartmans' lives had changed forever.

She also remembered her mother complaining about Mark's father when he would contact her whenever he needed ironing done, which was something Alli's mother had done on occasion to earn extra money. Mildred Lind had often said that Nathaniel Hartman was a cold, heartless and bitter man who hadn't shown anyone—not even his two sons—any love or affection.

When Mark had returned to Royal and contacted her about becoming his secretary, she had been hesitant about working for him, thinking that if he was anything like his father, she would not want him as an employer. Eventually she had decided not to prejudge him. She had worked for him only a couple of weeks before discovering that, although he was a private person, he treated her with kindness and was fair. But it was evident there were demons eating at him.

More than once, especially around the holidays, she had caught an expression of pain and grief in his face and a part of her had regretted all the sadness he had endured in his life. Most of the people in town had heard about the tragedy that had happened to his wife, prompting him to return to Royal. She'd also heard that Mark blamed himself for her death and establishing the studio to teach women self-defense was a way to relieve some of that guilt.

And speaking of guilt, she couldn't help but remember the phone call she'd gotten from her sister that morning. Kara had been all excited about a guy she had met the night before at the library. Alli had listened to her sister go on and on about what a hottie he was and that he had asked her to a party this weekend. Upon hearing that, red flags had gone up in Alli's head, especially after remembering Kara had mentioned earlier in the week how much studying she had to do for a big exam she had next week. Alli had ended up giving Kara some sisterly advice, which included a reminder of how important getting a good education was. Evidently that had been the last thing Kara had wanted to hear and, needless to say, had ended the call quickly. Alli was left wondering if perhaps she had reacted prematurely and laid the lecture on too thick. Kara had concentrated fully on her studies during her first year at Texas Southern and Alli just didn't want her to lose focus now. And Alli especially didn't want this "hottie" to interfere with Kara's studies.

Alli took a deep breath as she brought her car to a stop in front of the huge ranch house with the sprawling front porch, and couldn't help but smile when the door opened and Mark stepped out with Erika in his arms.

Mark had heard the sound of a car approaching and when he had glanced out of the window and saw it was Alli, he had breathed a deep sigh of relief. He had seen her briefly that morning, long enough to introduce her replacement before returning to the ranch to relieve Christine of Erika.

As soon as he stepped onto the porch and watched Alli get out of her car, he was besieged again with thoughts that having her here wasn't a good idea. But it was the only option he had. "Glad you made it," he said, coming to a stop near the steps. She smiled up at him and, although he didn't want it to, his insides felt warm all over.

It didn't help matters when he got a whiff of her perfume. He had long ago accepted that it was the most seductive scent he'd ever come in contact with. She was wearing her hair down around her shoulders, the way he liked. The sunlight slanting on her head made the strands appear more chestnut than dark brown in color.

"I'm glad I made it, too," she said coming to meet him and automatically taking Erika out of his arms to hold her against her shoulder. His niece remembered Alli from the times he had brought her to the studio and went willingly, but then she did the same thing to everyone. It often bothered him how friendly Erika was and knew when she got older he would have to make sure he taught her not to be so open to strangers.

"You need help with your things?" Mark asked, seeing the boxes in the back seat of her car.

He studied the older vehicle and hoped she would use the bonus she would be getting to purchase another one. Recently he had overheard Christine telling Jake how the car had broken down on an isolated road leading into town one night and that Malcolm Durmorr had stopped to offer help.

Malcolm, known around town as a shiftless lowlife who was always on the brink of some kind of disaster, was said to be a distant cousin of the Devlins, although it seemed they weren't eager to claim him. There were a number of things about him that Mark didn't like, especially the get-rich-quick schemes Malcolm had pulled on a couple of innocent, unsuspecting people in Royal.

Mark recalled how Malcolm had come into the Royal Diner one afternoon and had sat eating his dinner while gazing at one particular waitress by the name of Valerie Raines as though he would have preferred having her on his plate instead of the pork chop. The lust in the man's eyes had been disgusting and the thought that Malcolm had been the one to help Alli hadn't set too well with Mark.

Mark suddenly lost his train of thought when Erika, fascinated with the gold chain around Alli's neck, reached inside Alli's blouse to pull out the topaz pendant attached to it, providing Mark with a generous view of Alli's cleavage as well as the top of a black lace bra. Upon realizing what the baby had done, Alli quickly switched Erica to her other shoulder and snatched the blouse back up in place. When Alli met his gaze, an embarrassing tint flushed her cheeks.

Mark thought it best to pretend he hadn't seen a thing instead of standing there wishing he could get an instant replay. He cleared his throat. "If you give me your keys, I'll bring your stuff inside so you can get settled in," he said as warning bells clanged in his ears.

He had to fight his attraction to Alli no matter what, but already things were getting off to a heated start. With her dressed in a blouse and a pair of slacks wasn't helping. He had decided after the first time he had seen Alli in pants that she'd had the most well-defined, enticingly shaped butt of any woman he'd ever seen. In fact, he didn't know of anyone who even qualified as a close second.

She always dressed professionally while in the office. The only time he hadn't seen her dressed that way was when she had signed up to take his class. He remembered how, like the other ladies, she had shown up wearing shorts. In addition to teaching her the art of self-defense, he had taught himself the art of self-control.

His thoughts returned to the present when she handed him her car key. "I didn't bring over much since I'll have time to do more packing this weekend," she said shifting her gaze from him to Erika. "Has she eaten dinner yet?"

Mark laughed. "Yes. If she was hungry, you would know it. That's the only time she's in a bad mood."

Alli gave herself a mental shake. Mark's laugh threw her, since she had never heard him laugh before. This was the first time she had ever seen this side of him. He was being so pleasant and human. Not that he walked around being a tyrant, but he'd never been in her presence and not acted with reserve and reticence.

He must have seen the strange look on her face because he eyed her for a moment as his expression went from curious to concern. Then he asked, "Is something wrong?"

She shrugged. "No, nothing's wrong." Cautiously, she added, "I just don't ever recall the two of us ever holding a conversation for more than five minutes that didn't have anything to do with business."

Mark leaned against the wooden column and thought for a moment. Neither had he. Even yesterday while they had discussed the arrangements of her becoming Erika's nanny, it had been business. "Well, you're doing me a huge favor by being here. Away from work I'm more relaxed and at ease so get prepared to see another side of me. Believe it or not, I can be a friendly guy."

"It's not that I thought you weren't friendly," Alli rushed to say, hoping she hadn't offended him. "But you—"

He held up his hand. "Hey, there's no need to explain," Mark said chuckling, thinking he liked how Alli looked when she was flustered, which was something he rarely had seen. "Come on in, let me show you around. I'll get the things out of your car later."

She gave him her usual shy smile and said, "All right."

Erika began murmuring words Alli couldn't quite make out as she followed Mark into the house. This was her first time inside. The last time she had been here he had stepped out onto the porch to sign the papers she had delivered.

She glanced around as Mark took her from room to room. She couldn't help noticing how each one was richly furnished with leathered pieces of a rustic, western design. Erika's bedroom was another matter. It was wallpapered with Snow White and her seven dwarfs, and a beautiful white convertible crib sat in the middle of the room. The room's decor was colorful, bright, fit for a little princess, and the bedding accessories matched a miniature chair and ottoman that sat near a window in the room. A huge stuffed bear had been placed in the chair. Alli couldn't help smiling. "It's beautiful in here, Mark."

He turned to her. "Thanks. I hired a professional decorator for this room. I was a bachelor with no experience with kids when I got Erika and had to learn everything and fast."

He automatically took Erika out of Alli's arms when his niece reached for him. He nodded toward all the furniture in the room "The first thing I found out was that a child's room should grow with the child and not the child having to grow with the room. I spend a lot of time in here with Erika since this is also her play room," he said, tipping his head toward the huge toy chest that sat in one corner. "That's the reason for the recliner-rocker over there. When I first got her I would sit in that chair and rock her to sleep. Now I just sit back and watch her play."

Alli nodded as she studied the chair, seeing the image of Mark kicked back, relaxed, while keeping a protective eye on Erika. Another vision suddenly came to mind: one of her sitting in that chair with him, in his lap, while the two of them watched Erika together. She could actually see herself as she cuddled close to him, her body curled to his with her head resting on his shoulder, while the warmth of his breath fanned her face.

She blinked and swallowed deeply, not believing she had allowed such thoughts to enter her mind.

"Alli, are you okay?"

She snapped her head around and met Mark's curious eyes. "Yes, I'm fine."

It seemed that he focused his gaze on her for the longest time before saying, "Okay, then let me show you the room that you'll be using."

Before they walked out the room they passed a framed

picture sitting on the dresser. Alli stopped and picked it up. It was a photograph of an attractive couple who were smiling and holding an infant.

"That's Matt and Candice when Erika was only a few months old," Mark said softly.

Alli stiffened slightly. She hadn't been aware that he was standing so close. He was leaning down to peer at the picture and she could feel the moist warmth of his breath against her neck. His closeness was causing a sensation she had never felt before to slowly inch its way up her spine. There was also the heat she felt pooling her belly.

She forced herself to stay focused on the picture, fearful that if she turned her head even the slightest inch, her lips would connect to his. "They were a beautiful family and look happy together," she finally said, forcing the words out while keenly aware the heat had moved from her stomach, traveling lower down her body.

"Yes, they were happy together and they loved each other very much. I always envied what they had."

Noting that Mark had taken a step back, Alli turned slightly and met his gaze. He'd sounded so heartrending. She couldn't help looking deep into his eyes, and then she saw it clearly—pain. He was still hurting. But for whom? His brother and sister-in-law? His wife? For all three?

Her gaze shifted to the rest of his features. They were prominent. Handsome. He had beautiful brown skin, thick eyebrows, a nose that was the perfect shape and size for his face. And then there were his lips...

She couldn't help but study his lips. They had a seductive shape to them and had such a smooth texture. They looked soft, which seemed odd for such a rough man. A part of her yearned to figure out the contrast for herself. It wouldn't take much for her to ease her mouth to his, take her tongue and go from corner to corner and lick the—

"Da-da! Down da-da!"

Erika's words snapped Alli around. She had no idea just how long she had been standing there mesmerized by Mark's mouth. What had he thought of her staring at him like that? Heat flooded her cheeks and, instead of meeting his gaze, she placed the picture frame on the dresser.

"No, I can't put you down, sweetheart," she heard Mark say to the baby. "We still have to show Alli around."

Feeling more in control, Alli turned but kept her gaze focused on Erika and smiled when the little girl reached for her. She scooped her out of Mark's arms and planted a kiss on Erika's cheek, liking the sound of her giggle. "She calls you dad."

"Yes, but I prefer that she didn't do that."

The agitation in his voice made Alli's head jerk up, not being able to avoid eye contact with him any longer. She saw the deep frown that marred his handsome features. "Why?" she asked.

"Because I'm not her daddy."

Alli lifted an eyebrow in confusion. "I know you're not her daddy, Mark, but calling you that is as natural and familiar to her as eating and sleeping. You represent a permanent fixture in her life. She might or might not remember her parents and—"

"I want her to remember them, Alli. That's the reason I have this picture in here. When she gets older I want her to know about them. I want her to know they were her parents and that I'm her uncle who's nothing more than her caretaker."

Alli tried not to glare at him but felt herself doing so anyway. What he'd said sounded too detached and she knew that wasn't the case. Anyone could see how much he loved and adored his niece. Alison had been in his office when he had received the call regarding his brother's and sister-in-law's deaths and his being named as Erika's guardian. That had to have been a tailspin for any carefree bachelor.

She would never forget the day he had flown to California to bring his niece home. And it was obvious he was fiercely protective of Erika, otherwise Alli wouldn't be here.

Pursing her lips, Alli studied Erika's features then met Mark's gaze. "She favors you a lot. You both have identical hazel eyes, the same skin coloring, and her mouth is like yours, just a smaller version. She could be your daughter."

He stuck his hands in the pockets of his jeans and rocked on his heels. She had worked with him long enough to know the first signs of his anger. "But she's not. You saw the photograph. Matt and I looked alike but there was a lot about us that was different. We were both Nathaniel Hartman's sons so there were some things that couldn't be changed, but Matt inherited a lot of Mama's ways. Although the old man tried making him hard, Matt had a soft spot. And he always wanted to grow up and have children. I never did."

Mark's words surprised Alli. He was sharing more with her now than he had before. "But how could you not want kids? You were married."

Mark stared at her in silence for a moment, reached out and absently took Erika out of her arms. He moved to put space between them. Moments later he said, "Getting married had nothing to do with it. Patrice knew I never wanted kids, which was fine with her since, because of a medical condition, she couldn't have them."

Alli felt her pulse go still and she inhaled a deep breath. It appeared that this was a touchy subject with Mark but she wasn't ready to put it to rest. She crossed the room to join him and Erika. "Now that Erika has broken you in, what do you think about fatherhood?"

His head shot around and hazel eyes collided with hers. Too late she realized what she'd asked was a mistake. "I'm Erika's uncle, let's keep that clear, Alli. Matt entrusted her into my care and I will do the best that I can by her. She will never want for anything. And as far as me ever wanting kids of my own, nothing has changed. I still don't want any."

Alli's chest tightened as he placed Erika in her arms and she watched him walk out of the room.

Chapter 3

It was the most stunning room, Alli thought, as she followed Mark into the bedroom that was conveniently located across the hall from Erika's.

Besides the huge four-poster, cherry-oak bed that sat between two huge windows, the other furnishings included double nightstands, a mirror dresser, a chest and an accent bench. All in all the elegant-looking accessories, from the floral bedspread and matching window treatments to the massive brick fireplace, and she felt it was a room fit for a queen. What was even nicer was the fact that she had her own bath, a rather nice modern one that had a separate shower and a bathtub. It was apparent some renovations been done since the original house had been built.

"I hope you like this room."

She swung around and the swift movement made Erika

happily squeal loudly. "Oh, Mark, it's perfect. Did you hire a professional decorator to do this room as well?"

He nodded. "Yes, when I moved back I found the place needed a lot of repairs." He took Erika out of Alli's arms and continued saying, "After the repairs were taken care of I started doing renovations. I wanted to give the place a whole new look and I didn't want anything here to remind me of before."

A part of Alli wanted to reach out and throw her arms around him. She regretted he did not have memories of a happy childhood. Although her father had deserted them and her mother had eventually worked herself into an early grave, Mildred Lind had done the best she could to make sure her daughters had childhoods filled with many fond memories. There hadn't been a lot of money to spend but there had been a lot of love to go around. Too bad Mark had missed out on that.

"I'd better get your things out the car," Mark said, handing Erika back to her.

Alli chuckled as she held Erika against her shoulder. Mark lifted an eyebrow in confusion. "What's so funny?"

"Have you noticed what we've been doing? I bet Erika has never been passed back and forth before between two people so much in her life."

A smile touched the corners of Mark's lips. "You're probably right. I hadn't noticed."

Alli smiled at Erika before dropping a kiss on her cheek. "But you noticed didn't you, sweetheart, and you enjoyed every minute of going from arm to arm, right?"

"That's something else she isn't used to."

Alli switched her gaze to Mark. "What?"

"Being kissed. You've done it three times since you've been here."

Forcing her gaze back to Erika, Alli asked, "You're counting?"

He shrugged. "I can't help but notice. I didn't know you were such an affectionate person."

There's a lot you don't know about me, Mark Hartman. She looked at him, wanting to tell him that she had more than enough affection to share if he was interested, but she knew that saying that wouldn't be a good idea. "Well, when it comes to babies, I'm as affectionate as anyone can get."

"You want children one day?"

She grinned. "You would have done better just asking me how many."

After studying her thoughtfully for a brief moment, he said, "Okay, how many?"

"A houseful. I'll even make room in the barn if I have to."

Evidently the image of that played out in Mark's mind and he chuckled. "I hope your husband will be able to afford all your kids."

"I hope so, too." Automatically and without thought, she kissed Erika's cheek again, making the baby giggle with pleasure.

When Alli glanced up she saw that Mark's gaze was focused on her lips while he absently wet his own with his tongue. She became aware of the tension that suddenly filled the room and the pulsing heat that was forming between them. As if his lips were dry, he licked them again and at that moment she was dying to know how his kisses tasted.

Alli was mortified that such thoughts had entered her mind and knew she should dismiss them, but she couldn't. Even if she were to kiss him until the cows came home, he would never be out of her system…or out of her heart. He was still staring at her mouth the way she was staring at his. The beatings of their hearts could be heard as a throbbing tempo in the room and even Erika's babbling couldn't drown it out.

Heat flowed all through her when she could see the guarded expression that he always wore was gone and he was staring at her as if he finally was seeing her as a woman. At that very moment, whether it was his intent or not, he made her feel desired. She wanted more than anything to curl up in his arms while he kissed her in all the ways she had dreamed about.

Her breath caught in her throat when he took a step closer, leaned forward and came within inches of capturing her mouth in his.

"Da-da. Play."

As if snapping out of a daze, Mark straightened, took a quick step back and ran a hand down his face. "I better get your things out the car," he said, turning quickly.

Emotions tightened Alli's throat. He had almost kissed her. After two years, he had shown some sign that he was attracted to her.

"You do remember about my Cattleman's Club meeting tonight, right?"

His question jarred her from her thoughts. "Yes, I remember."

"And don't worry about dinner. Mrs. Sanders was here yesterday and prepared enough dinner for today as well."

"Mrs. Sanders?"

"She's my housekeeper and cook, and she usually comes a couple of times a week."

Evidently seeing the question in her eyes, he went on to say, "She cooks and cleans but is quick to inform you that she doesn't do babies. She's fifty-seven, has five kids of her own and doesn't relish the thought of taking care of another child. She's one of those grandmothers whose kids can't just drop the grandkids off and keep going. Her philosophy is, and I quote, 'I raised mine, now you raise yours.'"

"I'm looking forward to meeting her," Alli said as she continued to stare at Mark. She thought it was a darn shame for any man to look that good. He took her breath away. She needed him to leave so she could breathe normally again.

He smiled warmly. "And I have a feeling that she's looking forward to meeting you as well."

And then he was gone.

"I hear you've solved your babysitting problems, Mark," Logan Voss said as the two of them entered the bar of the Texas Cattleman's Club and proceeded to the private meeting room.

Out of habit, Mark's gaze went to the Leadership, Justice and Peace motto on a far wall before meeting his friend's eyes. "Then I'm also sure you've heard that Alli is Erika's nanny."

Logan chuckled. "Yes, I did hear that."

"What did you hear?" Jake Thorne asked curiously as he greeted the two men and watched them settle into the leather chairs.

"That Alli is Erika's nanny," Logan responded.

Jake smiled. "Yes, and knowing what a responsible person Alli is, we can safely say that Erika will be in good hands."

Mark nodded. At the moment, he would have given anything to know just how good those hands were; just as he would have loved sampling that mouth of Alli's. Luckily for him, when he had returned to the room with her things, she hadn't been there. She had placed Erika in her stroller and had taken her outside for a walk. He was grateful for that time alone to pull himself together. Never in his life had he wanted to kiss a woman so badly.

He had spent a long time in the shower berating himself for his weakness of coming within inches of kissing Alli. By the time he had gotten dressed for the meeting, he had decided that hell, he was only human, and any man would have wanted to kiss her given the way her lips were made, not to mention how alluring her perfume was. The total package would have any man interested and he was definitely a man.

Damn, he had to stop thinking about her. Thoughts of her had consumed him on the drive to this meeting and they were consuming him now. He hoped like hell that she'd be asleep when he returned home. But just in case, it might be a good idea if he didn't return to the ranch immediately after the meeting. Maybe he could interest a couple of the guys in a game of poker.

He glanced around. He knew Thomas Devlin and Gavin O'Neal were standing outside talking. But where the hell was Connor Thorne? He was the one who had ribbed Mark the most whenever he had shown up late due to babysitting issues. Mark wondered if Connor also had heard that his problem was solved.

Mark glanced over at Jake. "Where's Connor?"

Jake smiled lazily, his blue eyes shining brightly. "I am my brother's brother, but I am not my brother's keeper," he replied jokingly. He then glanced at his watch. "We have seven minutes to go. He'll be here."

Mark nodded and then asked, "How's the campaign going?" Jake's opponent in the mayoral race was Gretchen Halifax. In her mid-thirties, Gretchen was intelligent, sophisticated and had a large circle of influence in town. But what she didn't have was a clue about what Royal needed. If Gretchen became mayor, there was no doubt in Mark's mind that, with her proposed tax plan, the town would lose businesses to other areas.

"I'm playing by the rules and sticking to the campaign issues," Jake said. "But it seems Gretchen doesn't want to play fair."

Logan, who had stood to remove his jacket, sat and chuckled as he leaned back in his chair. "Now why doesn't that surprise me?"

The three men glanced up when Connor Thorne, Tom Devlin and Gavin O'Neal walked in. They could tell by the look on Gavin's face that the news he had to share wouldn't be good. As a relatively new sheriff, he had his hands full trying to figure out a murder as well as a number of suspicious happenings around town.

"We might as well get started," Gavin said, dropping into one of the leather chairs. Connor and Tom, who had recently joined the club, did likewise.

When Gavin was certain he had everyone's attention, he continued to speak. "We still don't have a clue who fired that shot at Melissa Mason," he said to everyone, although the guys knew he was really answering the question Logan hadn't asked yet. Melissa was Logan's fiancée and the attempt on her life had riled him to say the least.

"So we're still operating on the theory that since Melissa was driving one of Logan's vehicles, the sniper thought it was Logan and was trying to dissuade him from going to see Lucas Devlin?" Connor asked, leaning forward.

"Yes. In my opinion someone is trying like hell to keep the Devlin and Windcroft feud going," Gavin said somberly.

"Hmm, but who would benefit from such a thing and how does it all tie in to Jonathan's murder?" Jake asked, as if thinking out loud.

"That's what we need to find out," Gavin said, sighing deeply. He glanced over at Mark. "I need you to go talk to Nita Windcroft to see whether her allegations are founded or she's blowing things out of proportion to stir up trouble. I'm fairly new to the area but what I'm hearing is that she's pretty damn headstrong and if she thinks we're not taking her seriously, she might take matters into her own hands. Heaven help us all if she does that. My deputies claim she has one hell of a temper and is as stubborn as they come."

Mark nodded. "All right. I'll talk to Nita."

Gavin then glanced over at Jake and smiled. "I thought I'd better give you a heads-up. Rumor has it around town that Gretchen is trying like hell to tie you to the vandalism of the Halifax Exhibit. She claims you're running a negative campaign and that's one example of your unsavory tactics."

Jake shook his head and chuckled. "Thanks for letting me know but if anyone is using unsavory tactics, it's Gretchen. But she'll eventually hang herself since the people who know me won't believe a word of it."

"What about the woman captured on tape stealing the map? Any new leads?" Tom Devlin decided to ask, his silver-gray eyes alert. Since he was relatively new to town, he was quickly finding out about the feud that involved the family he only recently had discovered he had.

"No, there's nothing new," Gavin said. "I showed the video around and no one seems to recognize the woman, so it's still a mystery." He glanced down at his watch. "That's all I have to report tonight. I'm sure you're all aware that word has gotten around that Jonathan was murdered by some sort of lethal injection and everyone has an idea of who did it." He shook his head. "You wouldn't believe how many people stopped me today with the list of their own suspects."

Mark lifted an eyebrow in amusement. "Any particular name that's heading the list?"

Gavin sighed. "Yeah, Nita Windcroft's, but only because of the feud. But then everyone was quick to add that more than likely she didn't do it because she would not have let poor Jonathan linger. If he had made her mad enough, she would have taken a gun and shot him on the spot."

Connor grinned. "She doesn't sound like a woman I would want to tangle with."

Tom chuckled. "From what I'm hearing, no one would."

Gavin smiled. "Well, that ends tonight's meeting. We'll get together again next Wednesday. At that time, Mark, you can tell us what you've found out after talking with Nita."

"Sure thing," Mark said." When the men all stood, he asked, "Anyone interested in a game of poker tonight?"

Jake smiled and shook his head. "Sorry, I have a lady waiting for my return."

"And so do I," Logan said, grinning as he put back on his jacket. His gray-green eyes had the quiet, determined intent of a man who knew just where he was going and didn't plan on wasting time getting there.

Mark studied the two men who were rushing for the door. "Hmm, I can distinctively remember a time when there were no ladies in your lives."

Jake paused in the doorway and chuckled. "Well, you know how it is." After studying Mark for a brief moment he said, "Then again, my friend, maybe you don't. But I have a feeling that one day soon you will." Then he was gone with Logan right on his heels.

Mark frowned and turned to look at Tom, Connor and Gavin. "What the hell did he mean by that?"

Gavin shrugged. "I'm through figuring out things for the night. I'll leave that one for the three of you to ponder." His brown eyes seemed to smile when he added, "I'm headed over to the diner for a cup of coffee." And he rushed out the door as well.

Mark, Connor and Tom shared a knowing look between them. They knew of Gavin's fascination with a certain waitress at the Royal Diner.

"The least he could have done was invite us to come along," Connor said jokingly.

"Yes, he very well could have. However, since he didn't, we can only assume he felt that four was a crowd," Tom replied laughing.

Mark nodded, amused. "Maybe I better warn Gavin that he's not the only one who has the hots for Valerie Raines. I've noticed Malcolm Durmorr giving her a lusty eye more than once when I happened to be in there."

Connor sat and folded his arms over his chest, rolling his blue eyes heavenward. "Malcolm? That lowlife?" He glanced over at Tom. "Sorry. I forgot he's a distant relative of yours."

Tom shook his head. "From what I understand, the Devlins try to forget that fact as well."

Connor seemed to understand. He then gave Mark a sly grin. "If I were you, I wouldn't tell Gavin anything about Malcolm's interest in Valerie Raines. Competition is good for the soul and it will keep our sheriff on his toes."

Mark smiled. "Maybe you're right." He glanced at his watch. It wasn't nine o'clock and chances were Alli hadn't gone to bed yet. He looked at Connor and Tom. "A game of poker anyone?"

When the two men agreed, Mark's smile widened. Good. He'd been saved by a poker game.

Holding Erika in her arms, Alli walked over to the rocker-recliner and sat. She could not believe that it was almost nine o'clock and the little girl was still wide awake. She couldn't help but smile down at the big, beautiful hazel eyes in that round little face that was staring up at her. Her dark curly hair framed her face and a little pink ribbon sat on top of her head.

Alli smiled as she shook her head thinking that every time she'd seen Erika her hair had been fixed the same way, which was probably a convenient style for Mark. She decided that she was going to introduce Erika to some cute new hairdos and thought a mass of braids would look rather nice on her.

"So, your uncle is short on affection and you still love him anyway, huh?" Alli said as she began rocking the chair. "Well, I know just how you feel, so welcome to the club."

When the baby gave her a grin that showed a few sprouting teeth, Alli returned the gesture. "I guess it's going to take the two of us to give him a lesson in love, wouldn't you say?"

As Alli continued to rock, she thought that, affection or no affection, Mark was evidently doing something right for his niece to adore him so much. She had noted earlier while feeding Erika a snack that even the slightest sound had Erika glancing toward the kitchen door as if anxious to see her uncle walk through it. And a couple of times she had wandered around the living room chanting "Da-da" as if saying it would make Mark appear.

Okay, so he didn't go for all that kissy stuff, but he was

bestowing affection on Erika in ways that Mark himself probably didn't even realize.

Like this rocker-recliner chair for instance.

He had mentioned how he used to rock her in it. An affec-
tionless person would not have bothered doing that.

Alli sighed deeply. After what had almost happened between her and Mark in the bedroom, she had needed distance
and a chance to escape. Spotting the stroller in Erika's room,
she had decided it would be a perfect time to go for a stroll
around the Hartman property.

She had never imagined the ranch consisted of that much
land. It seemed she had walked endlessly, enjoying the beauty
of the landscape and wondering how Mark had ever moved
away since every tree, shrub and patch of grass was so beautiful. And Erika seemed to have enjoyed being outside, breathing
in the rich Texas air and appreciating the warmth of a sunny
September day.

Alli glanced down at the little girl who was still fighting
sleep, although it seemed she wasn't winning as much as she
had been earlier. "You have your uncle's heart and he doesn't
even know it. He's so slow. A typical man," she whispered as
she continued to rock.

Moments later she glanced down and saw that Erika had
fallen asleep, but Alli wasn't ready to put her down yet. So
she kept rocking and slowly her own eyes closed as thoughts
of a very slow, typical man by the name of Mark Hartman
filled her unconsciousness.

It was close to eleven o'clock when Mark returned to the
ranch. As habit, he went straight to Erika's room to check
on her and was surprised to find the light still on in her bed-

room. He was further surprised to see Alli holding Erika in the rocker-recliner and they were both asleep.

He had seen Erika sleeping many times but this was the first time he had ever seen his administrative assistant anything but wide awake and fully alert. For a moment he couldn't move, too mesmerized by the beauty of her sitting there with her eyes closed. So he took the time to study her.

His gaze first went to her hair—thick, shoulder-length and dark brown. A vision entered his mind of him running his fingers though the silky strands while he was kissing her. His gaze then shifted to her face and took in the creaminess of her brown skin, the perfection of her naturally shaped eyebrows and the faultless precision of her chin. But what his gaze zeroed in on was her mouth. Even from across the room it looked moist, tempting, inviting.

He swallowed. His own lips suddenly felt hot, dry, parched and he was convinced that the only way to bring relief to them was to mate them with hers. Without questioning the wisdom of what he was about to do, he slowly crossed the room to her.

He leaned over and softly whispered in Alli's ear. "I'm putting Erika in her bed, Alli."

He watched as Alli's eyes flew open the moment he scooped his niece out of her arms. "Mark, you're back," she whispered and the low, throaty sound, as well as the sigh that followed, sent a riveting sensation all the way to his gut. And the sensuously seductive scent of her wasn't helping matters.

Holding Erika, he straightened and met Alli's eyes. "Yes, I'm back. Let me put her in bed."

He turned quickly and crossed the room to lay his niece down. Covering her with the blanket, he watched her for a moment to make sure she was all right and checked the monitor that was attached to the crib before turning his attention back to Alli.

She was standing and his throat tightened when he saw she was no longer wearing slacks but had changed into shorts. His desire was instantaneous and his gaze moved over her. Their eyes connected and he studied the darkness of her brown eyes and felt the same intense heat that he was feeling radiating from them. The same heat that was burning his insides with desire.

"I had meant to put her down earlier but fell asleep rocking her," she whispered.

"Did you?" he asked softly.

"Yes."

He slowly began walking over toward her.

Alli's pulse raced. He was looking at her that way again. The way he had earlier, which was the way he always looked at her in her dreams, especially the one he had awakened her from moments earlier. She knew she should be happy, thrilled and elated that after two years he was finally noticing her, but a part of her questioned the wisdom of becoming involved with Mark, although she was hopelessly in love with him.

When he came to a stop in front of her, his eyes leveled on hers. He reached out and lifted her chin with his finger. "You are a very beautiful woman, Alli."

She blinked, startled. She hadn't expected him to say such a thing. At first she didn't know what to say, then she decided to say something flippant, although being flip wasn't the norm for her. But it seemed that tonight neither she nor Mark was acting normally.

She smiled and tilted her head to the side. "So, it took you two years to notice, Mark?" she asked jokingly.

His eyes seemed to darken when he said, "No. I noticed the

first day I met you, which is the reason I came pretty damn close to not hiring you."

His words wiped that glib look off her face. She then nibbled nervously on her lower lip. "I didn't think you noticed me."

He tilted her chin up more. "Oh, trust me, you've been a distraction, Alli. In fact, for two years I've been fighting my attraction to you. And that night at the Anniversary Ball was the hardest, I think. You looked so damn beautiful in that gown and more than once I started to ask you to dance but stopped myself. The last thing I wanted when I returned to Royal was to become seriously involved with anyone, especially an employee."

Alli nodded. She hadn't known he had paid her any attention at the ball and knowing that he had filled her with happiness. "And now?" she asked quietly.

"And now I want to kiss you so bad I ache."

"Oh."

That was the only word he gave her time to say before he embraced her as his mouth descended on hers, stealing her next breath. At the same time, he swept his tongue into her mouth. And she accepted it with the same ease that he gave it to her.

Alli had never been kissed this way. If the truth were known, at twenty-five she had never really been kissed at all and was puzzled by how effortless it was to follow Mark's lead. Taking care of Kara had been a full-time job and left no time for dating. But she'd figured she had not missed out on anything...until now. She seriously doubted that anyone would have been able to blow her away with a kiss the way Mark was doing. He had the ability to turn on all her buttons and was sending new sensations zinging all through her. She wondered if he knew how much of a novice she was at this.

He did.

Mark had detected it the moment his tongue had entered Alli's mouth and he had felt her body go tense at the invasion, as if she hadn't been expecting such intimacy. He had kissed a lot of women, some more experienced than others. He wouldn't go so far to say that Alli had never been kissed before, but evidently the other men hadn't done it right.

Not only did he intend to do it right, but he also planned on taking it to another level. He pulled back slightly and whispered against her moist lips. "Wrap your arms around my neck, Alli."

She did as he asked and, the moment she complied with his request, he captured her mouth again and deepened the kiss while one of his hands stroked through her hair and the other wrapped around her waist, bringing her closer to the fit of him. He heard her moan softly and felt the way her heart was racing with her chest pressed so tightly to his. He also felt the firm tips of her breasts, which made his pulse quicken.

He knew the moment she became aware of his erection and, when she deliberately rocked into him, he released a low groan and automatically thrust his hips against hers. He had asked her to place her arms around his neck but now she was clutching his shoulders, kneading her fingers deep into the muscles as if to keep her balance. The way she was returning his kiss was robbing him of any control he might have had. He lowered his arms from her waist to mold her curvy buttocks more intimately against him.

The sound of Erika whimpering in her sleep made Mark withdraw his mouth and inhale deeply. It also brought about a semblance of self-control. He took a step back and stared at

Alli's swollen mouth, thinking this woman was all fire and danger. At the moment he didn't want to tangle with either. Kissing her had definitely been a mistake. Not only she was an affectionate person, but she was a passionate one as well. And it had been obvious from their kiss that her sensuality hadn't been tapped yet.

He dragged in another deep breath and with it came a whiff of her perfume. Seductive. Alluring. A total turn-on. Needing to put distance between them, he crossed the room to Erika's crib to check on her.

"Mark, we—"

"Made a mistake," he said briskly, finishing what he knew she was about to say. "Go on to bed, Alli. I'll see you in the morning," he all but snapped.

Out of the corner of his eyes, he saw how Alli's spine stiffened. He was tempted to go to her and start the kissing all over again. But he knew he couldn't do that.

Mark didn't turn around until he heard the sound of the door closing. It was then that he sat in the rocker-recliner and dropped his head into his hands, thinking that he finally had given into temptation. And as a result, he definitely had made a mess of things.

Chapter 4

He owed Alli an apology.

Mark awakened with that thought and quickly glanced at the clock on the nightstand beside his bed. It was still early, barely five in the morning. Chances were she was still sleep so, for the time being, there was nothing he could do.

He rubbed his hand down his face when the memory of kissing her seeped into his mind. Damn, she hadn't been in his house for a full night and he had acted like a stallion in heat. That had been unfair to her.

She was here to take care of his niece, something he appreciated her doing. But he had shown his gratitude by pouncing on her the first chance he'd gotten and would have continued kissing her if they hadn't been interrupted by the sounds Erika had made in her sleep.

Although he didn't want to, he found himself again thinking about the kiss they had shared. He had wanted to taste

Alli, and had gotten more than he'd bargained for. Her lips had fit perfectly to his, as if they had been made just for him, and they had felt soft and had had such a seductive flavor. And when he had deepened the kiss, he had wanted more than anything to pick her up, take her into his bedroom, place her on his bed, undress her and then slide inside of her, between her long shapely legs...

Mark muttered a curse as he threw back the covers to sit on the side of the bed. Since it seemed that going back to sleep was out of the question, he decided to get up. Although it was early, there were a number of things he could do before leaving for the studio. And no matter how many appointments he had on his calendar, he intended to give Nita Windcroft a call to determine the best time he could drive over to the Windcroft horse farm to talk to her.

But first thing this morning, as soon as he saw Alli, he intended to apologize for his actions last night.

Sitting on the accent bench in her bedroom, Alli closed her eyes when she found herself still shivering from the sensations that had gripped her the night before. She barely had been able to sleep, so instead she had decided to get up and think. However, she found that all she could do was mentally replay every single detail of being in Mark's arms.

An undefined ache still throbbed between her legs, and all during the night while trying to sleep she had shifted positions in an attempt to ease it. Whenever she had closed her eyes she had felt the pulsing heat from his erection pressed so intimately against her while he kissed her in a way that had melted her insides.

"This isn't good," she said softly with a sigh as she leaned back on the bench. She loved Mark but she wasn't sure she was ready for the degree of passion that he invoked.

Like his toe-curling kiss, for instance.

And although he had definitely left a lasting impression on her, she was convinced that she hadn't left any on him except possibly the question why a twenty-five-year-old woman knew absolutely nothing about the pleasures that men and women shared. He had even gone so far to admit that kissing her had been a mistake. But she didn't see things that way. What had been a mistake to him had been pure enjoyment to her.

Did he also see her being here as a mistake? Did he feel there was no way she could stay on as Erika's nanny since it was obvious that her presence was causing problems? What if he intended to take it further and ask her to quit her job as his assistant as well, since their employer-employee relationship had been breached? Panic tightened her throat. She couldn't lose her job now when Kara was depending so much on her.

Heaving a troubled sigh, she rose and walked back over to the bed. Feeling exhausted from lack of sleep, she decided to close her eyes and try to rest a while before Erika awakened for breakfast.

The last thing Alli wanted was to see Mark this morning, but she knew that was something she would not be able to avoid.

"Da-da. Eat."

Alli snapped her eyes open when the sound of Erika's voice seemed so close to her ear. She quickly turned over and remembered the monitor that Mark had installed in her room the day before. She smiled. Evidently Erika was awake and hungry.

Quickly getting out of bed, Alli slipped into her robe and, after tightening the belt securely around her waist, she opened her bedroom door only to collide with the solid wall of a male's chest.

"Oops."

"Sorry."

Mark caught her when she nearly lost her balance and the sensations she had been fighting all night intensified with his touch. As soon as he released her, she took a step back. "Thanks. I heard Erika."

He nodded. "So did I."

Alli noticed that his chin was covered with shaving cream, which meant he had been about to shave. She also noticed—although she wished she hadn't, but there was no way to avoid it—that he was bare-chested. The only thing covering his body was a pair of jeans and the towel wrapped around his neck. The top button of his jeans was undone and the dark mass of hair on his chest went down toward his abdomen and disappeared beneath the waist of his jeans. The one word that immediately came to Alli's mind was *sexy*.

When he leaned back against the wall and grinned, she frowned in confusion and wondered if he knew what she'd been thinking. "What's so funny?" she asked when he continued to grin.

"This," he said before reaching out and touching her cheek. He held up his finger.

"Oh," she said when she saw the shaving cream. She lifted a corner of her robe to wipe it off but he stopped her.

"No, let me."

Before she could stop him, he used his towel to wipe off

her cheek. His touch was gentle and soft and the towel held his manly scent. She tried averting her gaze but found herself meeting his anyway. When she locked on the hazel eyes staring at her, she gulped, almost losing her breath. The heat that flared between them was instantaneous, absolute, blinding. And when he slid his gaze to her mouth, she had enough sense to know that she was in big trouble.

Deciding to head it off, she took another step back. "I need to go check on Erika."

He nodded and took a step back as well while placing the towel back around his neck. "We need to talk later, Alli."

She sighed deeply. "Yes…I know."

"But first I need to apologize about last night."

Stunned that he was placing the blame all on himself, she could only stare at him for a moment before finding her voice to say, "And I need to apologize as well."

He lifted an eyebrow. "For what?"

She shrugged. "For whatever you're apologizing for and for the fact that you evidently found me lacking."

Mark frowned. Apparently exhaustion was impairing his hearing. There was no way she could have said anything about him finding her lacking…was there? He leaned forward. "Lacking?"

"Yes." And without saying another word, she spun around and quickly entered the baby's room.

Totally stunned, he watched as Erika's door closed behind Alli. Seconds later he threw up his hand. *He found her lacking?* Where in the hell did she get a crazy idea like that? The last thing he thought was that she was lacking in anything. If the truth was known, he was convinced that she had an over-abundance of everything, especially sensuality and passion.

And he had a good mind to follow her into Erika's room to tell her that.

Okay, he quickly decided, now was not a good time to have that sort of a discussion with her. He needed time to think and he'd already told her that they needed to talk. He realized that they needed to do more than just talk. He definitely needed to straighten her out on a few things.

"Ah, just look at you," Alli whispered to Erika after putting the finishing touches on her hair. "Your uncle won't even recognize you."

Alli sighed. She'd had a lot of time to think while getting Erika dressed. Mark was right, they needed to talk. After what had happened last night and if he was uncomfortable with her being here, then she definitely would leave once he found someone to take her place. The same held true with the studio. If he felt their kiss had left it impossible for them to work together, then she would resign. It would be that simple.

She shook her head. She was fooling herself if she thought anything involving Mark Hartman was simple. But then she had known that living under the same roof with him wouldn't be easy given her feelings for him.

She inhaled a calming breath. Maybe it was time that she realized that nothing could, or would, ever develop between her and Mark. She could now admit that for the past two years she'd been waiting for a fairy tale to happen to her. A part of her had actually wanted to believe that one day she would walk into Hartman's Self-Defense Studio and Mark would see her with different eyes and realize she was capable of being more than just his dependable and efficient administrative assistant.

Well, okay, he had admitted that he thought she was beautiful. But she'd heard from several sources that men thought most women were beautiful; especially women they were interested in sleeping with. But now that Mark realized she couldn't kiss worth a damn and lacked the skills to pleasure a man, she was quite certain that any interest he might have had had died a sudden death.

And maybe it was for the best. If nothing else, her father's actions should have taught her that most men didn't deserve a woman's heart. All she had to do was remember the pain Arthur Lind had caused her mother to know that was true. In addition to that, Mark had told her yesterday he didn't want children. She, on the other hand, had made it pretty clear that she wanted several, which meant the things they wanted or didn't want out of life were vastly different.

At least with things ending this way she saved the humiliation of him finding out that she was in love with him. This way she could move on, concentrate on helping Kara finish college and then continue to live a peaceful existence for the rest of her life. It was time she began being practical and levelheaded.

Picking Erika up off the dressing table, Alli left the bedroom accepting the fact that handsome millionaires didn't fall in love with plain old regular folk like herself and it was time she got rid of any foolish romantic notions that such a thing was possible.

Mark could not stop staring the moment he walked into the kitchen. Both Erika and Alli looked different. It was quite obvious that Alli had taken the time to fix Erika's hair another way but the difference in Alli's appearance was a bit more startling.

She was wearing jeans.

Forget about the western shirt she also had on; his concentration was on her jeans and just how good she looked in them. He always thought she looked good wearing pants, but nothing—and he meant nothing—compared to her wearing jeans. Maybe it would not have been obvious if, when he had walked in the room, she hadn't been leaning over while searching inside the refrigerator.

Transfixed, he watched her move around his kitchen, unaware that he was watching her. Everything was shapely about her, lushly so, and the way the jeans fit her butt had him swallowing hard. And that wasn't the only thing that was feeling hard. He could actually feel his blood heat up, shooting hot fluid through all parts of his body, especially one particular stop. He shifted his position when he felt his erection strain against the zipper of his own jeans.

He couldn't help wondering how on earth he and Alli would maintain an employer-employee relationship now. Kissing her was bad enough, but having lustful thoughts about her was worse. Oh, as he had told her last night, he had wanted her for two years, yet had managed to keep his desire in check. But that was before he had tasted her and knew just how sweet and delicious she was. Now he would be hard-pressed to call her into his office without wanting to have his way with her on his desk.

"Da-da!"

Erika's outburst made Alli swing around, her gaze meeting his. Damn. He'd been caught staring. And when she reached up to get something out of his kitchen cabinet, causing the cotton shirt she was wearing to stretch tight across her breasts, he almost swallowed his tongue.

"I didn't hear you come in," Alli said in a breathless

whisper that didn't help the erotic thoughts flowing through his head.

"Sorry, didn't mean to startle you," he said and walked over to where Erika was sitting in the high chair. The little girl automatically reached for him. "Da-da."

"Mark," he tried correcting her as he picked her up. He looked forward to the day when she would understand who he was and his role in her life. When she merely giggled and said, "Da-da," again, he shook his head. He studied the way her hair was styled and smiled. He liked it.

He glanced up to find Alli watching him, evidently waiting to hear his opinion. "I guess braiding her hair is better since it was getting all tangled. She was beginning to make a fuss whenever I combed it."

Alli nodded. "Yes, it will be more manageable this way." She turned back around to the stove. "Would you like something for breakfast? I'm fixing pancakes, eggs and bacon."

Mark wished she hadn't turned around, giving him a view of her delectable backside. Her curves were out of this world and he couldn't help but appreciate just how snugly her jeans fit.

"Mark."

He blinked when she turned back and met his gaze. He had been caught staring again. "Ah, thanks for the offer but I have several appointments this morning. I had planned to come back here for lunch but I need to go out to the Windcroft horse ranch and talk to Nita."

Alli nodded. "The Texas Cattlemen are finally taking her seriously?"

Mark placed Erika on his shoulder while he leaned against the counter. He lifted an eyebrow. "You know about what she claims is going on over there at her farm?"

Alli shrugged. "I know what she's told me, and I have no reason not to believe her. I've known Nita a long time, ever since Kara was small and Nita gave her riding lessons. There's no way she would make that stuff up."

Mark nodded as he returned Erika to the high chair. It was apparent that Alli had an idea that the Texas Cattleman's Club did more for the community than hosting fund-raisers, but he wasn't at liberty to disclose everything they did and felt the best thing to do would be to change the subject.

"How is your sister doing at college?" He watched as a frown puckered Alli's forehead.

"She was doing just fine until a few days ago when she met this guy at the library.

Mark heard the concern in her voice. "Is something wrong with her meeting guys?"

Alli's gaze narrowed. "She's at college to get a higher education, Mark, not to meet boys. She'll have plenty of time for a social life after she finishes school. Right now that's the main thing I want her to focus on. She's been making the dean's list every semester and I want her to continue to do so."

Mark nodded, wondering if perhaps Alli was expecting too much from her sister, but he decided it wasn't his business to mention that fact. Alli had begun working for him the summer before Kara had started college and he had met Kara several times when she had dropped by the studio to visit with Alli. Kara was a beautiful teenager who, in his book, was a younger version of Alli. Kara had been valedictorian of her senior class and her manners had been exemplary, which was a pretty darn good indication that Alli had done a great job raising her.

One of the reasons he had offered Alli so much money to

work for him was that he'd heard about the extra expenses she would be putting out to assist her sister.

"I'll be at the studio if you need to reach me," he said, grabbing his hat off the rack. "You also know my mobile number."

"You haven't forgotten that I have class tonight have you, Mark?"

He dug into his pocket for the keys to his truck. "No, I haven't forgotten. I'll be home for dinner. Mrs. Sanders should be here around noon. If she asks, please tell her that I'd like to have some of her fried chicken, mash potatoes and gravy. She makes the best."

Alli smiled. "All right, I'll tell her."

Mark looked down at Erika and lightly pinched her cheek, making her squeal with laughter. "See you later, kid." He then looked at Alli and forced the thought from his mind of how much he wanted to walk across the room and kiss her goodbye. "I'll see you later, too," he said then headed for the door."

"Will we have our talk when you come home later?"

He stopped, turned around and met her gaze. "Yes, we'll talk then."

"So you're the new nanny?"

Alli smiled at the older woman who had shown up precisely at noon just as Mark had said she would. Erika had been fed lunch and was taking a nap, and Alli decided to take that time to do the baby's laundry. She was sitting at the kitchen table folding clothes while keeping the older woman company.

"Yes, but only on a temporary basis. I work as Mark's administrative assistant at the studio. He needed someone to fill in here and asked me to do it for a while."

The older woman shook her head as she tossed chicken in the bag to be floured. "I'm glad. Someone needed to help that boy with the baby."

Alli lifted an eyebrow, remembering what Mark had told her. "But you wouldn't," she decided to point out to the older woman.

Still shaking her head, Mrs. Sanders smiled over at her. "No. I had my reasons and they went deeper than what I told Mark. I felt he needed time to bond with his niece. When he brought her home he was a nervous wreck. Had I pitched in and helped, he would have depended on me and would have practically ignored that child. But I saw what was needed."

Alli leaned back in her chair. "And what was needed?"

"Time for him to get to know the baby, to remember who she was and why she was here, to figure out things about her care on his own."

The older woman paused to peer into a pot that was cooking on the stove. In addition to making the dishes Mark had requested, she had decided to cook a huge pot of vegetable soup. She turned and met Alli's gaze. "Erika was such a precious thing when she first got here, but like most babies she was a little fidgety, crying all the time and whimpering. Mark didn't know how to do anything, not even change a diaper. I taught him the basics and told him the rest would come naturally. He'd learn as he went along. He caught on quick and is doing a wonderful job with her."

Alli nodded. She had to agree with that. "Have you known Mark long?" she asked as the woman began peeling potatoes.

"Practically all his life. I came to work for his pa off and on after his mother died. Mark was only seven at the time and Matt was five. Losing their mother was like losing their best friend. Carolina Hartman was a fine woman and to this day I never knew what she saw in Nathaniel. He was cold and heartless. All he ever cared about was this land and the oil that was on it. He wouldn't show affection of any kind, claimed it was a sign of weakness and punished his sons if they ever slipped and showed such an emotion in front of others. I remember Mark and Matt going to bed plenty of nights without supper after their mother died."

She joined Alli at the table. "Matt got punished all the time since he was so much like his mother he couldn't help it. Mark, on the other hand, learned to roll with the flow and did what the old man wanted so he wouldn't get into trouble. Hell knew no fury like Nathaniel Hartman's temper. That's the reason both Mark and Matt got the hell out of here as soon as they finished school. Mark left for the marines and two years later Matt left to attend college out west. Both swore they would never return to Royal while the old man was living and they kept their word. The only time they came back was for the funeral to see their pa laid to rest. I was so happy for Mark when he told me that he had met someone and planned to marry. Then I was so sad when I heard what had happened to his wife and he was left all alone. Too bad they never had any children. Mark had told me at his father's funeral that he didn't ever plan to have any. And he was pretty adamant about it, too."

Alli who had just folded one of Erika's shirts, glanced up and met Mrs. Sanders's gaze. "Why do you think he is so unyielding about it?"

The woman shook her head sadly. "Mark thinks he will grow up to be cold and heartless like his pa. Of course I don't believe it, which is why I wanted him to play a big part in

Erika's care, just to prove him wrong. He needs to see that he's nothing like his old man. I'd watched him with that baby and he's given her so much love, affection and attention that at times I don't think he realizes that he's doing it."

Alli had to agree, thinking of him playfully tweaking Erika's cheek before he left. "It's sad that Mr. Hartman treated his sons that way. I remember hearing about it from my mom when I was younger and—"

"Your mom?" Mrs. Sanders asked with her bushy eyebrows arched.

"Yes, my mother used to do the ironing for Mr. Hartman years ago."

Rearing back, Mrs. Sanders sat in silence for a moment while staring at Alli, as if she were trying to make a connection to her last name as well as to her features. Then Mrs. Sanders's eyes lit up. "You're Mildred Lind's daughter?"

"Yes." Alli was surprised the woman would remember her mother.

The older woman laughed as she stood and walked over to the sink. "Well, I'll be. Now isn't it a small world? I knew your mother. We attended the same church for a while when she first married your father. My husband and I moved away for a few years. When we returned, instead of moving back to the city, we bought us a piece of property in the country since we needed a bigger spread to raise our kids."

She met Alli's gaze and regretfully shook her head. "I heard your mother had passed some years ago and I was sorry to hear about it. She was a good woman and a hard worker."

"Thank you." Alli paused, feeling a moment of unease when she wondered if Mrs. Sanders would bring up the incident involving her father at the time of her mother's death. News had gotten around about it when it had occurred eight years ago. It wasn't something most people would forget; at least she knew she never would.

Arthur Lind, who had deserted his wife and daughters years before, had shown up on the day of the funeral anticipating that he would inherit the house his wife had purchased without him. He actually had gotten ticked when he'd discovered she had willed it to her daughters. He had filed a lawsuit claiming since he and his wife had never divorced, he deserved at least half of whatever assets she had accumulated.

Luckily for Alli and Kara, by the time the judge ordered her father to pay the back child-support payments he owed her and Kara, the amount was well over the equity he felt he was due from the house. In fact, he was ordered to pay an additional five thousand dollars, which he never did, and neither Alli nor Kara had heard from him again.

"You have no reason to thank me since I'm speaking the truth," Mrs. Sanders said as she resumed peeling the potatoes and glanced up for only a second. "How's your baby sister doing?"

Since it seemed that the older woman already had had a glimpse into her past, Alli spent the next ten minutes telling her how Kara had adjusted over the years and how well she was doing with her studies at college. Inwardly, she hoped her sister continued to do so. They hadn't talked since Kara had told her about her upcoming date for this weekend. Kara had dated some in high school but had never taken any of the guys seriously. But there had been something in her voice when she'd told Alli about the library guy that Alli had never heard before whenever the two of them had any discussions about the opposite sex.

"Something smells good in here."

Upon hearing Mark's voice, Alli whipped her head around and stared at him in surprise. She hadn't expected to see him until dinnertime. She took a deep breath and slowly exhaled. Seeing him again was turning her insides to mush. She may not have experienced the pleasures a man and a woman shared but being around Mark had her body yearning to do so. The memory of their kiss just wouldn't leave her alone.

He must have read the questions lodged in her eyes and said, "My last appointment canceled so I thought I'd drop by to see how things were going."

Before Alli could open her mouth to respond, Mrs. Sanders replied as she checked on the food she was cooking, "Things are going fine. Erika is sleeping, and Alli and I were taking the time to get to know each other."

"Hmm, you don't say?"

Alli decided not to say anything. Instead, she went about folding the last piece of Erika's laundry. She glanced up, however, when Mark came to stand beside the table.

"Do you think Erika will be sleeping for a while?" he asked.

Alli shrugged as she held his gaze. "It's hard to say. She's been sleeping for half an hour. I'd think she'll have another hour or so to go. Why?"

"I came by to see if the two of you wanted to take the ride with me over to Nita Windcroft's place."

"Oh."

"You two can go on. I'll keep an eye on Erika."

Alli stared at the older woman, surprised at her offer. Evidently Mark was surprised as well and said, "I thought you didn't take care of babies."

Mrs. Sanders flapped her hand before she lifted the lid of her pot. "I don't. But Erika is sleeping and chances are she'll stay that way for a while and if not, then I'll make an exception and handle things. No big deal."

"B-but, I—I'm sure he wanted Erika to go, too. This would have been a good outing for her," Alli sputtered, not sure she was ready to be alone with Mark. That would give them the perfect time for the talk they needed to have; something she wasn't looking forward to.

Leaning against the sink, Mrs. Sanders gazed at both her and Mark. "Well, Erika can't go because she's sleeping and I doubt you'd want to wake her. She's a fuss box if she doesn't get her rest." Frowning, the woman then dipped her chin as she stared at Mark. "Besides, I got the feeling that Mark just wanted some company."

Alli stole a quick glance at Mark. He was shaking his head, smiling while holding Mrs. Sanders's gaze, as if he knew what she was up to. Evidently there was a private joke going on that Alli wasn't privy to.

Mark then turned and met Alli's gaze. "Yes, I'd love the company if you'd like to go with me, Alli."

Inhaling a calming breath, Alli silently told herself that Mark was just being kind in asking her to go. The smart thing to do would be to turn down his offer. But then, as much as she wasn't looking forward to it, they needed to talk, and putting things off wouldn't help matters.

"Okay, I just need to put these things away and grab my jacket." She stood and, without looking at either him or Mrs. Sanders, walked out of the kitchen.

Alli took the time to do more than grab her jacket. She brushed her hair and applied some lip gloss. She also changed blouses since Erika accidentally had spilled some syrup on it at breakfast.

Moments later, she stared at her reflection in the mirror, deciding that she looked decent. She sucked in a deep breath as she left the bedroom and decided to quickly check on Erika. Alli stopped dead in her tracks when she found Mark in the room standing over the crib staring down at the sleeping baby.

Alli wanted to give him a private moment with his niece. She was quietly backing out of the room, more than certain he hadn't heard her, when he turned his head and met her gaze.

She opened her mouth to apologize for the untimely intrusion when he placed a finger to his lips and beckoned for them to step outside the room. After following her into the hall, he closed the door behind them.

"Sorry, I thought I'd check on her before we left," Alli said softly, trying not to notice how close together they were standing. She could see the irises of his hazel eyes as well as smell the masculine scent of the cologne he wore.

He smiled in understanding. "I thought I'd check on her, too. For some reason I like watching her sleep. She seems so at peace," he murmured.

Alli returned his smile. Earlier today she had thought the same thing. "She's that way when she's awake as well. Erika is a happy baby."

Mark lifted an eyebrow. "You really think so?"

Alli chuckled. "Yes. She has such a good temperament and is a joy to take care of."

Mark couldn't help but be pleased at what Alli had said. "Her father was that way. No matter how bad things were around here, nothing could break Matt's spirit, although the old man tried. My brother was always able to look on the bright side."

Alli felt a tugging at her heart. She couldn't help but recall the conversation she'd had with Mrs. Sanders and could only imagine Mark and his brother as young boys dealing with a father who thought it was wrong for him or his sons to show emotions.

"Ready to go?"

Mark's question jarred her out of her reverie. She stared at him for a moment and then asked, "I know you're visiting Nita on Texas Cattleman's Club business. Are you sure you want me to come along?"

He nodded his head. "Yes, I'm sure. Besides, this will give us time to talk."

Alli nodded. That's what she'd been afraid of.

Chapter 5

Mark glanced over at Alli as they walked out to his truck, not able to suppress his full awareness of her. He could feel her nervous tension and wondered if it was because of him.

He knew that kissing her had been a mistake, although, heaven help him, he wanted to do it again. The desire for her wouldn't go away. It was as if the lust that had been building and accumulating for two years was demanding to break free. They had crossed the boundary of what was acceptable between an employer and his employee and he couldn't help wondering what she thought about it. His actions last night had put him at risk of losing the best assistant he'd ever had.

But as much as he tried, he could not ignore her presence. He had dated some since his return to Royal but never had he let any woman get close to him. In fact, other than Erika, Mrs. Sanders, Christine Travers, the interior decorator and the other piss-poor nannies he'd hired, no other female had been allowed across the threshold in his home.

He was suddenly pulled from his thoughts when, to avoid coming into contact with the branch of a shrub, Alli moved closer to him and innocently touched her arm to his. He stiffened when a jolt of awareness shot through him. Just being around her was murder on his self-control.

How in the world could she think that she was lacking in anything? he wondered again. Although he could tell she wasn't an experienced kisser, that hadn't had any bearing on how she had made him feel. In fact, he had found her inexperience totally refreshing and unique. There weren't too many twenty-five-year-olds who hadn't been in and out of numerous affairs. After thinking about it most of the day, he realized that during the two years Alli had worked for him, he'd never known her to go out on a date, not that he was privy to everything there was to know about her personal life and how she spent her free time.

Hell, for all he knew she could have had a boyfriend, several of them. How did he know for sure that she didn't have one now? She was a beautiful woman, a real head-turner no matter where she went, so it was possible she *was* seeing someone. For some reason, he was disturbed at the thought that there might be a special man in her life, although he had no right to feel that way.

He sighed deeply. Instead of his mind being focused on Alli and whether or not she was involved with someone, he should be concentrating on his meeting with Nita Windcroft.

But he knew he couldn't put it off any longer. He and Alli needed to talk.

* * *

Mark and Alli rode for about four miles before either one of them spoke.

"It won't be much farther now," Mark said, glancing over at her.

"Yes, I know." Alli turned from looking out the window and glanced over at him, barely seeing his eyes because of the wide brim of his Stetson. "You said that we would talk." She had decided that if she needed to look for other employment, the sooner she did so, the better.

"Yes, I did." He glanced back over at her again. "About last night. I think you misunderstood the reason I was apologizing."

She lifted an eyebrow. "Did I?"

He gave her a lazy smile. "Yes, I think you did."

She took a deep breath, reminding herself that lately she and Mark weren't on the same wavelength, so she decided to let him do the explaining. "I don't understand what you're saying, Mark."

She blinked when she saw he was pulling to the side of the road, and once they were stopped, he turned off the engine of his truck. He turned in his seat to face her, tipping his hat back. In a way, Alli wished that he hadn't done that. Now she could see his eyes and the intensity she saw in them made her breath catch.

"The reason I apologized, Alli, was because I'm the one who initiated the kiss and I was out of line to do so. When I said that we made a mistake, what I meant was that the kiss should not have happened. I told you that I wasn't ready to become involved with anyone. But last night I gave into a weakness I've been fighting for two years."

Alli blinked in surprise. "Two years?"

He smiled warmly. "Yes, for two years. I've wanted to kiss

you for a very long time and my apology had nothing to do
with your lack of experience."

Alli wanted to believe what he was saying. "I wasn't sure
since I haven't dated much. Over the years, even while I was
in high school, taking care of Kara occupied most of my time
and there wasn't time for dates."

There was no way she was going to tell him that once Kara
had left for school she could have started dating, but by that
time she had fallen in love with him and no other man had
interested her.

"I don't want to become involved with you, Alli."

She pursed her lips and raised her chin. "And I don't want
to become involved with you, either."

"Good. I'm glad we agree on that. Another kiss would be
asking for trouble."

"I totally agree."

He leaned back in his seat. "If we were to kiss again it will
be hard for us to go back to having a strictly professional relationship."

"I concur with that as well."

"We will be living together for a while and since we know
what's the most sensible thing to do, which is the only thing
that we can do, what do you suggest?" His gaze slid to her
mouth. She saw it happen and her pulse quickened.

"I could leave here today and, if you want, I'll even quit
my job at the studio."

"No. That's not what I want, Alli." Mark rubbed his hand
down his face. He needed to rid her of the notion that he preferred she leave.

"I need you here, Alli, and when I find a nanny who I can

depend on, I'll need you back at the studio. In no way am I suggesting that you stop working for me."

"Then what are you saying?"

His muscles tightened at the memory of what had happened to Patrice and the months of endless guilt he endured following her death. Never again would he set himself up for such heartbreak. The quicker he established some distance between Alison and him, the better things would be for both of them.

His eyes met hers. "What I'm trying to say is that I need to practice more self-control when it comes to you. But it won't be easy. I need your help. We both need to accept that we're attracted to each other. It's an attraction that will lead nowhere, since I don't ever intend to get serious about a woman again." He held her gaze intensely. "Do you understand what I'm trying to say, Alli?"

She nodded, fighting the tightness in her throat. He was telling her in a nice way that he didn't want her. Ever. "You want to keep things as they have been between us for the past two years, a strictly professional relationship. Is that what you want?"

Mark nodded. "Yes, that is exactly what I want."

"We're here," Mark said, glancing over at Alli. She hadn't said more than two words to him since they'd had their talk. More than once he had tried to strike up a conversation with her but in a polite yet distant way she had let him know she wasn't prone to chitchat. In fact, she was doing exactly what he'd asked her to do—establish a strictly professional relationship between them.

And already he didn't like it.

He glanced out of his truck's windshield and stared at the

main house of the Windcrofts' horse farm. The structure was very modern with a lot of tall windows and a stone facade. The primary stable was located close to the house and an older farmhouse—probably the original family dwelling—was set back in the distance. There were also four corrals, stallion pens as well as a training pen.

From his early days of living in Royal, Mark recalled that Will Windcroft's wife had died when his two daughters, Nita and Rose, were small children. The Windcroft girls were as different as day and night. It had always been Rose's dream to leave Royal and pursue a career in the big city. Nita never wanted to leave and had looked forward to continuing her father's horse-breeding farm. In recent years, as business had increased, she'd begun assuming a greater role in running things.

"I've always liked this place."

Mark jerked his head around. Alli had spoken without being prompted. It suddenly occurred to him how much he liked hearing her voice. Even while at the studio when she was going over reports, he would be more in tune to listening to her voice than concentrating on the subject they were discussing.

"My dad used to purchase his horses from Mr. Windcroft and I've always liked it here, too," he said. "You come here often?" he asked, wanting to keep her talking. Just because they had agreed to have a strictly business relationship was no reason they had to act like total strangers.

"Not as often as I'd like to. When I was a little girl, Mr. Windcroft taught me how to ride my first horse, and later when Nita took over the running of things, she taught Kara. Even now there are days on the weekend when I'll come and get one of their horses and ride for hours, although not as often as I used to."

Mark gave her an incredulous look. Though he knew most people in Royal could ride, he never gave it much thought that she could. For some reason, he could not imagine her sitting on the back of a horse. She seemed too prim and proper for that. "I have horses at my ranch. You're welcome to take one out whenever you want. John Collier is my foreman. He'll be glad to saddle one up for you."

She glanced at him as she brushed her hair back from her face. "Thanks."

Before he could say anything, she opened the truck's door and hopped out. He figured she was putting distance between them again. He inhaled deeply as he opened his own door. And for the second time he had to remind himself that he was getting just what he'd asked for.

She wasn't trying to be difficult, Alli tried convincing herself. What she was doing was trying to make the best of a difficult situation. Mark had made things pretty clear. In order to keep her job, she needed to keep her distance and he would keep his. Although it would be challenging with them living under the same roof, she intended to do it.

She smiled when she saw Jimmy, the Windcrofts' foreman, approaching. However, she tensed when she felt Mark's presence beside her. She hadn't wasted any time getting out of the truck because of the desperate need to catch her breath and gather her composure. She was sure Mark wasn't aware of it, but each and every time he looked at her for too long or got too close to her, her insides filled with heat. She walked away from him to meet Jimmy, needing desperately to escape his presence.

"Ms. Lind, how are you?" Jimmy greeted her, smiling brightly. "It's been a while since you've come out for a ride."

She returned the man's smile. "Yes, I've been pretty busy lately. How is everything going?"

Before Jimmy could respond, his gaze moved to Mark, who had joined them. "Jimmy, do you know Mark Hartman?" Alli asked. "He's here to talk to Nita."

The two men regarded each other as introductions were made and handshakes exchanged. "I don't think we've ever met, since I was hired on here after you left Royal years ago," Jimmy was saying. "You own the Hartman place, right?"

Mark smiled. "Yes, that's right."

"You have a mighty fine spread."

"Thanks. Is Nita around?"

"Yeah, she's out back near the stables with a few of the hands. I'll be glad to take you to her," Jimmy said. He then glanced over at Alli. "Are you coming, too, Ms. Lind?"

Alli shook her head. "No, I think I'll go inside and visit with Will and Jane. Is she in?"

Jimmy chuckled. "Now you know Jane isn't going anyplace," he said of the Windcrofts' housekeeper. "In fact, there's a rumor floating around the farm that she's baking a ton of pies today, so you came to visit right in time."

"That's wonderful. I love Jane's pies," Alli said chuckling. She made a move to step past Mark and he reached out and touched her arm. Although she tried to remain unaffected, every part of her tingled from the contact.

"I'll see you again in a little while," he said huskily, the depth of his gaze holding hers.

She gave him a strained smile. "All right." And then she quickly walked off toward the main house.

When they reached the stables, Mark looked around. Several ranch hands were crowded around the training pen watching one of the hands break in a horse. The animal was a beauty. He was also mean and it was obvious that he intended to throw the rider. However, the rider was showing the animal that he wasn't going anywhere. There was nothing like seeing man tame beast... or vice versa.

Fascinated, Mark walked to the corral and joined the onlookers. Everyone was cheering the rider on and, from the way the man was handling the horse, it appeared he was definitely up to the challenge, even with the horse not making it easy for him bucking all over the place.

The longer Mark watched, the more fascinated he became with the rider's skills. Moments later when it became evident the cowboy was the victorious one, a loud cheer went up. "What a way to go, Nita!" the crowd called out.

Mark blinked. "Nita?"

He stared at the rider who was getting off the horse and, when her feet touched the ground, she pulled off her hat, spilling a mass of black hair that she'd tucked underneath. She smiled and waved to the crowd.

"Damn." That was the only word Mark could think to say at that moment. How could he have forgotten that Nita Windcroft could outrace, out rope and outride just about any male?

He watched as the slim woman glanced his way after Jimmy said something to her. Without a hint of any smile on her face, she walked toward Mark. When she reached him, instinctively he held out his hand. She took it, although a deep, dark frown had settled on her face.

She met his gaze. "Hi, Mark. It's about time one of you guys decided to pay a visit."

Mark nodded. He knew she had expected them to drop everything and come running the first time she'd come to them claiming that the Devlins were causing mischief. "Any new developments, Nita?" he asked.

She placed her hands on her hips and glared at him. "Like poisoned feed, broken fences, cut lines, spooked horses and threatening notes aren't enough?"

Mark sighed deeply. The Texas Cattleman Club had seen the so-called threatening notes and thought they were too vague to actually take seriously, and although Nita had disagreed, there was no evidence that indicated the Devlins were involved. "Have you received another threatening note?"

"No."

"Then things have gotten back to calm around here?"

Nita narrowed her eyes. "For now but I'm not going to hold my breath it will last."

Mark nodded. "I'd like to take a look around."

"That's fine. I'm just glad to see you guys are finally taking me serious."

Mark sighed, choosing not to tell her it hadn't been decided if they were taking her seriously or not. "It might be a good idea if we have a list of names of anyone and everyone you do business with. It could come in handy later."

Nita nodded. "All right. It will take me a few moments to print it off the computer."

After Nita left, Mark checked out the other areas of her property, looking for anything that could give him a hint of who might be responsible for the activities going on at her place.

Mark had circled around the back of the stable when suddenly something lying on the ground near the barn caught his attention. He kneeled down for a closer look. Lying in the grass near a shrub was a syringe, the kind typically used in hospitals to give injections.

He sighed deeply. It was probably the same kind, or pretty similar, to the one used to kill Jonathan Devlin.

Chapter 6

"I'm leaving for class now, Mark."

Mark glanced up from the printout of names he'd gotten from Nita Windcroft to Alli as she walked into the room. Ever since their talk earlier that day, things had been strained between them. They had barely said two words to each other on the ride back from the Windcroft farm.

He glanced out the window. It was already dark and the thought of her going out alone at night bothered him. He remembered the incident with her car breaking down and stood to fish his car keys out of the pocket of his jeans. "Here, use my car."

Alli stared at the keys he held out to her. She then looked up with a puzzled expression on her face. "Why?"

"Because I rarely drive it since I mostly use the truck and it's in a lot better shape than yours."

Alli frowned. Well, of course his car was in better shape,

for heaven's sake. Her car was eight years old and his brand new Maxima probably hadn't hit one hundred miles yet. Although what he said was true, she didn't appreciate him pointing out that fact. "Thanks for the offer but I prefer driving my own car."

From the expression on his face, she could tell he didn't like her response. "Why?" he asked.

She managed a smile when she said, "Because I just do."

Immediately she could tell he liked that response even worse. He crossed his arms over his chest. "I prefer that you take mine."

Her frown deepened. "Again thanks for the offer, Mark, but I prefer driving my own car."

She watched as he took a deep breath and glared at her. "You need a new car."

Again what he said was true but she resented him telling her that. "I plan to get a new one this weekend when Jake has the time to go with me to the dealership."

His dark eyebrows arched. "Jake?"

"Yes, Jake. Christine thought a man should go with me when I pick out a car since some salesmen have a tendency of taking advantage of female customers." She turned to leave.

"You could have asked me to go with you," Mark snapped angrily.

Alli stopped and turned around. She met his glare as calmly as she could and wondered just what his problem was. "No, I could not have asked you to go with me, Mark."

A confused look covered his face. "Why not?"

"It would not have been ethical. Jake is a friend. You're

my employer. Good night." She then paused long enough to bend down to give Erika a kiss on the cheek before walking out the room.

With an agitation that he felt all the way down to his toes, Mark sat on the sofa across from the television as he flipped though several channels before muttering a curse and tossing the remote aside. He stood and began pacing the floor.

It was one of those rare nights that Erika had fallen asleep early, and although there were a number of things he could be doing, he could barely concentrate.

Alli had really ticked him off. The nerve of her asking Jake instead of him to go with her to pick out a car. Mark would have been glad to assist her in making a selection. Then for her to say she hadn't asked since he was her employer really grated on his nerves.

He was about to go into the kitchen for a beer when he heard a knock at the door. He glanced at the clock on the wall. Alli's class wouldn't be over for another hour and she had her own key. Fear gripped his gut. Was someone at the door to tell him something had happened to her? Had her car broken down by the side of the road and…

He inhaled deeply as he rushed to the window and looked out. He quickly let out a deep breath of relief when he saw it was Gavin's SUV out front. He had totally forgotten that he had called Gavin earlier and asked him to stop by.

He walked over to the door and opened it. "Evening, Sheriff." Mark was tall but Gavin O'Neal was taller, which was something Mark couldn't help but notice when the man walked into the house.

"Mark. Sorry it took so long for me to get here but I had to transport a prisoner to Midland. You indicated when you called that you may have found something out at the Wind-crofts' place today."

"Yes," Mark said as he crossed the room to retrieve the bag he had placed in his desk drawer. "Like I told you, it's a syringe. I know syringes are used in the breeding of horses but this one is the kind used in hospitals for human injections."

Gavin took the clear plastic bag Mark handed him and studied the syringe inside of it. "Did you mention you had found this to Nita?"

Mark shook his head. "No, I didn't mention it to anyone. Luckily I was alone when I found it."

Gavin nodded. "Good. The last thing we need is word getting out and people speculating whether or not it's connected to Jonathan's murder since it's all around town that he was killed with some sort of lethal injection. The lab is closed tonight but I'll have it to them first thing in the morning. It shouldn't take long for them to analyze it and get back to us. I hope to have their report at our club meeting on Wednesday night."

"Here's a list of names of Nita's entire clientele, which includes anyone using her breeding services, those she's giving riding lessons to, as well as everyone who boards their horses in her stables."

Gavin let out a whistle as he accepted the pages from Mark. "It seems she does a lot of business."

"Yes, which is the main reason she wants us to do something to stop what's going on. If word gets out that she's being harassed, she can start losing business. People will be afraid to patronize her."

"You have a point there," Gavin said, glancing down at his watch. "I hate to run but I need to get by the Royal Diner for a cup of coffee before they close."

Mark lifted an eyebrow knowing that a cup of coffee wasn't the only interest Gavin had at the diner. He tried hiding his smile when he said, "You're in luck, Sheriff. I just made a fresh pot and you're welcome to a cup if you like."

Gavin shot him a quick apologetic look, and then said, "Ah, sorry, no offense, I'm sure your coffee is decent but I like the diner's coffee better. Thanks for the offer though." He quickly headed for the door.

Mark chuckled as he locked the door behind Gavin, thinking that, whether or not Gavin realized it, he was definitely acting like a man smitten.

Alli opened the door and breezed through it still feeling elated. She had gotten an A on her paper tonight and she was thrilled. Professor Jones was a stickler for grades and she was trying hard to make it through the end of the semester without getting on his bad side the way a lot of the other students were doing.

Taking classes part-time was bad enough and she didn't envy her sister one bit with her full load, which was one of the main reasons she didn't want Kara to lose focus on her studies. The only good thing, Alli thought, about her own personal situation was that she could finally see a light at the end of the tunnel. Taking two classes for the next four semesters—even though it meant going to school year-round—and she could be graduating in December of next year.

"You're back."

Alli whirled around clutching her chest. Mark had practically scared the living daylights out of her. She watched as he straightened away from the wall and emerged out of the shadows to stand in front of her.

She met his gaze as she forced her heartbeat back to normal. "Yes, I'm back."

She stared at him. He was wearing a pair of blue silk pajamas and a matching bathrobe. "I didn't expect to see you," she said quickly as she tried not to stare, but she'd always thought that blue was his color. "I thought you'd be in bed."

"I was but my throat got dry and I decided to get up for a glass of water."

"Oh."

"And how was class?"

She wanted to say that her class was none of his business. But since Hartman's Self-Defense Studio's tuition-aid policy was paying a percentage of her college expenses, he did have a right to know how the investment was paying off. "Class was great tonight and I got an A on my paper," she said excitedly.

He smiled. "That's great."

"Thanks."

"You, Erika and I will have to celebrate."

Alli lifted an eyebrow. "Celebrate?"

"Yes. I think it's something worth celebrating. It's not easy to get an A on a paper in college these days."

"Yes, but—"

"Then it's settled. Erika and I usually eat at the Royal Diner on Friday evenings and we invite you to join us."

Alli stared down at the floor as she thought about his invitation. She looked up and met his gaze. Her mouth tightened briefly. "How does dinner with you and Erika fall under the category of an employer-employee relationship?"

A smile touched the corners of Mark's lips. "That's easy enough to define," he said simply. "I've hired you to take care of my niece and as her nanny you'll be there enjoying a meal with us." He held her gaze for a moment, then he asked, "Does that suit you?"

Alli inhaled deeply. No, that didn't suit her, not after he had made it absolutely clear that he wanted distance between them. Having dinner with him tomorrow night was not keeping distance. "If I remember correctly we agreed that I would have Friday and Saturday evenings off," she said, reminding him of that fact.

He slanted her a glance that looked as if he might argue the point. Then he said, "You're right. I had forgotten about that. The three of us will have to celebrate some other time, perhaps."

"Perhaps. Now if you'll excuse me, I want to check on Erika before I go to bed."

Without giving him a chance to say anything else, she quickly walked out of the room.

Mark lay in bed and sucked in a sharp breath as soon as he heard the shower come on in the bedroom next to his. It didn't take much to visualize Alli undressing—first, taking off the dress she had worn to school, followed by her slip, bra and panties. Then stepping beneath the pounding spray of warm water as it cascaded over her body, soaking her face and running rivulets down her neck to flow over her breasts.

He further imagined that at some point she would grab hold of one of those bottles of shower gel that he had seen her unpack yesterday and dab an ample amount in the palms of her hands to rub generously over her body, starting with her flat stomach, then moving upward to her breasts, making circles around her nipples, coming back lower to massage her curves, before reaching down to her thighs and then the area between her legs and…

He bolted up, unable to handle the vision any longer. Why couldn't he follow her lead and accept what he himself had decreed regarding their relationship? *Strictly professional.* She had accepted his dictate and moved on. It seemed that he was the one who had issues. Such as with Jake going to the dealership with her to purchase a new car instead of Mark.

He dropped back down in bed thinking, *Fat chance of that happening!* She was his employee. He was the one who had given her the bonus for the down payment on the car. If anyone deserved to be there when she purchased a new vehicle, it was him. Satisfied he had reached that conclusion, he decided he would contact Jake tomorrow…on behalf of his employee. And what was the problem if she considered him a friend as well? A lot of bosses had friendly yet professional relationships with their staff.

Mark lay down, wondering why that thought hadn't occurred to him before. Probably because over the past two years he had been too busy fighting his attraction to her. What he should have been doing was getting to know her as a friend on a professional level. There was no law that said she couldn't be his assistant as well as his friend. It would definitely relieve some of the tension he felt when they worked together, and it would contribute to a more comfortable environment regardless of whether it was at his home or at the studio.

So, as far as he was concerned, there was no reason the two of them couldn't get better acquainted while she was staying in his house, as long as they established boundaries. And the first thing he had to do was get rid of any and all lustful thoughts about Alli that were plaguing him.

With that decision made, he felt a lot better and snuggled

under the covers, pulling the pillow over his head. As sleep came down upon him, his earlier imaginings returned and invaded his unconscious mind.

It was the vision of Alli in the shower.

Alli stepped out of the shower and grabbed a towel to dry herself. She had been excited about her grade from Professor Jones until Mark had made the suggestion that she join him and Erika for dinner tomorrow night. There was no way she could do that and have people speculating that she had designs on her boss. She had loved him secretly for two years without anyone having a clue and she intended to keep things that way.

She knew after what he'd said on their way over to the Windcrofts' place that nothing would ever develop between them. He saw her as his employee and nothing more. At least she would have memories of the one and only time they'd kissed—how he'd held her in his arms, how his mouth had moved over hers and how her mouth had parted instinctively when he had inserted his tongue. And when he had deepened the kiss, taken her mouth with a skill and a mastery she hadn't known existed, she had felt sensations and emotions unlike any she'd had before. And now, although she was still damp from her shower, she could feel heat flow through her belly and settle right smack between her thighs.

She sighed so deeply it was almost a moan deep in her throat. She would always remember the taste of him, a taste she was dying to sample again, but knew there was no way that she ever would.

She would have to be satisfied with her memories.

Chapter 7

Mark walked into the kitchen the next morning in a much better mood than he'd been in the night before. Immediately his eyes lit on Alli. She was standing in front of the high chair, showing Erika how to hold her spoon properly, and was dressed in a T-shirt that advertised Hartman's Self-Defense Studio and a pair of black walking shorts.

He shook his head and smiled. Even now, she was trying to keep her attire modest and professional. He had discovered a long time ago that it didn't matter what type of clothing Alison Lind placed on her body—she would still look delectable. The red-and-white T-shirt was tucked inside her shorts and emphasized her small waist and curvy hips. And her shorts showed enough of her long, slender legs to remind him of the visions that had taken over his dreams last night. In all his twenty-eight years, he had never dreamed about a woman taking a bath.

His dream had alternated with visions of her bath and of him kissing her. He had kissed her so much that she had begged him to make love to her. And he'd been about to do just that when his alarm had gone off.

Sighing deeply, he forced his gaze from Alli to his niece. Erika seemed to be enjoying Alli's instructions. He couldn't help but notice how his niece was dressed. Since Alli's arrival two days ago, Erika's hair was combed differently, in a cute little style, and she wore ribbons and bows to coordinate with whatever outfit she had on that day, not to mention the matching socks.

As he leaned against the wall, he had to admit that the way Erika was dressed was just one of many noticeable changes Alli had made in less than seventy-two hours. His niece seemed to smile even more. She ate home-cooked oatmeal instead of the instant kind, and Alli had no problems cooking a full-course breakfast whenever his niece muttered the word *egg*.

Then there was the scent that always emitted from Alli's bedroom whenever he passed it. It was a feminine scent. A woman's scent. More than once he had paused in the hallway outside her door to get his bearings and to remind himself that a woman was now in residence…as if he really needed reminding. There was no way he could forget that Alli was in his house.

"Da-da!"

He couldn't help but smile when two pairs of eyes lit on him. From Alli's expression it was plain that she was surprised to see him. Had she forgotten that he lived here? "Good morning," he said coming into the room.

"Good morning. I thought you were gone," Alli said still

eyeing him strangely. "When I got up and looked out the window I saw your truck driving away."

He nodded, now understanding her confusion. "John is using my truck to pick up supplies. His is in the shop getting repaired."

"Oh." She then turned her attention back to Erika. He felt dismissed and ignored when she began talking to Erika and telling her how good oatmeal was for her.

He walked across the room and his niece's attention switched from Alli to him and she extended her arms for him to pick her up. "Da-da."

He gently tweaked her cheek, then said, "No, sweetheart, I'm Mark. And Alli needs to feed you so you can grow up to be big, strong and healthy like your daddy was."

"She won't understand the name thing until she gets a little older, Mark," Alli said, standing beside him. He glanced at her. Instead of looking back at him, she kept her gaze focused on Erika, but he didn't miss the guarded look on Alli's face, as if she were protecting herself from something. He couldn't help wondering just what that something was.

She walked toward the sink. "I'm taking Erika with me on an outing today," she said over her shoulder.

"Oh? Where are you ladies going?"

She turned around. The guarded look had been replaced with a bright smile. "Car shopping. I thought I'd take the time to look around today so that when Jake meets with me tomorrow I'll have an idea of the type of vehicle I want."

He nodded. "That's a good idea, however there's a problem with that."

She lifted an eyebrow. "What?"

"I spoke to Jake earlier this morning about TCC business, and he mentioned all the things he has going on this weekend. It seems that someone has pulled up his campaign signs and he and his workers are going to be busy tomorrow going around town replacing them."

Seeing her disappointed look, he added, "I told him you would understand and that since I was free tomorrow I'd be glad to go with you."

"But, but I thought that—"

"For me to go car shopping with you is perfectly fine," he rushed on to assure her. "No matter what, we still need to maintain a friendly working relationship, right?"

"Yes, but—"

"Then it's settled. I'll go with you tomorrow and I don't want you to worry about a thing. All right?"

Reluctantly she nodded.

"Good. Now I hope you ladies enjoy your day."

He smiled as he quickly walked out of the kitchen, not giving her the chance to say anything.

Mark looked at the sporty SUV and then at Alli. He raised an eyebrow. "Are you sure this is the vehicle you want?"

She smiled brightly. "Yes, I'm sure. Erika and I saw it yesterday and the man was nice enough to let me give it a test drive and I love it. I know it doesn't look like me but this is what I want."

She was right. It didn't look like her. He hadn't pegged her as the sports-utility-vehicle type. She looked like someone who would drive a car similar to the one she had now—a low-key four-door sedan. The vehicle she had selected, with its leather seats, sunroof, state-of-the-art sound system, just to name a few of the features, was definitely sporty.

Sighing, he turned to the salesman who'd been waiting patiently. "This is the one she'll take. And I want you to work up the best deal along with the best payment terms. Understand?"

The man smiled eagerly. "Yes, Mr. Hartman. Mr. Cross said you were a personal friend of his and to make sure we take care of you right."

Mark nodded. He and Stan Cross had gone to high school together and Mark had been glad when Alli had mentioned the vehicle she wanted was at this particular dealership. "Now we have two reasons to celebrate and I would like to invite you to dine with me and Erika at the Royal Diner."

"I thought you and Erika ate at the Royal Diner yesterday," she said, placing Erika back into the stroller. Alli had stayed at her own house last night to do some more packing, and had been glad to see Erika when she had arrived at the ranch this morning. And although she didn't want to admit it, she had been glad to see Mark as well.

"No matter how often you eat there, the food is always good," Mark said grinning. "So how about it? After spending so much fun time with you, I believe Erika is beginning to peg me as a bore. Whenever I look after her, she goes to bed early."

Alli held his gaze and her pulse quickened at the teasing warmth she saw in his hazel eyes. She would love go to out to eat with him and Erika but she didn't want to cause problems regarding their working relationship. "Are you sure it will be okay if we were to go to dinner together?"

Mark nodded. A part of him regretted he'd ever had that conversation with her. "Yes, I'm sure. So how about if we finalize the paperwork for your new vehicle and then we can meet up at the diner?"

Alli smiled. "All right."

* * *

The tinkle of the little gold bell that hung over the entrance door of the Royal Diner signaled Alli's arrival. The diner was your typical family café that didn't serve alcoholic beverages. The waitresses wore pink short-sleeve polyester dresses with well-above-the-knee hems and tailored collars and small white aprons.

The diner wasn't the best-looking place in town, with its worn and cracked dull-gray linoleum floor and the faded red plastic booth seats, as well as the scratched chrome strips that edged the tabletops, but the food—thanks to a cook by the name of Manny Reno—was mouthwateringly delicious.

Alli could almost smell his famous coconut-cream pie the moment she walked through the door. She glanced around and saw Mark waving to get her attention. She couldn't help but grin when she saw Erika following her uncle's lead and waving as well. Alli made her way around the long Formica counter toward the booth in the back.

The jukebox was playing a Ray Charles tune and, as expected, the diner was packed. It seemed that regardless of whether you were rich or poor, the Royal Diner was the place to be on Saturday evening and Manny's sinfully juicy hamburgers and coconut-cream pie were the hot items on the menu.

As Alli glanced across the room at Mark, she thought he was hot off the menu. She may not know a lot about the intimacies men and women shared, but she could recognize sexual tension and it seemed that whenever the two of them were together the air was full of it.

Every time she saw him, no matter the time or the place, she was reminded of their kiss, the feel of his mouth on hers, and how she had returned the kiss with everything she had, becoming rocked by sensations that still flooded her.

And she was frightened by them.

She didn't want to think about what might happen if those sensations continued to consume her. Now that she and Mark had had their talk, she wanted to do the right thing, which meant she needed to stop thinking about the one time they had made a mistake, as he'd put it, and crossed over boundaries that they shouldn't have.

Mark stood when she reached the booth. "Sorry, I'm late but I wanted to cruise awhile and try out everything," she said taking the seat across from him. Erika was sitting in a toddler seat next to Mark.

Mark sat back down and grinned. "And how does it drive?"

She gave him a cheeky smile. "Like a charm. I love it and it's so easy to maneuver. I can't wait for Kara to see it."

He smiled at her. "When will she be home?"

"I'm hoping next weekend. She's carrying a full load this semester and has a lot of studying to do." A few moments later she said, "I miss her."

Mark leaned back in his seat. He knew how close Alli and her sister were. "I may not have ever told you this, Alli, but I think you did a remarkable job raising her. I'm sure it wasn't easy."

"No," she agreed, "it wasn't. But if I had it to do all over again, I would. Kara was such a swell kid, but that didn't mean we didn't have our moments," she said grinning. "I thought I would never talk her out of getting her nose pierced." Alli didn't want to think of what could turn out to be her next crisis with Kara. Alli couldn't wait until she talked to Kara tomorrow to see how her date with the hottie had gone. "But

I can't see Erika ever getting her nose pierced, do you?" she asked teasingly as she put thoughts of Kara from her mind.

Mark's eyes flashed with amusement as he glanced over at Erika, who was busy playing with a toy one of the waitresses had given her. "No, but I wonder what the fad is going to be when Erika reaches her teen years."

"Trust me, you don't want to know," Alli said chuckling.

Mark laughed. "You're probably right. We'll just have to wait and see."

Alli's heartbeat quickened. He had said it as though he expected her to be around during that time. Did he think she would still be working for him then? She didn't have time to ponder that question when a waitress walked up to take their order.

"Good afternoon, everyone."

Alli looked at the attractive waitress with the golden-blond hair and periwinkle-blue eyes who handed them plastic-coated menus. "Hello."

When the woman leaned over to fill their glasses with water, Alli noticed that a pendant that had been tucked inside her dress slipped out. Alli thought the piece of jewelry, a heart that was etched with two intertwining roses, was simply beautiful. When the waitress walked off, Alli couldn't help wondering if the pendant had sentimental value like the one she was wearing, which had belonged to her mother.

"Gavin has a thing for her."

Mark's words jarred her attention. "For who?"

He smiled. "Our waitress. Her name is Valerie Raines and she arrived in town a few months ago. Gavin has a thing for her."

Alli lifted an arched eyebrow. "Sheriff Gavin O'Neal?"

Mark chuckled. "Yes. He makes sure he comes here every

night for coffee. Before she arrived in town he didn't consume it as much as he does now." He chuckled again. "If he's not careful he might be headed for an addiction of another kind."

Alli nodded. She wondered if there was a particular woman out there that Mark had a *thing* for. She was well aware that he dated occasionally since she often screened the phone calls he received at the studio. He'd been known to date a number of gorgeous women and just last year his name had been linked to a senator's daughter. But all that had changed after he'd gotten Erika. His social life had practically become nonexistent.

"Do you have any idea what you want to order?"

She looked up from the menu. "I think I'll get a hamburger, a peach milkshake and for dessert, a slice of Manny's coconut-cream pie."

Mark set aside his menu. "I think I'm going to have the same."

"I think we wore her out," Mark said as he entered his home with a sleeping Erika in his arms.

"Hmm, it seems that way doesn't it? I think the circus did it."

As they were leaving the diner, Manny had called Mark over and given him tickets to the circus that was in Midland. Since Midland wasn't too far away, Mark thought it would be the perfect opportunity to put Alli's SUV on the road to break it in.

Instead of leaving his truck at the diner, he had left it in the Cattleman's Club parking lot. It was the first time Mark had been a passenger while Alli was a driver. On the way back, he had done the driving and had made a number of positive comments on how impressed he was with the way she had handled her new vehicle.

"Let me get her ready for bed," Alli said, taking Erika out of his arms. They touched in the process and the sexual tension that had been humming between them all evening increased.

"Do you need help with her?" Mark asked throatily, hoping Alli would say no. He needed to put distance between them to get his bearings. The conversation during the drive to and from Midland had been enjoyable, but he had been fully aware of the chemistry that stirred whenever they were together, and being in such close quarters hadn't helped. The spark he'd felt just now when she had taken Erika from him was almost too much.

"No, I can handle her all by myself," Alli said, cradling the sleeping baby in her arms. "Thanks for going with me to pick up my truck and thanks, too, for dinner and the circus. I had a wonderful time."

He nodded. "And I had a good time, too."

He wouldn't admit that he had spent most of his time watching her. As usual, she looked good and the skirt and blouse she was wearing emphasized her curves to perfection. The hem of the skirt was short enough to show off what he considered the best-looking legs he'd ever seen on a woman. He hated admitting it, but during the entire evening his mind had been filled with erotic fantasies of those legs wrapped around him while they made love. To his chagrin and dismay, he had been thinking about that a lot lately. Despite his effort, the fact that she was his employee was slowly fading to the background.

"Good night, Mark. I'll see you in the morning."

"Good night, Alli. I'll see you in the morning as well. "

As soon as she entered Erika's bedroom and closed the

door, he quickly moved down the hallway, desperately needing the privacy and seclusion that he would find in his own bedroom.

Mark couldn't sleep. He had tried counting sheep, pigs, cattle and even little lambs, and nothing did the trick. It didn't help matters that earlier he had heard the sound of the shower in Alli's room again, and those visions that had played havoc on his mind two nights ago came storming back. At least the house was quiet, which meant she had settled down and one of them was getting some sleep.

But it seemed that sleep wasn't coming his way. He was sentenced to lie in bed wide awake and fight this overpowering physical attraction that he felt for her. Physical attraction, hell! What he was beginning to feel was need, deep-in-the-gut need that a man felt for a woman he wanted. Alli was intensely woman, seductively female. No matter how much he tried, he couldn't ignore the way his body, his entire being, was craving another taste of her. It didn't take much to remember the feel of her mouth beneath his, soft, hot, delicious, and the texture of her skin, smooth and creamy, whenever he touched her. Then there had been the feel of her breasts, lush and firm, when they had pressed up against his chest. And last but not least, there was something about her smile. He was inherently drawn to it. The one she gave Erika was different than the one she gave him, which wasn't as easy and open, but nevertheless, it did things to him.

He changed positions and tried rearranging his pillows. Tomorrow was Sunday and with Alli in the house to take care of Erika, he would get to sleep late. But a part of him didn't want to sleep late. He wanted to get up and see Erika and Alli, have breakfast with them and spend time with them.

He didn't want to admit it but he had enjoyed their company today, and Alli's presence had been like a breath of fresh air. Unlike other women he'd dated, she didn't try to impress him. She had been able to make an impact by merely being herself.

Seeing that sleep was impossible, he got out of bed, slipped into his pajama bottoms and decided to go into the kitchen to get something to drink.

Alli couldn't sleep and decided to get up to check on Erika. She was easing out of the baby's room, closing the door behind herself, when she stopped, the cool wood floor beneath her bare feet suddenly feeling warm. She tensed, abruptly turned and her gaze collided with Mark's as he walked out of his bedroom.

For a long moment their gazes held, connected, interlocked with a fierce tension. Even from the few feet that separated them, she could smell his scent, and seeing him dressed in a pair of low-slung gray pajama bottoms wasn't helping matters. Not when his bare chest reminded her of when they had collided that morning he'd been about to shave.

And now, like then, her body tingled with full awareness of him as a man.

"I thought you were in bed asleep," Mark said, almost in a whisper.

She swallowed, trying to get both her brain and her mouth to function, and knew she needed to stop staring at his chest, especially the way a thin, hairy line made a path downward to disappear in the waistband of his pajamas. "I decided to check on Erika," she somehow managed to say.

Concern touched his features and he covered the distance

to stand in front of her. "Why? Was something wrong? Is she okay?"

Erika is fine. I'm the one about to go up in flames, she wanted to say, meeting his gaze. "No, she's okay. I couldn't sleep and decided to check on her."

"Oh, I see."

Alli doubted that he did, but that was okay. Right now she needed to escape to her bedroom and fast. "Well, I'd better go back to bed. Good night."

"Good night, Alli." He stepped back to let her pass but then, driven by a need he didn't understand, he reached out and touched her arm.

Mark felt it the moment their flesh connected, that spark. He heard the quick intake of her breath and knew she had felt it, too. And if that wasn't bad enough, the air around them seemed to change. It got thicker, overpowering, and pulsated with sexual energy of the most potent kind. He could breathe it, smell it, almost taste it.

The same way he desperately wanted to taste her.

Acting on something greater than instinct and driven by a need that suddenly took control of his entire body, he leaned down and captured her lips, urging and coaxing them to part under his, then tempting her tongue with his own. His fingers tangled in her hair as he held her immobile, determined to get his fill of what had been the cause of his sleepless nights.

His tongue took hers in firm strokes and when he heard a whimper from deep within her throat, he deepened the kiss, pulled her closer to the fit of him, flexed his hips and rocked hard against her, wanting her to know just what she was doing to him.

He refused to ease the pressure he was placing on her mouth and with each fragmented moan she released, he deepened the kiss more, fighting the thought that although this kiss was as good as it got, there was something else here, something he was feeling that went beyond sexual.

The sudden need to breathe overrode his urgency to continue tasting her and he slowly let go, but he didn't pull back, nor did he stop kissing her completely. His tongue made slow, teasing strokes to each corner of her mouth and he felt the deep shudder that passed through her.

"We broke the rules again, didn't we?" she said softly, releasing a shaky breath and burying her face in his chest.

He inhaled deeply as his arms tightened around her. She sounded so disappointed, so sad, and her entire body was trembling.

"I'm sorry, Mark. I allowed things to get out of hand again. I'll pack my things and leave in the morning."

Her words infiltrated his heat-infested mind and the beating of his heart almost stopped. Did she actually blame herself for this?

He sighed deeply and pulled her closer. No one was to blame, especially not her. Yes, they had broken the rules again, but at this point it didn't matter because he intended for them to keep breaking them. He didn't care about the strictly professional relationship they were supposed to have anymore. He knew that he might be making one of the biggest mistakes of his life, but he wanted her, this woman, in his arms, his bed. He wanted her to have an in-depth, intimate knowledge of him and he wanted an in-depth, intimate knowledge of her.

"Alli, look at me," he whispered softly.

It took a while but she finally lifted her head and met his gaze. "Now tell me, what do you see?"

Alli silently searched his face. What she saw was a very

handsome man; a man with a big heart and a lot of love to share. But he was trying desperately to keep that love shut up inside. He was a man who could love with a passion if only he allowed himself to let go. He was also a man who cared but was determined to keep his emotions buried and unexposed. But what she saw more than anything was the man she had fallen in love with two years ago. A part of her wanted to expose those hidden emotions within him, bring them out in the open and destroy the heart-wrenching pain that engulfed his world. Then it hit her. She felt it and couldn't ignore it. Absurd as it might seem, for the moment, she believed it.

Mark needed her.

She inhaled deeply and finally responded by making him think about his own question. "You tell me what I *should* see, Mark."

Time stood still as he gazed at her, saying nothing, then after drawing in a ragged breath, he said, "You should see a man who doesn't give a damn about rules right now. A man who will have no regrets tomorrow. What you should see is a man who desperately wants you, who has wanted you for a long time and at this moment he can't breathe another breath unless he has you, in his arms, in his bed."

Knowing he had to be completely honest with her, he continued to speak. "I can't make you promises and I won't. I don't want, nor am I looking for, a serious, lasting relationship, which is the main reason I never wanted to become involved with you. But if you allow me, I'll introduce you to all the pleasures that a man and a woman can share. Pleasures you've denied yourself and pleasures I've denied myself as well. I haven't been with anyone for over a year, Alli, because every woman I dated I wanted to be you. I've wanted you that much."

Emotions clogged Alli's throat. In no way was he saying that he cared anything about her. In fact, he was letting her know that commitment of any kind was out of the question. But what he'd said touched her. He wanted her, and although there weren't promises of forever, she felt drawn to him nonetheless.

"I know that considering everything I've just said, I don't have any rights to ask anything of you, so I won't," he said, reclaiming her thoughts. "I'm going back to my room so you can think about what I'm offering. If you decide to accept my terms, then come to me. You don't have to knock, just open the door and walk on in."

He swallowed deeply and then said, "If you decide not to come, I'll understand. The decision is yours."

Before Alli could say anything, he had turned, reentered his bedroom and softly closed the door behind himself.

Alli breathed deeply. Mark was wrong. The decision wasn't hers. It belonged to her heart.

Chapter 8

She wasn't coming.

Mark blinked, realizing that his gaze had been riveted on his bedroom door ever since he had left Alli standing in the hall. He glanced at the clock on the nightstand. Twenty minutes had passed.

His stomach tumbled in disappointment, but he accepted her decision. After all, he wasn't offering her anything except pleasure and for her that might not be enough.

But that was all he could give her.

He had made sure he thoroughly explained that, not wanting to take a chance on there being any misunderstandings. A misunderstanding would not be a good situation for either of them. He had wanted her to know the score.

Knowing sleep was impossible, he threw back the covers and got out of bed to walk over to the window that overlooked the back of his property. From the moon's satiny glow, he could see the outlines of the meadows and valleys that were Hartman land. As a child he had loved it here, but as a teenager he had counted the days before he could leave. Both he and Matt had sworn never to return as long as their old man had lived. And they never had.

Mark's body jolted to attention when he heard his bedroom door opening and he held his breath, too afraid to turn around for fear he had just imagined the sound. But moments later when he heard the soft sound of bare footsteps touching the wood floor, and inhaled the scent that was distinctively Alli, he knew he wasn't imagining things.

With his pulse racing a mile a minute, he forced back the surge of desire that rammed his body as he slowly turned around. His gaze went to her face and watched as a nervous smile touched her lips.

"I'm here," she whispered softly, and the seductively quiet voice sent his pulse racing even more.

His breath hitched and the only words he could manage to say while his brain seemed not to be functioning were, "Thank you for coming."

His gaze then took in what she was wearing. She had changed from the tea-length nightgown and matching robe she'd had on earlier to a more seductive outfit. Now she was wearing a very short, red silk sleep shirt that did more than just complement her chocolate-brown skin. And with her five-eight height and long, gorgeous legs, the outfit looked both feminine and sexy on her.

"I didn't think you were coming," he said huskily, abruptly aware that the room was filled with the sound of their uneven breathing.

She smiled wryly and he saw the nervousness begin to

ease from her features. "I wanted to put on something that I thought would be more appropriate."

Doesn't matter since I plan to remove every stitch from you, he thought, slowly dropping his gaze to rake it over her. Moments later he was staring back into the beautiful face that had haunted his dreams for nearly two years; whether he had wanted it to or not.

Is she sure about this? he wondered, as he swallowed the lump that suddenly appeared in his throat. He had to be certain. "Are you positive this is what you want?" he asked in a slightly hoarse voice.

"Yes, I'm positive." She lifted her chin and what he saw almost took his breath away. The same desire that he knew was lining his features was also lining hers. Tonight she had more to lose than he did, since he was fairly certain, could probably bet his ranch on it, that the woman standing before him was still a virgin. It all made sense. The way she always seemed unsure of herself when they kissed and how she would let him take the lead and eagerly followed. But then he had to admit, tonight would mean a lot to him as well. He had never introduced sexual pleasures to a virgin and hoped that he went above and beyond her expectations.

He decided to set the tone for what was about to follow. "If you're absolutely certain, come here."

With her gaze still holding his, she padded over to him. "Closer," he whispered as her soft feminine scent filtered into his nostrils. He watched her swallow, saw the thickness in her throat when she took another couple of steps, bringing her nearly face-to-face with him. But as far as he was concerned, that wasn't close enough.

"Closer," he whispered lower still.

She lifted an eyebrow, obviously confused. If she took another step, she would be all on top of him. A smile touched the corners of his mouth. That was the idea.

Mark watched as she drew a quivering breath and when she took another step, he automatically widened his stance and, as he'd known, she fit perfectly, positioning herself between his legs. He wanted her to feel the size of his erection and this way she couldn't miss it. And from the sudden look that appeared on her face, she hadn't.

The feel of Mark's erection pressed large, hard and throbbing against her middle sent a deep ache through Alli's body. It was an ache for something she couldn't name but wanted just the same. When she had eased between his open legs, her nightshirt had risen up past her thighs, beyond what was decent, and provided a provocative glimpse of her matching bikini panties. A surge of heat ripped through her and all she could think about was the degree of passion he was making her feel. To want him this much and be this close to having him were things she had only experienced in her dreams. Now she had to concede that reality was a whole lot better.

She had decided to do this, to become his lover for tonight, tomorrow, for however long he wanted. He might think of it as animal attraction, lust, an uncontrollable yearning or overwhelming desire, but for her she knew it was love. She loved this man with every ounce of her being and if this would be all they would ever share, then she was willing to make do. But just as he had given her a choice tonight, when it was time for her to leave she would give him the chance to make a choice as well. She believed that behind the stone wall surrounding his heart was the loving kindness of the man she knew he was.

"Feel it?"

His question jolted her to attention. She met his gaze. It was intense, hypnotic, arousing. She didn't doubt for an instant just what he was asking. "Yes, I feel it."

"Would you like to have it?"

She hesitated a second; not that she wasn't sure that she wanted it, but because she was surprised he would ask. She sucked in a deep breath when it seemed the throbbing tempo of the erection pressed against her increased and the size of it got larger. She tilted her head. "Yes, most definitely."

She watched as a smile touched his lips. "I hope you know what you're getting into because I plan to get all into you," he whispered huskily, before leaning down and kissing her with an urgency that almost made her swoon.

The way his tongue was taking her had desire—as potent as it could get—seeping into her pores, making her want things she never had before. And not knowing how it was possible, he pulled her closer to the fit of him as silk rubbed against silk, flesh against flesh, heat against heat. She felt it the instant he slid his hands up her thighs while deepening the kiss at the same time. She felt his fingers work their way beneath her shirt then inch toward the edge of her panties.

While changing clothes, she had been tempted to leave them off, which would have had her completely bare to his hands at this point. But it seemed nothing was going to stop him and he intended to have her bare anyway. And when his fingers eased past the waistband on her panties and he touched her intimately, she knew how it felt to place oneself in a man's hands.

She was wet, drenched, Mark thought as his fingers found their mark and gently eased inside of her. He shifted positions, widening his legs, as well as hers. He fought for control, clung to his last ounce of willpower when the moans she began making filled the room. The scent of her aroused body was permeating the air and it was like an aphrodisiac, stimulating every cell within him and amplifying his libido.

And then she did something he hadn't expected and wasn't prepared for. She shifted her body, reached out and wiggled her small hand into the opening of his silk pajama bottoms and grabbed hold of him. He could tell she was just as surprised by her actions as he was. But in no way did he intend to discourage her. Unlike her, he didn't have on a stitch of clothing beneath and all he could think about was the feel of her soft hand on his hard shaft. When she began running her fingers down the length of him, as if she needed to find out for herself what his erection was all about, he almost lost it.

With an animal groan that erupted deep from within his throat, he swept her into his arms. Never in his life had he ached so much for a woman and, clinging to his last shred of self-control, he carried her over to his bed.

Alli buried her face into Mark's hair-covered chest, now fully understanding how if felt to be swept off her feet. From the moment she had walked into his room, he had made her feel like the most desired woman in the world. Now being engulfed in his strong arms, she felt doubly so.

When he placed her on the bed and joined her there, she knew her endurance was about to be tested. He reached out and began unbuttoning her shirt and then removed it from her body, leaving her clad only in her panties. She wondered if he realized that he was staggering her senses.

He raised high above her, after letting his gaze roam over her near-naked body, his hazel eyes locked on her face. "If I do or suggest doing anything you aren't comfortable with, promise that you'll let me know," he whispered huskily as he brushed her hair aside and moved his lips closer to her ear.

"I promise."

Her body began shuddering when the palm of his hand moved slowly down her bare arms at the same time his warm breath trailed over her neck. "And I want you to promise if I tell you *not* to stop that you won't," she whispered, feeling herself lose what little control she'd been holding on to.

She felt the imprint of his smile against her neck. "You sure about that?"

"Positive."

"I don't think you know what you'll be asking for," he said, swathing her neck with a series of wet butterfly kisses.

"Yes, I do," she whispered when his mouth started moving lower. "I'll be asking for more of you."

He lifted his head, met her eyes and penetrated them with a deep intensity. "I promise," he whispered. And then, as if in slow motion, he connected his mouth to hers.

In Alli's mind this kiss was different. Using the tip of his tongue, he invaded, teased and explored every corner, nook and crevice of her mouth, especially those areas she hadn't been aware were insanely sensitive until now. And with every movement of his tongue, he elicited her reaction; he seemed to feed on it and, in no time at all, he had her moaning out sounds she wasn't aware she was capable of making.

The multitude of what she was feeling stunned her, captivated her and filled her with a need that was all consuming.

As slowly as he had entered her mouth, he was pulling out, but didn't go far. He trailed kisses down her neck, easing down her chest and, when his lips came to her breasts, he pulled her close and took one into this mouth, licking, sucking and nibbling, one then the other.

No man had ever touched her there, let alone kissed her, and the feel of Mark's mouth on her nipples—as well as what he was doing to them—had her sucking in deep breaths. Winding her arms around his neck, he intensified his mouth tugging on her, making her feel erotic sensations all the way to her toes. He had a very talented mouth, she quickly concluded, and when he finally pulled back, she suddenly felt a deep sense of loss.

"You taste good," he whispered, the intensity in his eyes making her even hotter. "And I want to get inside of you, Alli."

The heat of his words, uttered so close to her ear, made her skin vibrate and her stomach quicken in anticipation. "And I want you, Mark," she whispered back, still swooning from the drugging sensations of his kisses to her mouth and breasts.

"I want to make sure you're completely ready for me, baby."

She met his gaze, wondering why he would do that when her body was already overheated. "Remember your promise," he whispered softly as he leaned down and his lips began skimming softly, gently, heated over her bare flesh. He stopped when he reached her navel and plied it with wet kisses that brought her to complete awareness.

While Mark had her full attention, Alli was aware that he was removing her panties, and he pulled back slightly to ease them down her legs. Then he stood and she watched as he eased his pajama bottoms from his body, and they became a puddle at the foot of the bed. The lamp in the room gave her enough light to see him and she began breathing hard. Never had she thought that a male's body could be so beautiful, so well defined and so masculine. She had thought he was built before, but now, seeing him completely naked sent a delicious shiver all the way through her.

She wanted to reach out and touch him, run her hands down the expanse of his hairy chest, along the muscles of his shoulders, and as her gaze moved lower to that part of him that she had brazenly touched earlier, she inhaled deeply at the size, wondering how on earth…

She blinked when he moved and reached over to the nightstand, opened the drawer and pulled out a condom packet. Anticipation ran rampant through her as he put it on.

Then he lifted his head and their eyes met. The way he looked at her made erotic sensations engulf her. He joined her on the bed again. Leaning back on his haunches, he continued to look at her. Instead of making her nervous and embarrassed about not having on a stitch of clothing, she was eagerly anticipating his next move.

He made it.

He leaned down and slipped his hand between her thighs, touching her intimately. She sucked in a deep breath when he gently inserted a finger inside of her, and instinctively her hips moved, her thighs opened to accommodate him.

If she thought he had a talented mouth, then his fingers were a close second. She began feeling dazed at the way he was making her feel with each movement. The feelings it was evoking within her were beyond belief and, when he drove a little deeper and touched an area inside of her that had to be some type of pleasure point to make her body feel this way, she felt a gush of blood rush through all parts of her, centering right where his finger was located. The intensity of it caused her moan almost to become a sob. Never had she been so unreservedly aroused before.

"I think you're ready for me now."

She met the intensity of his gaze, thinking that she'd been ready…for nearly two years. Long ago she had made up her mind to have him if he ever made the move. She was tired of living a lonely unexciting life. She wanted to share this most intimate and personal act with the man she loved. And although he might not love her, tonight he was making her feel wanted, desired and beautiful.

Before she could think another thing, he eased over her, positioning himself between her open thighs, supporting his weight on his elbows. The heady thought of what they were about to do sent shivers racing through her. He must have felt them and looked down to meet her gaze.

She closed her eyes, but he whispered, "Open them. I want to be looking at you the entire time. I want to see your reaction, your response to my loving you this way, Alli."

She opened her eyes and wound her arms around his neck. Then she felt it, his attempt to ease inside of her, but struggling to do so because her body was too tight. He eased out a little and then tried again, the huge tip of him hot and eager at her entrance.

Alli watched perspiration forming on his forehead, his gaze still holding hers. "We're going to try this again. Hold on, baby."

She did.

And she breathed deeply as she felt him entering her once more, this time not letting the barrier get in his way. Inch by sensual inch, he continued going deeper, breaking through, overwhelming her with his size as well as his possession. She felt the pain and tried not to show it on her face but knew she did anyway. And when a tear she couldn't control eased from the corner of her eye, he paused.

Apprehension about what she knew he was thinking about doing ruled her mind. Still holding his gaze she whispered,

"Don't stop." And when he still hesitated, she added, "Remember your promise."

She watched as he breathed in deeply, and then he was slowly penetrating her again, moving deeper, painfully so, until he was completely sheathed inside of her.

"Are you okay?"

Looking into his eyes, she nodded, seeing the concern and the caring there. She noticed the pain was going away and what she was beginning to feel was a deep driving need right in the place where their bodies were joined. He must have felt it, too, because she felt him move, slowly at first, gentle, long, even strokes that started a heated flame escalating through her, as if feeding on what she needed. Feeding on it as well as intensifying it.

Her body began writhing at the sensations she was feeling and all she could think of was having more of him, him going deeper inside of her, touching every part of her that existed. He increased the tempo, the intensity of it took her breath away. He stroked deeper, thrusting back and forth. She cried out at the tension she felt building inside of her and the only thing she could think about was how much she loved him and how he was making her feel. Mark had captured her heart and was initiating her into the throes of womanhood in its truest form.

Then something happened. Something snapped inside of her and her first instinct was to scream but she knew doing so would wake the baby. Instead she groaned and moaned out loud as sensations racked through her and she muttered his name from deep within her throat.

"Mark!"

"That's it, baby, let go. I'm here with you all the way."

And he was.

He grabbed her hips as he continued to thrust inside of her, over and over again, completely filling her with him and taking everything she was offering. He shuddered one, twice, a third time then called her name, the sound a deep wrenching moan from his lips. She felt his body jerk, the same way hers was, and knew that what they were experiencing was an orgasm of the highest magnitude, the most explosive kind.

Their moans of pleasure filled the room and when he lowered his mouth to hers, the joy of what they were sharing brought more tears to her eyes. She knew that she would love Mark Hartman forever, no matter what.

Some time during the night, Mark woke up and glanced down at the woman snuggled against him. After making love to her that first time, he had picked her up and carried her into the bathroom where he'd run bathwater for both of them. In his huge whirlpool tub, he'd washed the soreness from her body, glorying in them sharing such an intimate act as bathing together.

Then he had wrapped her in a huge towel and taken her back to his room to dry her and had slipped her nightshirt on her. Evidently assuming she was being dismissed, he had reached out to capture her wrist when she had headed for the door. After kissing her deeply, to show her how wrong that assumption was, he had picked her up in his arms and taken her to bed with him, cuddling her gently beside him until they had gone to sleep. He could even admit that he had gotten the best sleep he'd had in years.

He would never forget the expression on Alli's face when she had experienced her first orgasm. That sight would remain in his brain forever. She had come apart in his arms the same way she did everything else, with breathtaking enthusiasm.

They had broken the rule of maintaining a strictly professional relationship, but that didn't bother him. In fact, he was waiting for her to wake up so they could break the rules again. He smiled, not ever remembering wanting a woman so much.

He closed his eyes and pinched the bridge of his nose, refusing to think where all this could lead…and where it couldn't lead. How would they go back to spending hours in the office together without him needing to touch her, spread her out on his desk and enjoy a little afternoon delight? How in the hell was he going to control his deep craving for her? It was different when he just had his fantasies, but now he had sampled what he considered the most delicious morsel he'd ever had the pleasure of tasting.

And that included Patrice.

Patrice had never really enjoyed making love and only did so because she felt it was her duty. But Alli was totally different. She had to be the most passionate woman he knew and he could tell she thoroughly enjoyed making love with him. He was going to enjoy tapping into her passion.

A sudden thought unnerved him. What if now that he had unleashed her sensual side, she decided that making love with him wasn't enough? What if she decided that since he wouldn't commit to her, dating other men was the thing to do? His jaw tightened at the thought of her in bed with another man, another man holding her in his arms this way, another man making her scream out his name.

Mark inhaled in a deep breath. He would have to make sure that while Alli lived under his roof and worked at the studio, he was the only man she needed. The only man she wanted.

Satisfied with that decision, he shifted positions, reached out and held her in his arms as he drifted off to sleep.

* * *

Alli slowly opened her eyes and glanced up. Mark was lying beside her and had been resting on his elbows looking at her, evidently watching her sleep…or waiting for her to wake up.

"Good morning, Alli."

The sound of his voice, deep, rich and ultra sexy, sent shivers through her. She tilted her head and glanced at the clock on his nightstand. She guessed that technically it was morning although it was just five o'clock. "Good morning," she said, trying to rid her voice of that drowsy sound.

"I've been waiting for you to wake up," he said, leaning down, close to her lips.

"You have?" Her pulse began racing, especially when he shifted positions slightly and placed his leg over hers. The contact of flesh on flesh sent more shivers escalating through her.

"Yes. I want to make love to you again."

She swallowed. "You do?"

He chuckled. "Oh yes, I do." And then he was kissing her and she forgot everything except how he was making her feel.

The only thing she remembered after that was him pulling back long enough to remove her nightshirt and his pajama bottoms and put on a condom, then him using his hands to drive her to what had to be the highest sexual peak. It was at that moment that he eased his body over hers and slowly entered her, not finding the impediment he had the night before.

As he continued to kiss her and thrust back and forth inside her body, his tongue did likewise, moving back and forth between her parted lips. She felt emotions in every part of her as he deliberately drove her over the edge. When she lost control and exploded in what seemed like a thousand pieces, she cried out his name. With a deep animal groan, he followed her and she felt the tremors that slammed into him ram into her as well.

And when he pulled her closer as he continued to pump into her as they groaned out their pleasures, she had a feeling that Mark Hartman wasn't through with her yet.

And wouldn't be for a long time.

Chapter 9

Mark walked into Erika's bedroom and saw Alli and Erika sitting on the floor going through his niece's toy box.

The sheer beauty of everything they had shared left him breathless when he thought about it. After making love to her again that morning, once, twice, he had been driven to make love to her over and over again until they had both succumbed to total exhaustion. And when they heard the sound of Erika's voice coming over the monitor, exclaiming she wanted to eat, he had encouraged Alli to sleep a little longer while he took care of his niece. It was halfway through breakfast when Alli had walked into the kitchen, looking utterly gorgeous and apologizing for having overslept. He had taken great pleasure in pulling her into his arms and kissing the apology right off her lips.

"Da-da!"

Automatically, as if it were the most natural thing in the

world to do, he crossed the room to them and crouched down to place a kiss on Alli's lips.

"Kiss me, Da-da," Erika said, wrapping her arms around his neck so he could pick her up. Her request caught him up short. He had never gone far in showing that sort of affection to his niece. "Kiss me, Da-da," she said again. A little more adamant this time.

Not wanting to disappoint her, he placed a kiss on her cheek and she let out a shriek of happiness. He quickly handed her to Alli. "I just wanted to let you know I need to go to the studio for a second. I'll be back in an hour."

Alli nodded. "How is the temporary help working out?"

He shrugged, deciding not to mention the mix-up in appointments the woman had made on Friday. "She'll do until you get back. I'm hoping to hear something from Mrs. Tucker in a couple of weeks whether or not she'll be returning to Royal."

"Do you think that she will?"

"I'm hoping that she does. That would be the best thing that could happen."

To Alli, the best thing that could happen was for Mark to fall in love with her and want to keep her around, but she knew that was really reaching for the stars. "What do you think about grilling something for dinner?"

Mark raised his eyebrow. "We usually eat whatever Mrs. Sanders prepares on Friday."

Alli smiled. "I thought it would be nice if you grilled hamburgers or hot dogs. Something simple. I'd be glad to prepare all the trimmings."

"Trimmings like what?"

"Potato salad, corn on the cob, baked beans."

Mark smiled. "Sounds delicious."

Alli returned his smile. "Then it's settled. I'll have everything set up when you get back."

"Okay." Then he leaned over and kissed her before turning and walking out the door.

"So how was your date last night, Kara?"

"Do you really want to know, Alli, or are you calling to lecture me again like I've never gone out on a date before? I know more about dating than you do."

Alli opened her mouth to say something then changed her mind and closed it. In a way Kara was right. How could someone who'd never dated give anyone advice about it? And spending a night in Mark's arms didn't really count.

"I'm sorry, Alli. That was tacky of me to say such a thing. Tacky and thoughtless especially when you sacrificed your social life for me."

Hearing Kara's apology she said, "Hey, it's okay and you're right, I'm no expert. So how was the date?"

She spent the next few minutes listening to Kara tell her how the hottie named Cameron took her to a fraternity party on campus and what a perfect gentleman he'd been. Kara also mentioned that they had another date this weekend and would be going to the movies.

"Look, this might not be the best time to remind you, but you were coming home this weekend," Alli decided to say.

"Oh my gosh, I forgot all about that." Moments later she asked. "Do I really need to come home?"

Alli sighed deeply. This would be Kara's first visit back since school had started and Alli wanted to see her. Besides, she hoped to have a surprise for her. The extra money she was making as Erika's nanny meant that she could swing the payments for a used car for Kara and had wanted to surprise her with it . "No, not if you don't want to."

"It's not that I don't want to come home, Alli, but I forgot and told Cameron I'd go to the movies with him this weekend. Please don't get upset with me about it."

Alli considered Kara's words. She knew that she and her sister loved each other but even the strongest loving relationships could suffer from the strain of opposing opinions about things. "I'm not upset and I understand you wanting to stay there and go out with your new friend."

"Thanks for understanding, Alli. You're the greatest and I love you."

Alli smiled, not really understanding. "And I love you, too, kiddo."

After hanging up the phone, Alli walked over to the window and looked out. Was she being unfair to Kara by expecting more of her than she should? It was natural for girls to be interested in boys and vice versa. Although Kara had dated while in high school, she'd never let anything, especially boys, interfere with her studies.

Alli turned when she heard the gentle knock on her bedroom door. "Come in."

Mark entered the room looking as gorgeous as usual. "I finally got Erika off to sleep. She was determined to play all night." He grinned. "If I didn't know better, I'd think that applesauce you gave her was laced with some sort of energy booster. She's been a live wire all afternoon."

Alli couldn't help but agree. When Mark had returned from the studio, she'd been busy in the kitchen preparing the trimmings. It hadn't taken him any time to put the hot dogs and hamburgers on the grill. He'd even cooked a couple of steaks. Afterward, they had sat outside on the patio. For a handful of seconds while sitting across from him, it had run through her mind just how much of a real family they seemed to be. When he'd mentioned something about Gavin calling a Cattleman's Club meeting for tomorrow night, she had been reminded of just how outside of his world she really was.

She watched as he stepped farther into the room. "I was wondering if you wanted to eat a slice of apple pie with me," he said. "And I know I've already told you, but I have to tell you again how good the pie was."

She smiled at the compliment. "Thanks. And thanks for inviting me to have another slice of pie but I don't think I can eat anything else." She tilted her head and looked at him. "I'm wondering how you can."

He chuckled. "Well, it was just that good. You knew apple pie is my favorite, didn't you?"

"Yes."

He leaned against her bedpost. "And how did you know that?"

She chuckled. "Mark, I'm your assistant. I'm supposed to know these things. Besides, I asked you once when Mrs. Gallant wanted to bake you that pie for giving those self-defense classes to the ladies at that senior-citizens center the first of the year. Don't you remember me asking you about it?"

He shook his head. "No." Evidently, that had to be one of those times when he'd been concentrating on her and not on what she'd been saying, he thought.

"Will you be available Tuesday for Erika's doctor's appointment?"

Her question jarred his attention to her. He raised his eyebrow. "Erika has a doctor's appointment?"

"Yes, the doctor's office called last week as a reminder. It's for her routine checkup." Alli smiled. "She'll be celebrating her first birthday next month."

Mark sighed. Had it been nearly three months already? Erika had been a bouncing eight-month-old baby when he had flown to California to get her. "I've never gone to her doctor appointments. Mrs. Tucker always took her and afterwards told me what the doctor said. I prefer doing things that way."

Alli nodded. She knew it was another technique he was using to keep a semblance of distance between him and his niece. "I would think you'd want to meet her pediatrician and hear what he has to say about Erika's health."

Mark frowned. "Why? You think there might be something wrong with her?"

Alli heard the panic in his voice. She wondered if he was hearing it. "No. Like I said it's a routine checkup. She'll probably get a vaccination of some sort."

Mark nodded. "Then there's no reason for me to be there. I'm sure you can handle things."

She opened her mouth to push the issue, then decided not to push now. She would push later. If nothing else, she was determined to make him see just how deeply he cared for his niece.

Mark continued to gaze at Alli, getting turned on by the minute just looking at her. She was wearing the tank top and cutoff jeans she'd had on earlier, which meant she hadn't taken her bath yet.

Deciding that he was a man of action, he walked across the room to stand in front of her. "If I can't interest you in eating a slice of pie with me, can I interest you in something else?"

He could tell that her curiosity was piqued when she lifted an arched eyebrow. "Something else like what?"

"A bath."

She chuckled as she slumped back against the windowsill. "Are you suggesting that I need one?"

"No," he said, taking a closer step to her. "I was suggesting that you take a bath. With me."

A smile curved her lips. "And just what will I get out of such a venture?"

He shook his head, chuckling, remembering. "Do you have to ask after last night and this morning?"

Mark saw an intense look appear on her face and he knew she was reliving the memories just as he was. "So, are you game?"

Alli knew she was more than game. She was becoming putty in his hands and she didn't have any regrets. "You're going to have to convince me it's something that I should do," she said, knowing she was giving him a challenge—a challenge he wouldn't hesitate in meeting.

"Convincing you is no problem, Alli," he whispered softly, reaching out, taking hold of her wrist and pulling her closer to him. His hands slid under her tank top, finding her bare, just as he thought. He hadn't been able to take his eyes off her chest while eating, seeing how the tips of her nipples were pressing against her top. He'd known that she was braless.

He watched her eyes as he caressed those same nipples, rubbing his fingers over the protruding tips, feeling them harden. "Remember how my mouth was on them last night, Alli, and how my tongue teased and tasted them?" He continued to let his hand fondle her, making her feel what he was feeling, getting her as aroused as he was. "Do you remember?"

"Yes, I remember," she answered in a raspy voice.

He liked the sound of it. "And do you remember how I kissed you and the number of times I kissed you?"

"Yes."

"Good, because I want to kiss you now. Part your lips for me, Alli, and let me in."

The moment she parted her lips, he leaned closer and his tongue slid heatedly over hers and the moment she released a deep moan, he went inside her mouth, kissing her with a hunger that she felt all the way to her toes. Pulling her closer to him, she couldn't help but cradle her thighs against the hardness of his aroused body.

She shuddered when sensations seeped through her pores, blood gushed through her veins and her pulse escalated to a point that had her sighing in pleasure. He kept kissing her until she was almost weak in the knees. It was only then that he pulled back.

He dropped his hands to his side. "Now will you take that bath with me?"

They stared at each other. Alli knew what her response would be, but she decided to show him rather than tell him. She leaned closer, framed his face with her hands, then kissed him with the same intensity that he had kissed her earlier.

Suddenly he broke off the kiss and he led her by the hand out of her bedroom into his. The first thing she noticed was the wood blazing in the fireplace. It had been warm earlier that day but the night had brought in cooler air.

He didn't stop until they reached his bathroom. She watched as he began running the bathwater in the tub that could fit two people easily. He turned to her, and without saying a word, began removing her clothes. When she was completely naked, she eased up to him to get some of his heated warmth. He gently lifted her and placed her in the tub.

She watched him remove his own clothing as his gaze locked on her with restrained hunger. She eased into the bubbles, thinking they might offer relief for her overheated body. She raised an eyebrow when he placed several condom packets on the edge of the tub.

"Lesson number two," he said, as his smile widened. "We have the freedom of making love at any time and any place on this ranch as long as we're protected from prying eyes." He joined her in the tub, grabbing the scented soap and lathering up his hands.

When he pulled her to face him, curving her legs around his waist and began rubbing the bubbles all over her, she let out a sigh. "We do?" Her breathing escalated at the way he was rubbing his soapy hands over her stomach, arms and breasts.

"Yes, we do," he whispered. His gaze held hers so she could see the intense desire in his eyes. "Now let me prove it."

And it didn't take long for him to do so.

Sheriff Gavin O'Neal glanced around the table, meeting the gazes of all the men present. Their Texas Cattleman's Club meeting was scheduled for Wednesday, but he thought he should share the lab's report with everyone as soon as possible.

"As all of you know, Mark found a syringe on the Windcrofts' ranch. The lab report came in today and their findings indicate it contains traces of potassium chloride, the same drug used to kill Jonathan."

It was Jake who spoke. "That makes Nita Windcroft a prime suspect."

Gavin nodded. "Yes, but I'm also looking at the possibility that someone might be framing her."

Logan leaned in. "Who?"

"Whoever is responsible for killing Jonathan. What could be better than to plant evidence on a major suspect? And if that's the case, then the person who put it there expects us to fall for it."

"And when we don't?" Connor Thorne asked.

Gavin met his gaze. "Then there's the likelihood they'll try again to make it seem like Nita did it."

Mark sat back in his chair. "Shouldn't we tell Nita so she'll know what to expect?"

Gavin shook his head. "No, because for now there's still a chance she might be guilty and want us to think she's being framed."

Mark sighed deeply. "Just so you'll know, last night Alli asked me about the rumors that are going around that Nita might be responsible for Jonathan's death. Alli went with me out to the Windcroft ranch and got to talk to Nita. According to Alli, Nita has heard the rumors and maintains she is innocent. Alli knows her better than I do and she believes her. She says there is no way Nita could have done it."

Gavin nodded again. "Then it is up to us to catch the right person and prove Nita Windcroft's innocence. This is a listing of all Nita's clients," he said, passing copies of the list around the table. "As you can see she has plenty of them. I want all of you to take a look at it and at our next meeting we'll discuss anyone who we might want to add to the suspect list."

"Hey, Jake, I see your opponent's name on the list. Can you believe Gretchen Halifax owns a horse that she keeps boarded at the Windcrofts' farm?" Connor said, chuckling. "I thought the lady-who-wants-to-be-mayor was too dignified to mount a horse."

"Yeah," Logan said, joining in. "And can you believe her horse is named Silver Dollar?"

Mark shook his head, smiling. "Figures."

Gavin shifted in his chair, deciding to bring the meeting back to order. "There's another reason I called this meeting tonight. The map has been returned."

"What?" The exclamation was uttered by five men.

"Yes, I got a call from Aaron Hill, the director of the Royal Museum. Hill says the map mysteriously returned today with a note."

"What note?" Thomas Devlin asked.

"A handwritten note of apology."

"Did the person say why they stole it in the first place?" Jake asked, shaking his head.

"Yes, the reason given was to keep it out of the hands of the real thieves," Gavin replied, placing the note in the middle of the table.

Logan chuckled. "At least we know for certain the person who stole it was really a woman. Only a female would see the logic in that."

The other five men at the table nodded in agreement.

"I had the handwriting on this note compared to those threatening notes that have been sent to Nita Windcroft. According to the lab, this note was definitely written by a woman and the notes Nita received were written by a man."

"Is there anything you need for us to do, Gavin?" Mark asked, checking his watch. He was looking forward to spending time with Alli again. He was still having memories of the bath they had shared last night and the lovemaking that had followed.

"No, that's about it other than to keep both your eyes and

ears open and report anything. I won't rest until the person responsible for Jonathan's death is brought to justice."

"And just so you guys will know," Connor said, looking around the table. "I'm leaving to go out of town for a while. I have business to take care of in Virginia, but I hope to be back in a few weeks."

Gavin rose. "Well, that ends tonight's meeting." No sooner had he said those words, Mark was out of his chair headed for the door.

"You're in a hurry tonight, aren't you, Mark?" Jake called out.

"Yes, I guess you can say that," Mark replied over his shoulder without stopping or looking back.

Mark swung around and faced Alli, his eyes locked on hers. "What do you mean you can't take Erika to her doctor's appointment this morning?"

He tried not to notice how much of her thigh he saw when she crawled out of his bed and how her hair was tumbled around her face. When he had gotten in from the meeting last night, Erika had been asleep and Alli had been awake waiting for him…in his bed. And this was the first opportunity she'd had to get out of it.

"I know this is last minute and I do apologize, but I got a call from the bank yesterday reminding me that I needed to be there first thing this morning to sign those loan papers."

He lifted an eyebrow as she passed him on her way to the bathroom. He hurried after her. "What loan papers?"

She stared at him before walking into the bathroom where she intended to have a few private moments. "I'm getting Kara a used car. She could use one to get around on campus. Nothing fancy and definitely something I can afford since the payments on my new one will be low thanks to your friendship with that car dealer."

"I would have loaned you the money for that," he said as if he were in the habit of making car loans.

"Yes, well, I thought it best if I went to a financial institution, Mark, considering everything."

"Everything like what?"

"Our relationship. When Mrs. Tucker returns or when you find a permanent babysitter things between us will go back as they used to be. Besides, all I'm asking is for you to take Erika over to the doctor's office. Once I sign those papers I will join you there and take over. Now if you'll excuse me, I need to use the bathroom." She closed the bathroom door behind herself.

Mark's jaw tightened and his hands balled into fists at his side. He knew he was handling this badly, but he couldn't help it. First of all, he didn't want Alli reminding him that their relationship would be changing in a month or so. Secondly, he didn't want to take Erika to the doctor's office. He didn't want to sit in the waiting room with all those other people who would be parents and have them assume Erika was his daughter when he didn't know the first thing about being a dad. What if they tried making small talk about stuff he was supposed to know?

Damn, he wasn't looking forward to this particular assignment.

Mark sat in the doctor's office holding Erika in his lap. There were only a few people there and so far no one had been talkative. One woman had commented on how cute Erika looked. He had glanced down and noticed her pink coveralls, pink socks, white sneakers and the pink bows in her hair and had smiled proudly. She did look cute.

He glanced at his watch. Alli had said that she would be arriving around ten and it was almost that time. He hoped she got there before Erika's name was called.

"Erika Hartman."

"No such luck," Mark muttered quietly, glancing at the door beside the reception station and seeing a nurse standing there holding a patient's chart. "Looks like we're up, kid," he whispered softly, standing and holding Erika tightly as he maneuvered the diaper bag onto his shoulder.

"We're here," he decided to call out so the nurse wouldn't think they had disappeared.

The woman smiled when she saw Erika. "Well, hello little Miss Hartman. How have you been?" She then offered Mark her hand. "Hi, I'm Laurie, Dr. Covert's nurse. I don't think we've met."

And we wouldn't be meeting now if I'd had my way, Mark thought, accepting the woman's handshake. "No, we haven't. I won't be here with her long today. Her nanny is on the way."

Laurie nodded as she took Erika from Mark. "All right, but we can go ahead and get started. Follow me to an examination room."

Moments later, Mark stood on the sidelines as Laurie undressed Erika. "She's such a happy baby," the nurse commented. "I remember the first time Mrs. Tucker brought her in here. The poor thing was crying so much we had to calm her down before we could check her and that was only a few months ago. You've done well in helping her to adjust."

"Thank you."

Mark turned around when the examination-room door

opened, hoping it was Alli, but instead an older man he knew to be the doctor walked in. "Good morning, I'm Dr. Covert, and I understand it's time for this little lady's physical."

Mark continued to stand to the side and watched Erika get placed on a scale to be weighed, get her lungs checked and her head measured. "She seems to be developing nicely," the doctor said smiling.

The only bad moment was when the nurse had to give Erika a measles vaccination. She let out a loud wail but her tears quickly dried up when Laurie gave her a rubber ball to play with.

"Hmm, let's see," Dr. Covert was saying. "She's eleven months old so she should be standing alone—or at least trying to—responding to simple instructions, taking a few steps and saying mama and dada to the correct parent."

"She's not doing that," Mark decided to say.

The doctor lifted his gaze from Erika's chart and met Mark's eyes. "She's not doing what?"

"Saying those things correctly."

"She's not?"

"No."

The older man lifted a bushy eyebrow. "She's calling you mama and your wife dada?"

"No, I don't have a wife, just a nanny. And Erika's calling me dada but I'm not her daddy, I'm her uncle."

The doctor smiled. "That's natural. She sees you as a father figure, the one person who is constant in her life. Whenever she calls you dada just tell her your name, or the name you want her to call you."

"I've been doing that," Mark said, glancing at his watch again.

"Then just continue. She'll eventually catch on. Within the

next month she'll start forming other sounds and I'm sure she'll start calling you by your name or at least she'll make attempts to do so. Just be patient with her."

Mark nodded. "What else will she try to do?"

"She'll try responding to simple instructions."

Mark chuckled. "Hey, she's doing that now."

"Then you have a very smart girl on your hands."

Mark beamed proudly. "Yes, she sure is that. What about walking? She's standing alone and has even tried taking a couple of steps while holding on to something. Is there anything I can do to motivate the process?"

Dr. Covert chuckled. "Try not carrying her wherever she wants to go, that will usually work."

Mark nodded. "All right. Is there anything else?"

"No, that's it. Your niece seems to be in good health and after her visit next month we'll only need to see her every six months."

"What about foods? Is there anything she shouldn't have?"

The doctor spent the next few minutes explaining what foods were the best for Erika to eat and how they aided in her body's development, as well as those foods Mark should avoid giving her.

The examination-room door suddenly opened and Alli breezed in. "Sorry I'm late."

Mark waved away her apology and smiled. "That's fine. Things weren't so bad and Dr. Covert and I were having a little chat."

"Did you know we shouldn't give Erika honey until after her first birthday, and that honey can contain spores that cause botulism poisoning in babies?" Mark switched positions in bed to ask Alli.

Alli couldn't help but smile. It didn't take a Ph.D. to figure out that taking his niece to the doctor had certainly been an adventure for Mark. He hadn't stopped talking about it…at least he hadn't brought it up during the time they had made love. Now she didn't feel so bad about manipulating her time at the bank so he'd be the one to take Erika to the doctor once she'd discovered his calendar had been clear that morning.

"Yes, I knew it," Alli replied. "However, such a situation happening is rare."

Mark's expression turned serious. "Yeah, but it can happen. I'm going to have to remember that."

Alli shook her head smiling. She hoped he wasn't thinking of getting rid of all the honey in the house. "Erika is almost a year old now. She'll be able to have honey pretty soon."

"Hmm, I don't know," Mark said. "Just because she'll be a little older how do we know for certain she won't get that botulism stuff?"

"We won't. We just have to believe that the doctor knows what he's talking about."

"Yeah, I guess you're right." He reached out and pulled Alli into his arms, tight against his body. "I'm tired of talking. I want to do something else," he said, leaning over and placing small kisses along her ear and neck.

"Again?"

Mark pulled back slightly, his expression turning serious again. "Do you think I want to make love to you too often?"

Alli smiled. "No, I was just kidding." When he didn't move but continued to stare at her as if he hadn't believed her, she said, "Honest, Mark, I was just kidding. I want you as much as you want me and every time you want to make love I'm right there with you. Why would you think you want to do it too often?"

He sighed deeply and met her gaze. "Patrice always said I did. She didn't like making love with me."

His words stunned Alli. She couldn't imagine any woman not wanting to make love with Mark, especially the woman who'd been his wife. "But why?"

He shrugged. "She didn't like sex."

Alli reached out and wrapped her arms around his neck. "Well, I happen to like it, but only with you." She could tell her words pleased him.

"No kidding?"

"No kidding. Can I prove it?"

She could tell her question caught him by surprise. "Well, uh, yes, I suppose so."

"Good, then lay back and enjoy. Keep in mind that I still lack a lot of expertise in this, but I'm finding that I have an excellent teacher."

Mark didn't get a chance to say anything. Her mouth captured his as she got on top of him. Incredible, he thought, loving her taste and thinking that he would never get tired of kissing her, but evidently she had other ideas and slowly pulled her mouth from his.

And then she was kissing the area around his ear, taking her tongue and licking it while whispering just what she wanted to do to him, what she planned to do to him. Her words and the feverish pitch of her voice inflamed him and he felt himself getting harder. She must have felt it, too, and adjusted her thighs to cradle his, while at the same time thrusting her hips against him so he could feel the contact of flesh touching flesh.

"I remember the first time I got on a horse," she whispered. "Do you remember your first time?"

He was trying to maintain his control but the feel of the tip of her tongue sliding alongside his ear was driving him crazy, and the way her naked body was fitting intimately to his wasn't helping matters. "Yes, I remember."

"Do you also remember how it felt to have such a huge animal beneath you?"

When her soft hand slid down his body and she took hold of his aroused staff, he gasped, then said huskily. "Yes."

"I do, too, and being on top of you this way reminds me what it felt like and it makes me want to do something."

She was rubbing her fingers up and down him, as if she needed to know the shape, the texture and the degree of his heat. Her curiosity was pushing him over the edge. "Do something like what?"

"Ride you."

She reached over and took a condom pack off the nightstand and within minutes she had slipped it on him, almost driving him crazy in the process. "Now where were we?" she asked, shifting her body until she was over him again, locking his hips between her thighs. She braced herself above him and opened her legs wider.

Holding his gaze, she slowly eased her body down, taking him inside of her while listening to his labored breathing. Impatient, he thrust his hips upward, trying to hurry the connection, and since she was wet and slick, he drove easily into her to the hilt.

"I don't think you can go any farther," she panted, still looking at him. Their bodies were connected tight. But that didn't stop her from clenching her muscles around him, making him groan her name out loud.

"I'm dying," he whispered brokenly, not thinking he could last another minute. "I'm going to lose control."

"Not before I get a chance to ride."

It began. She withdrew partially, then plunged back on him again, taking him deeply inside of her. Over and over, thrusting her hips, rocking her bottom, slapping flesh against flesh, drawing up her knees and arching her body to ride harder. Each time she took him back inside of her, he seemed to go deeper still.

Mark grasped her hips, trying to hold himself inside of her but it wasn't working. She was determined to ride him and all he could do was give in and meet her movement for movement, thrust for thrust, stroke for stroke. His gaze locked on hers and what he saw in their dark depths sent even more heat rushing through his body.

He released her hips to curl his fingers in Alli's hair and gritted his teeth against the intense pleasure that was overtaking his body. He needed to kiss her, join her mouth with his but, before he could do so, she cried out his name. It was then that he let himself go and was thrown into a climax the depths of which he had never experienced before. His release kept coming and coming and she kept riding and riding.

She cried out his name again and threw her head back. Then after thrusting hard one final time, she collapsed on his chest. After a few moments, he felt her body go slack and could tell she was about to drift off to sleep. He wrapped his arms around her while trying to recover from what had to be the most exquisite experience of his life. He wanted to hold her in his arms for the rest of the night.

"How did I do?"

Mark groaned as a chuckle escaped his lips. "Sweetheart, if you would have done any better, I'd be a dead man."

All he could think about was the way she'd looked on top of him, riding him to her heart's content with the potency of her scent tantalizing his senses, her head thrown back, her firm and perfect breasts jutting forward, her hair tumbling wildly and swaying with every motion of her body as it moved up and down over his.

He took a deep breath as an overwhelming sense he'd never felt before caused his body to go taut and something inside of him came close to shattering. Closing his eyes and tightening his jaw, he forced the foreign feeling aside.

With a confused groan, he buried his face in Alli's throat as he fought to stop his control from slipping any further. He reminded himself that this was all he and Alli could ever share.

No matter what, he could not let her get past his defenses.

Chapter 10

A week later, Alli stood on the sidelines and watched Mark instruct a class of women on the art of self-defense. Her throat felt tight and her pulse escalated as she watched how he moved with precision, causing his broad shoulders to flex under his T-shirt. His firmly muscled thighs encased in a pair of sweats demonstrated incredible energy whenever he hunched down or let out a kick with lightning speed.

She swallowed thickly, amazed at how much Mark continued to appeal to her on a primal level. Intense heat rushed to pool between her thighs and she shifted positions to find relief. The cool air blasting from a vent overhead wasn't much help.

As she continued to watch him, she couldn't help but think of how things were between them. A smile tugged at the corner of her mouth when she remembered the picnic they'd had a few days ago. Mrs. Sanders had urged them to get out of the house and enjoy themselves while Erika was taking a nap and had gone so far as to pack a lunch for them.

Mark had driven them to a section of Hartman land near a huge lake, and after spreading a blanket on the ground under an oak tree, they had sat down. She had enjoyed eating the sandwiches while listening to him share his days of being in the marines and the close relationship he and his brother had with her. He even had talked about his mother and what a loving and thoughtful woman she had been. Alli noted that he avoided any conversation about his father or his deceased wife. But what she remembered most of all was them making love beneath the low hanging branches of that oak tree.

Alli's thoughts shifted to how she and Mark had gotten into the habit of sharing a bed every night. But a tinge of disappointment touched her heart when she thought of the shield he continued to keep not only with her but also with Erika. It seemed as though this boundary was elementally necessary for him to maintain a detached persona. But she had seen him let his guard down a few times, but quickly he would resurrect it.

"Da-da."

She glanced down at Erika who was sitting in her stroller getting excited at seeing Mark. No matter how many times Mark corrected his niece, Erika was intent on calling him daddy.

Alli hunched down to Erika. "He's busy now, sweetheart, but he knows you're here and will come over as soon he's finished." Alli had taken Erika shopping that morning for some winter clothes and while in town she'd decided to drop by the studio.

A few minutes later when class was over, Mark glanced over in their direction and smiled. The expression on his face indicated he was glad to see them. He ducked under the rope that kept the observers off the gym floor and walked over to them.

"Hello, ladies."

Alli smiled. "Hi, yourself." She felt her pulse go haywire again. God, but he smelled good. Only with him did sweat mix with a magnetic male force to produce a scent that was physically overpowering. She wished that for once he would defy proper etiquette and pull her into his arms—something he would do if they were behind closed doors.

"Erika and I were wondering if we could tempt you to have lunch with us at the Royal Diner," Alli said, forcing her brain to function normally.

He glanced at his watch. "I wish I could but I have a few things I need to do around here. Maybe some other time."

She caught her bottom lip between her teeth and glanced down at Erika to hide her disappointment. "Sure."

She glanced up to see him looking at Erika. That's when Alli saw it, a deep longing to pick up his niece, plant a kiss on her cheek and cuddle her close. But Alli knew that he wouldn't. To do so would show emotions and he had been taught as a child that to expose himself that way was a taboo.

He met her gaze, and at that moment, although she knew that he didn't feel anything for her, she felt all the love she had for him. The degree shook her to the core.

Realizing that they were standing staring at each other, she broke eye contact and returned her attention to Erika. "Well, I guess we'll be going."

"All right. Thanks for dropping by."

Alli glanced around. "Things seem to be running pretty smooth here without me."

He hesitated only the barest second and then said, "Don't ever think you aren't needed, Alli."

His words sounded breathy and Alli had to force herself not to put much stock in them. However, she couldn't resist cocking her head to the side and asking, "You sure?"

He nodded and said, "I'm positive."

Her heart suddenly lodged tightly in her throat. "We better be going. It will be time for Erika's nap pretty soon."

"All right."

"Da-da."

Alli couldn't help but smile. It seemed that Erika didn't intend to be ignored.

Mark hunched down. "You're ready for lunch, little lady? Uncle Mark can't go this time, but maybe next time."

Alli shook her head. Now it had gone from just *Mark* to *Uncle Mark*. "We'll see you at dinner, Mark."

He straightened and met her gaze again. "All right. Enjoy lunch."

"We will." She pushed Erika past him and kept walking without looking back.

Later that evening while Alli was giving Erika her bath, Mark came home. He had called to let Alli know that he would miss dinner. Nita Windcroft had contacted him. She had received another threatening letter and the Texas Cattleman's Club had met to discuss it.

"I can't believe someone is still harassing Nita," Alli said as she leaned over to take Erika out of the tub. Squealing at the fun she'd been having, Erika kicked up her legs and splashed water on both Alli and Mark.

Laughing, Alli wrapped Erika in a thick towel and handed her to Mark. "I washed now you can dry." She ignored the surprised look on his face.

"So what did the note say this time?" she asked, walking out of the bathroom to go to Erika's bedroom with him following behind.

"More of the same. The message is always vague. This one said, *Get out or else*."

Alli turned and raised an eyebrow. "If someone thinks a few notes and a little mischief will force Nita to leave her land, then they are crazy. I just hope you guys do something before Nita has a mind to take matters into her own hands."

Mark nodded as he continued to dry Erika. "I'm going to turn the note over to Gavin to see if the person who wrote this is the same one who wrote all the others."

He handed his niece back over to Alli. She'd noticed that lately Mark avoided any physical contact with Erika whenever he could, yet he had confided in her once that, when he had first gotten Erika, he would spend time rocking her in the rocking chair. It seemed to Alli that he had a tendency to put up a boundary when he found himself getting too close or when he felt his emotions were becoming involved.

"I left dinner warming for you in the oven."

"Thanks."

"Once I get Erika dressed for bed, I'm going to rock her for a while. You can join us if you'd like."

"Why?"

She shrugged. "I thought that perhaps you'd want to spend some time with her before she goes to sleep."

He looked at her for a moment, then at Erika and said, "No, that's not necessary." Without saying anything else he walked out of the room.

* * *

Alli walked through the French doors that led out onto the patio where the pool was located. She had put Erika to bed and had gone looking for Mark only to discover he had eaten and was in his office going over the ranch's accounting books. Deciding not to disturb him, she had gone to her bedroom to change into her bathing suit. She felt tense and thought a little swim might help.

She'd swum a dozen or so laps when she decided she'd done enough. Releasing a contented sigh, she climbed out of the pool and began drying herself with the huge velour towel when she glanced over and saw Mark standing in the doorway.

She met his gaze. "How long have you been standing there?"

"Long enough."

"Long enough for what?" she asked.

"Long enough for me to realize how much I want you."

Alli found herself melting under Mark's intense stare. There he stood, leaning in the doorway wearing a pair of stonewashed jeans and a T-shirt. She wondered if he knew he had a patent on the word *sexy*. Without batting an eye she asked, "So what do you plan to do about it?"

The wantonness of her invitation was so unlike her, but so were a number of her actions since she had moved into this house with him to become Erika's nanny. There was something about Mark that brought out something within her that she hadn't known existed. It was as though beneath the layers of flesh that covered her lived a passionate, insatiable being.

"Haven't you learned by now never to tempt me?" he asked, beginning to walk toward her.

As soon as he came closer into the light, she saw just how

much he wanted her. She could barely draw breath into her lungs. The lower part of his body that she knew would soon be connected with hers looked bigger than she'd ever seen it before. All from watching her swim?

He stood directly in front of her and reached out to take the towel from her hand and toss it aside. "I want you so bad I actually ache, baby," he whispered in her ear.

She was beginning to ache, too. The sexy sound of his voice, his breath hot against her skin wasn't helping matters. "Then I think I better help you find relief."

She lifted up his T-shirt, then smoothed her fingertips against the bare portion of his waist before easing them lower to the fastener of his jeans. She began undoing the zipper, and when that was done, she worked her fingers inside the waistband of his jeans. Her pulse increased at the feel of his hot, turgid flesh.

She caressed him, remembering the first time she'd done so and how aroused he'd gotten because of it. She moved her fingers back and forth, thinking there was something deliciously naughty and decadent about having him in her hands this way. She might be putty in his hands, but right now, at this very moment, he was the opposite of putty in hers. He was as solid as a rock.

"Your touch is driving me crazy," he whispered and seemed to grow larger in her hand. "I got to have you. Now!" he growled as if in pain.

Before she could draw her next breath, he had pushed her hand aside and snatched down the top of her bathing suit, freeing her breasts. But he didn't stop there. Determined to see her completely naked, he lowered his body to remove the suit entirely. Then he stepped back, ripped off his T-shirt, followed by the quick removal of his jeans and briefs. The sound of foil being torn rent the silence and she watched as he prepared himself, not for the first time wondering how such a small condom could fit over anything so big.

Heat of the highest intensity rushed to pool between her thighs when his hand suddenly reached out and went there, at the same time that he pulled her close to him and began sucking on her breasts. She shuddered, already so close to climax with the feel of his fingers stroking her between her legs and his mouth making a treat of her breasts. Her shivers became so intense that it was becoming hard for her to stand upright.

"Mark!"

"Not yet, baby, just hold on for a little while longer."

That was easy for him to say, she thought as his assault on her became more intense, more pleasurable. The feelings he was causing to flow through her were too great and she didn't know how long she would be able to hold on.

"Can't last until we get to the bedroom," he growled in her ear as he walked her backward until the backs of her legs touched the daybed and they tumbled on it together. She reached out to touch him but he shook his head. "No, not yet. There's something I have to do. It's something I've dreamed of doing to you for a long time."

Before she could ask what that something was, he dropped to his knees in front of her and curved her legs around his shoulders. He looked at her and she saw how his hazel eyes darkened and heard how deeply he was breathing just moments before he dipped his head between her legs, pressing an open-mouth kiss to her womanly core.

When the tip of his tongue touched her, she thought she was going to moan her throat raw, and when his tongue began twirling around inside of her, then licking and flicking out torture of the most sensuous kind, she threw her head against a huge fluffy pillow and instinctively raised her hips against his mouth. "Yes…oh yes."

What words she muttered after that she couldn't remember, but she was sure she said, *Please, don't stop, go deeper,* and *Yes, right there.* The intimate kiss grew more intense. It was as if he were hungry and planned to feast on her all night. She had heard about men and women engaging in this special form of lovemaking, but had never in her wildest dreams thought she would ever indulge in anything like this. Mark was proving her wrong. And when the swift signs of an orgasm began taking over her, she couldn't help but scream, grateful that Erika's bedroom was on the other side of the house.

"Mark!"

And then he was moving over her, parting the slick flesh that he had kissed greedily just seconds before. He entered her, sinking inside of her to the hilt and filling her completely.

"Hold on, baby. We're about to test this daybed's endurance," he said, pinning her arms above her head and smiling when her breasts jutted out. He began feasting on them at the same time the thrusts began. He pumped his throbbing arousal into her and pulled it back out again, over and over. And each time he filled her, he absorbed the shivers that hit her body with the impact. It seemed her womb was contracting with every stroke of his manhood.

Each time he withdrew, her hips followed him, almost coming off the bed, refusing to be disconnected from him, only to have him thrust back inside of her. When she heard him growl out her name, he let go of her arms and grasped her hips.

"Alli!"

She watched how he gritted his teeth, stretched his neck and threw his head back as an orgasm rammed through him.

He pulled out slightly but was thrusting back inside of her again, gripping her hips, refusing to sever the connection and she knew he was having yet another climax.

Watching his intense pleasure spurred her into another one and her fingers dug into the muscles of his shoulders and almost instantly she cried out. Words she had held back for two years found their way out of her throat and she heard herself saying, "I love you, Mark," just moments before another shudder worked its way through her body and she was entrenched in the throes of total fulfillment.

She had literally driven him wild and the shock of it jolted right through Mark. But what was even more detrimental were the words she had whispered while having an orgasm...*I love you, Mark.*

The sheer shock of her words had sent him into a panic. He didn't want her to love him. Want him, yes. Need him, yes. But love him, no.

Alli was the kind of woman a man could, and should, love but Mark wasn't the one to do it. He had issues to deal with and they were issues that the rest of his life wouldn't resolve. He looked down at her. So that both of them could fit in the daybed, her body was spooned intimately against his. She had drifted off to sleep. He studied her features and wondered how a sleeping woman could look as if she were ready for the next round of making love.

He sighed deeply. She was not supposed to fall in love with him. There was no place for love in his life, which meant there was no place for her in his life, either. He should have known, should have expected. Alli wasn't the type of woman who would give her body to a man without believing that her heart was involved. He had made a humongous mistake in letting his desire for her get in the way of his better judgment.

Long moments later, he listened to her even breathing and he knew what had to be done. Picking her up into his arms, he carried her into her bedroom and placed her in her own bed. After placing the covers over her, he stood back, deciding since she'd slept in the nude before, he wouldn't wake her to put on a nightgown.

Mark knew that the intimacy the two of them had shared during the past three weeks would always be a part of him. The thought that he was the first man ever to make love to her was truly special and at no time would he ever regret what they had shared. But there could never be anything lasting between them. He was a man who understood duty and not love.

After Patrice's death he had made a vow never again to let a woman matter to him and he meant to keep it.

The bedroom shone in the brightness of the morning sun by the time Alli awoke the next morning. She sat up and glanced around.

She was in her bed.

She lay back and drew in a ragged breath as she recalled in vivid detail what she and Mark had done just moments before she'd fallen asleep. She didn't need the fact that she'd slept in the nude to remind her. Ever since they had made love that first time, she had shared his bed so why had he brought her in here? She stared up at the ceiling trying to remember anything that could have happened to make him...

Then she remembered. She closed her eyes as she recalled the words she'd whispered to him while coming apart in his arms. She opened her eyes and pushed herself back up in a sitting position. Was this going to be his way of denying what she'd said? Did he think just because he wasn't one who was prone to show his emotions that she shouldn't show hers, either?

Alli winced at the thought that yes, that's exactly what he believed. He was no more interested in the fact that she loved him than he was in whatever was going on in Midland. And why should he when he had conveniently closed his heart ever to loving anyone again?

"Eat."

Alli forced her thoughts aside when she heard the sound of Erika on the monitor. Moving quickly, she got out of bed and headed for the bathroom. She and Mark would have a lot to talk about when she saw him.

She didn't see Mark at all that day and she was trying hard not to think that he was avoiding her, although deep down she knew that he was. Before, even when he would be away from the ranch for long periods during the day, he would call and tell her his schedule, and more than once he had surprised her and Erika by dropping by for lunch. But today he did neither.

The only highlight of her day had been a call she had gotten from Kara. Kara had told her all about her date at the movies. Alli had heard all the happiness and excitement in Kara's voice and it hadn't taken a rocket scientist to know that Kara was really taken with this guy.

Over the past couple of days, Alli had decided to let her sister live her own life and learn from her own mistakes. Alli was certainly learning from hers. It was true what everybody said about experience being the best teacher. And deep down she knew that Kara had a good head on her shoulders.

That night, Alli was in bed but not asleep when she heard Mark walk past her bedroom door going to his room after checking on Erika. At the sound of his bedroom door closing, she got out of bed and quickly slipped into her bathrobe. Leaving her room, she walked purposefully down the hall to knock softly on his door. When moments passed and he didn't answer, she knocked again, knowing he was there.

When he didn't answer after her second knock, she opened the door, stuck her head in and called his name. "Mark." She heard the sound of the shower running, figured he was in the shower and made the decision to wait.

He walked out the bathroom stripped down to his jeans at the same moment she walked into his room and closed the door. She tried not to notice the fact that his jeans were unsnapped.

"What are you doing in here, Alli?" he snarled.

She winced. In all her years of knowing him, this was the first time he had used that tone of voice with her. "I need to talk with you about something. I knocked twice and when you didn't answer, I thought I'd just come in and wait for you to finish your shower."

He leaned in the doorway of the bathroom. "Does what you want to talk to me about concern Erika?"

"No."

"Then whatever it is will have to wait until morning. I had a rather tiring day today and—"

"Why are you doing this, Mark?"

He tilted his head and looked at her. "Why am I doing what?"

"Casting me aside."

He crossed the room in a second flat, grabbed her wrist and stood looming before her. Anger was etched in his features. "Do you think that's what I'm doing? Casting you aside? Don't you know that I'm trying to be considerate of your feelings, Alli? I heard what you whispered to me last night, and knowing how you feel, how can you expect me to continue when I can't reciprocate those feelings? I want you, but I don't love you. As for Erika, what I feel for her is a sense of duty which I intend to carry out as long as there is breath in my body. I owe it to Matt. I care for both you and Erika but love has nothing to do with it."

Alli took a deep breath. No matter what Mark was saying, he loved Erika. He did more than care. Since living in his home, Alli had observed him with his niece and, although he wasn't quick with the kisses and cuddles, he'd always been there, helping her with Erika's feedings, baths. Why couldn't he see what was so obvious? And why couldn't he believe that over time he could love her as well? She knew loving didn't come easy for him but she refused to believe he couldn't find it in his heart ever to care anything about her. There wasn't a time when they'd made love that he hadn't made her feel loved, whether he knew he was doing so or not.

"You can love someone if you let yourself do so, Mark," she said, believing her words as she said them.

He stiffened, then let go of her hand and stared at her for a long moment. "Is this what you've been about all this time? Did you take the job as Erika's nanny because you thought doing so would be a way to get next to me? And that eventually I'd think differently about how I feel about love?"

When she didn't say anything but continued to look at him, he said in a sharp tone, "Answer me, dammit. Did you?"

Unable to believe he would ask such a thing, pain ripped through Alli. She glanced at the bed, where they had shared numerous passionate nights, before meeting his gaze. She swallowed, fighting back the emotions that were thick in her throat. "The reason I'm here as Erika's nanny is because you said you needed me, Mark."

She quickly looked away. "I guess I heard you wrong." She met his gaze again and then said, "There is no reason for me being here other than that. Good night."

Without giving him a chance to say anything, she brushed past him and swiftly walked out of the room.

Chapter 11

"Are you all right, Mr. Hartman?"

Mark opened his eyes and released his hand from the bridge of his nose, glancing across his desk at his temporary secretary. He had been in the middle of reciting a list of things he needed for her to do next week when thoughts of Alli suddenly had consumed his mind.

It had been almost a week since their argument, which was the last time he had seen her. He deliberately was gone from the ranch by the time she got up in the mornings and he didn't return until way past her bedtime. He would check on Erika every night when he got in, and a couple of times he had paused outside of Alli's door. But knowing the way things were between them was for the best, he had quickly moved on.

"Mr. Hartman?"

The woman was staring at him strangely. "Yes, Mrs.

Roundtree, I'm fine. I just had a tension headache. Let's finish this later, all right?"

She nodded as she stood. "Yes, sir. Buzz me when you're ready to get started again."

Mark heaved a deep sigh and leaned back in his chair when Mrs. Roundtree closed the door behind herself. He knew that his accusations had hurt Alli and he wanted to kick himself in the rear end every time he thought of what he'd said. But at the time, he still had been in shock at the thought that she could be in love with him.

Although he believed that letting her know how he felt had been the right thing, he owed her an apology for some of the other things he'd said. He had been wrong to suggest she'd had an ulterior motive for taking the job as Erika's nanny. He knew the only reason she was there was that he had asked her to help him out. He had told her that he needed her and he still did.

When he saw Alli again, he would give her the apology that she deserved. She was the type of woman he should be running away from. She had been pretty clear that whenever she married she would want kids and he'd been adamant about not wanting any. She always would be the type of woman who would expect her husband to love her and Mark was incapable of loving anyone. With Erika, he was there to meet her physical needs, be her caretaker and nothing more. Why was it so hard for Alli to accept things?

His thoughts were jarred with the ringing of his telephone. He quickly picked it up. "Yes, Mrs. Roundtree?"

"Jake Thorne is on line one, sir."

"Thanks. Please put him through."

As soon as the connection was made, Mark said. "Jake? What's up man?" He wondered if Jake's call had anything to do with them getting a possible lead on the Jonathan Devlin murder.

"I just left campaign headquarters and passed by the studio, saw your truck and wondered if you wanted to join me for lunch at the Royal Diner since Alli and Erika won't be at home."

Mark lifted an eyebrow. "They won't?"

"No, they're out shopping with Chrissie."

"Oh."

Jake chuckled. "Can't you keep up with your women-folk?"

"No, I guess I can't."

"Trust me, it'll get easier."

Mark doubted it. He checked his watch. "I can join you in half an hour."

"That's good timing. I'll stop by the sheriff's office and talk to Gavin to see if there's news on anything."

"Okay, I'll see you there."

"Oh, look Erika, this is such a pretty playsuit and it's going to look so nice on you. I can even see you wearing it on Christmas Day," Alli said as she folded the newly purchased item to place in the drawer in the little girl's room.

Too bad I won't be here to see you in it, she thought as a pain settled around her heart. She had made her decision and it was final. During the past week, Mark had withdrawn so much, retreated into a shell, that not only was he trying to avoid her, but in doing so he was avoiding Erika as well. Alli couldn't let it continue.

As painful as it had been, she had gone to the Royal newspaper office and placed an ad for someone to replace her as Erika's nanny. Once she felt comfortable the person Mark hired would work out, she would give him her resignation as both Erika's nanny and his administrative assistant.

She had decided that leaving Royal would be for the best. She had contacted a real-estate agent in Austin and, although she hadn't mentioned anything to Kara when she'd called yesterday, she was seriously considering moving there. With Alli's secretarial experience and good work record, it shouldn't be hard to find a job in Texas's capital. She had never lived anywhere other than Royal but felt that now it was time for a change. She hadn't told anyone about her plans other than Christine. Alli would tell Kara when she came home next weekend to get the car Alli had gotten for her.

The only thing Alli had to keep her going were the memories of the time she and Mark had spent together, alone and with Erika. Like the fuel she needed, she constantly replayed those special moments in her mind. And she believed that no matter what Mark thought, he was wrong. There was room in his heart for love but he was just too bullheaded to see it.

"Da-da."

Closing the drawer, Alli crossed the room and picked up Erika. "Your da-da hasn't forgotten you, little one. I know for a fact that he checks on you every night when he gets in. It's me he's trying to avoid, not you." She pulled Erika to her and hugged her tight. This little girl had come to mean a lot to her during the past three weeks and she would miss her dearly when she left.

But she had to do what she had to do.

Mark walked into the Royal Diner and glanced across the room. He saw Jake and quickly moved in that direction. Jake stood, stuck out his hand and Mark took it in a handshake.

"I was beginning to think you weren't coming, Mark,"

Jake said smiling. "I just finished talking with Chrissie and she says that Erika and Alli are back at your place. I might as well warn you that they spent a lot of your money."

"It was for a good cause I'm sure," Mark said pulling out a chair and sitting. Not wanting to discuss Alli and Erika any longer, he asked, "Did Gavin have any other news?"

A frown appeared in Jake's rugged face. "No, but he did mention that last note that Nita received was written by the same person who wrote the others."

Mark nodded. He was afraid of that.

"Excuse me, Mr. Hartman."

Both Mark and Jake looked up to see a young woman standing beside their table. She was not someone Mark recognized, and since she wasn't wearing a uniform, he knew she wasn't one of the waitresses. "Yes?" Mark said, rising from his chair.

"I was wondering about that ad in today's newspaper. Is the position still open?"

Mark's eyes widened in surprise. He knew nothing about an ad in the newspaper. "What position are you talking about?"

The woman looked at him strangely, then replied, "The one for a nanny. The ad said you were looking for someone and I've got a lot of exper—"

"There must be some mistake. I'm not looking for a nanny and I didn't place an ad in today's paper for one."

"Oh. The paper must have run an old ad by mistake then. Sorry to have bothered you."

Mark watched the woman walk off. Instead of taking his seat, he turned to Jake and said, "Excuse me for a minute. I need to snag Manny's newspaper to check out something." He returned a few minutes later with a deep frown on his face.

"Well?" Jake asked, leaning back in the chair. "Was it a mistake?"

Mark sighed deeply. "Evidently not. There is an ad in today's paper. I called the newspaper and they said Alli came in and placed the ad a couple of days ago."

Jake lifted an eyebrow. "She's quitting?"

"Apparently."

Jake tipped back his hat. "You really don't know what's going on with your womenfolk, do you? I found out the hard way that's the worst mistake a man can make."

Mark sighed deeply thinking that no, that wasn't the worst mistake a man could make. Being a total fool was. "I have to go, Jake," he said, already crossing the diner and heading for the door. The newspaper had to be wrong. Alli could not be leaving him.

"Where do you think you're going?"

Alli's hand flew to her chest. She had just walked out of Erika's room after placing her down for her nap, only to find Mark standing in the hall with an intense look on his face. "Mark, you scared me. I didn't know you were home."

"Answer my question, Alli," he said, struggling to control his temper.

Alli inhaled deeply. "Okay, we can talk in the kitchen."

He walked ahead of her and was pacing the kitchen by the time she got there. He stopped and glared at her. "All right, now where do you think you're going? We had a deal."

"Yes, and it's one I plan to honor so I'm not going anywhere, at least not until you find my replacement. Then I will be leaving. And just so you'll know, I'll be turning in my resignation as your administrative assistant as well. I've made a decision to leave Royal and move to Austin."

Her words were like a punch in the gut. He leaned against the kitchen counter to get his bearings. *She wasn't just leaving him, but was actually planning on leaving Royal?* "Why are you doing this, Alli?"

She took a deep breath as he continued to look at her. "To me it's simple. For two solid years I've loved you, Mark, and worked hard not to ever let you know it. It was my secret and my secret alone. I'd heard about what happened to your wife and knew there was a chance you might not ever get over her and it didn't matter to me if you didn't love me because I loved you and that's all that mattered."

She walked across the floor and sat at the kitchen table. "But that's no longer true. My feelings do matter to me. I came here to be Erika's nanny and it hurt that you thought I was manipulating the situation to be your lover. That wasn't the case, Mark."

He crossed the room to join her. "I know that, Alli, and I want to apologize for insinuating such a thing to you. I was still shocked at what you'd said the night before, although that's no excuse."

She met his gaze. "No, it's not an excuse and as far as my emotions are concerned, my feelings are my feelings, Mark, and nothing you do or say will make me change them. However, I respect and appreciate your honesty about how you feel. Therefore, I think the best thing for me to do is to leave Royal."

When he started to say something, she held up her hand. "No, Mark. You need to understand something. I've spent a large portion of my life taking care of Kara. When you came to town I fell in love with you, and I honestly thought that loving you secretly would be enough. Until I moved in here and became your lover, it was. I was even willing to sentence my sister to the same type of life I had, all work and no play. That would have been wrong. There's beauty in loving someone, sharing your time and life with that person."

She paused briefly before continuing. "Now that I know how wonderful it is to love someone openly with no boundaries, I've decided that's what I want. My only problem is the man I love doesn't want me or love me back. So the only thing left is to pick up my pride and move on. I'm not a woman who can be a man's lover and not want something in return. I have to have love. I can't change the way I feel no more than you can change the way you feel. That's why it is best for me to leave Royal and start a new life someplace else."

She took a deep breath and slowly released it as she stood. "Now if you don't mind, I want to get some rest while Erika is sleeping."

Not giving him a chance to say anything, she hurried out of the room.

Mark remained sitting in the chair long after Alli had left. Maybe leaving Royal would be the best thing for Alli since she deserved better. But why did the thought of her leaving cause a colossal pain to settle deep in his heart? The thought of never seeing her again was something he just couldn't bear. He thought about how his relationship with Patrice had been and knew what he'd shared with Alli had been so different. Was he going to go around blaming himself for the rest of his life for Patrice's death, knowing things might not have been any different had he been in the States? He and Patrice had begun living separate lives even while residing under the same roof. He had offered to teach her self-defense many times but she had refused his offer.

He thought of all the things he and Alli had shared. There was such a goodness about her that went beyond how she took care of Erika. It went beyond how she'd taken care of her sister and, more importantly, it went beyond how she had taken care of him.

And she had taken care of him. Since she had moved to the ranch, he had experienced some of the happiest and most joyous moments of his life. Suddenly he was struck with the reason why.

He loved her.

There was no sense denying it. As much as he hadn't wanted to fall in love with her, he had, and he could be honest enough with himself to admit he had probably loved her for as long as she had loved him. But since coming to live in his home, she had shown him love and how to express it, with her and with Erika. And he wanted to continue what they shared. It no longer bothered him that Erika referred to him as her father. When she got older, he and Alli would tell her all about her parents and how much they had loved her and that Matt had entrusted her in Mark's care because deep down his brother had known that eventually he would show her love and not expose her to the loveless childhood they had endured.

He stood, knowing what he had to do. He had to convince Alli that he loved her and wanted her as part of his life.

Alli had sworn she wouldn't cry but was doing so anyway, she thought as she wiped tears from her eyes. Moving away from Royal wouldn't be so bad. Austin was a big city with a lot of opportunities. She would make new friends and, who knew, she might even meet someone whom she could learn to love.

Fat chance! Her heart would always belong to Mark.

She lifted her head off the pillow when she heard a knock at her bedroom door. Knowing it could only be Mark, she ignored it. There was nothing left to be said. When she heard the knock again, she decided to see what he wanted. Definitely not her, she thought.

With a heartrending sigh, she crossed the room to open the door. "Yes?"

"I listened to what you said in the kitchen and now I'm asking that you listen to what I have to say."

Alli glanced down at the floor, not wanting him to see her red-rimmed eyes. Besides, she couldn't look into his face without seeing the man she loved more than anything. Feeling somewhat composed, she finally looked up. "I'm sure your message will be the same, Mark, so why bother?"

"Please hear me out, Alli."

Instead of saying anything, she backed up to let him in. He walked over to the window and looked out a long moment before turning around to face her. "The one special memory I have of my mom that I'll always hold dear to my heart was the day she took me and Matt for a walk. I believe it was the same day the doctor had given her the news that she only had a short time to live."

He looked out the window for a moment again and then his gaze returned to Alli. "She told us the story we'd heard so many times before about how our grandparents found oil making them rich. She also said that it was her dream that that legacy would continue with our kids. It wasn't until years later after she'd died and I was raised by a father who didn't know the meaning of expressing love that I decided I would never marry nor would I have children."

He walked across the room to lean against her dresser. "While serving in the marines, I met Patrice through a friend. Her childhood had been just as rough and unloving as mine, and because of a medical condition that had left her sterile, she couldn't have children. What we entered into was more of a partnership than a real marriage. Neither of us knew how to express our emotions and we were fine with it."

He looked down at the floor a moment then back at Alli. "I'd been satisfied until Erika came into my life. I kept wanting to give her more of myself but didn't think that I could. The one thing I didn't want was for her childhood here with me to resemble the type Matt and I had with our father. But it was only until you came to live here that I could see how much distance I'd put between me and my niece, even when I hadn't meant to do so."

He crossed the room to stand before Alli. "I'd never been my happiest, Alli, until you came to live here with us. I thought I could go the rest of my life without love but I see I can't. Knowing you might be leaving Royal has knocked some sense into me. I love you, Alli. I love both you and Erika, and I don't think I could handle it if you were to leave. Stay here, marry me and make this place a home for us. I want the three of us to become a family. I told you once that I needed you. At the time I didn't know how much. Now I do. If you will have me, I will never give you a reason to want to ever leave again."

Alli's mouth trembled and she swallowed a lump caught deep in her throat. She was speechless after Mark's declaration of love.

"I'll be good to you and our daughter. I promise."

Alli blinked back her tears. "Our daughter?"

"Yes, I want us to adopt Erika and when she gets older we will tell her all about Matt and Candice. I think they would have wanted things that way."

"What about other children? I want them but you don't, Mark."

"I do now," he said softly, meaning every word. "I want to give you my babies, Alli. As many as you want. I want to be a father to our kids, a good and loving father who won't be afraid to show them how much I love them every day of my life."

Alli squeezed her eyes shut to stop the flow of her tears and dipped her head. Mark's words were making her dream come true. He reached out and tilted her chin up with the tip of his finger. "I love you, Alli. Will you marry me and continue to show me love in its purest form?"

She met his gaze, saw the hopeful look in his eyes. "Yes," she said tearfully. "I love you, too, and I want to marry you so you, Erika and I can be a family."

He pulled her into his arms and held her close to his heart. "I love you, Alli," he said for the third time that day. "Everything will work out between us and we will be a family."

She smiled up at him. "Yes, we will be a family."

He pulled her into his arms, tasting the tears on her lips. And this time he put all the emotions he'd ever held back into this kiss, wanting her to feel the love that was flowing through every vein in his body. Desire ran rampant through his blood and he needed to make love to her, claim her as his, connect with her, and let her know just how much she was loved.

He picked her up in his arms, sweeping her off her feet, and carried her over to the bed. Without uttering a word, they undressed each other and, when they were both naked, he placed her against the pillows. He thought she was the most beautiful woman in the world lying nude before him with her hair spilled over the aqua bedspread.

She reached out for him. "Make love to me, Mark."

He came to her, drew her tongue deep into his mouth, sucking on it until she groaned out. His hand went lower down her body, past her stomach to settle between her legs and found her wet, ready, hot. Pulling back, he quickly sheathed himself with a condom and then moved his body in position over hers.

He met her gaze. Held it. And when he began entering her, he knew he had come home. When he'd gone as deep as he could, he kept his body motionless, needing to feel her around him, clutching him, loving him. Then with a loud animalistic growl, he withdrew, then thrust back into her again, feeling her body shiver and shudder at his onslaught. Over and over, he withdrew and went back in, knowing this would be his home for the rest of his days. And that she was his woman.

He spread her thighs some more, grasped her hips to part her farther, then threw his head back as flesh slapped against flesh, the sound heating up their desires and passion even more.

"Mark!"

She screamed his name, once, twice, three times and he continued to move within her. Then he gritted this teeth as a howl burst from his lips and he frantically rocked his body into hers, needing to go as deep as he could with the woman that he loved.

And he did.

Mark rolled off Alli to stare at the ceiling as he fought for breath. They had made love several times before, but never with this intensity. He pulled her into his arms. "I love you."

She looked over at him and smiled, fighting for breath as he was. "I love you, too."

"I want to get married next weekend, Alli."

She let out a soft chuckle. "Rushing things, aren't you?"

He grinned. "Yes, I suppose I am. Do you think it can be arranged?"

She sighed upon seeing he was dead serious. "I'll call Kara. She was coming home next weekend anyway to get her car so that time might be perfect."

"Good, and when Erika wakes up we'll go to the jeweler so you can pick out a ring. We're going to make it a family affair."

Alli smiled. "That sounds wonderful to me."

"Da-da. " Erika's voice could be heard through the monitor.

Alli smiled sheepishly. "Oops. My screams may have wakened her."

Mark chuckled. "Or it could have been the sound of this bed knocking against the wall."

"Mark!"

"Well, it's the truth," he said laughing.

"Da-da."

Mark leaned over and flipped on the speaker that was connected to Erika's room. "Your daddy is coming, sweetheart," he said with all the love in his heart.

He glanced over at a smiling Alli. An expression of love and tenderness consumed his features when he said, "And so is your mommy."

Four days later, a smiling Mark walked into the Texas Cattleman's Club to attend a meeting that had been called by

Gavin. It was a perfect Texas night and back home waiting for him were two perfect young ladies. Everything was set. He and Alli would be getting married this coming weekend. Her sister would be there as well as all of their friends. Mrs. Tucker had called two days ago to let them know she would be returning to Royal and would love to have her old job back as Erika's nanny.

Mark and Alli had jumped for joy and, since Mrs. Roundtree was working out just fine at the studio, he suggested that Alli attend school full-time to obtain her degree. When she finished, he wanted her to use the vacant space in the studio as her computer-engineering business office.

"Hartman, wipe that silly grin off your face so we can get down to business," Logan said when Mark took a seat at the table.

"Hey, don't get testy because I decided not to have a long engagement and move ahead and marry my woman. I expect all of you to be at the wedding on Saturday."

"We'll be there," Gavin said grinning. "Now let's get down to business. With this last threatening note to Nita Windcroft if things continue to escalate, one of us may need to start watching the Windcroft farm. I think Connor would be the logical choice. With his army ranger experience he will be the perfect person for the job."

Jake leaned back in his chair. "Have you broken this news to Connor yet?" he asked, thinking that his brother would have his hands full taking on Nita Windcroft. He wouldn't wish that nightmare on his worst enemy.

"No, and I don't plan to do so, either, until he returns from Virginia. This is something he needs to hear in person."

Everyone nodded in full agreement.

"Connor did indicate he wanted me to call him tonight and

husband to Alli and a wonderful father to Erika. He intended to spend the rest of his life showing both of his ladies just how much he loved them.

"Nita looks nice doesn't she?" Alli asked.

Following her gaze, Mark saw Nita Windcroft talking to Mrs. Tucker. She was wearing a light blue pantsuit. "Yes, she does and this is the first time I've seen her in anything other than a pair of jeans."

Alli nodded. This was the first time she had seen Nita wearing anything but jeans, too. Alli thought the pantsuit looked really good on Nita and couldn't wait for the day she got to see Nita wearing a dress—if that day ever came. "So, Mr. Hartman, are you ready to take time away from Royal for a while?"

"As long as I am with you, Mrs. Hartman, I am ready for anything." He leaned closer and kissed her, ignoring the cat-calls and applause.

When he released her, Alli glanced across the yard at her sister, who was smiling happily at her. Alli smiled back. Cameron, who had arrived in town with Kara to help her drive her new car back to Houston, was indeed a hottie. But after talking with him, Alli concluded that he was also a really nice guy. He had come from a family of attorneys and had plans to go to law school. She could tell he cared a lot for Kara and he told her that he and Kara had talked about it and had decided not to let their dates interfere with their schoolwork. Alli liked that decision. Even Mark had said he liked Cameron since he seemed to be a pretty decent and mature guy with a good head on his shoulders.

Moments later, when Mark escorted her back to their table

where Erika was sitting in her high chair, he leaned over and kissed his niece. Love ran swiftly through Alli's veins as she watched her husband. He was no longer afraid to show his emotions and for that she was thankful.

Hand in hand, they began walking around thanking their guests for coming and sharing in their special day. Happiness shone on their faces in knowing this was the beginning of their lives together and they intended to make every day exceptional.

"How about another dance, sweetheart?" Mark asked, pulling her into his arms and leading her toward the dance floor.

"I'd love to," she said, smiling up at him.

He leaned down and brushed a kiss across her mouth. "And I love you," he said softly, thinking he could never say it enough. Never had he dreamed someone so beautiful would come into his life and help him to overcome his past, and give him the love and the passion he'd always yearned for. He gathered her closer into his arms and couldn't wait for later that night when they would be alone.

"What are you thinking about, Mark?" Alli asked, leaning back slightly to look into his eyes.

His eyes—no doubt full of love—held hers. Deciding that what he was thinking about was for her ears only, he leaned closer and whispered to her.

What he said nearly took her breath away. He smiled and hugged her closer, burying his face in the curve of her neck and inhaling the scent that was so much a part of her. "You did ask."

A smile touched the corners of Alli's lips. He had just

whispered some very naughty things that he had planned for her later. "Yes, I did, didn't I?"

"Yes, you did," he murmured softly. And then he was kissing her again.

* * * * *

TAKING CARE OF BUSINESS

A special thank-you to the interracial couples
that I interviewed who provided the feedback
I asked for. It was deeply appreciated
and proves that true love is color-blind.

Live happily with the woman you love through the
fleeting days of life, for the wife God gives you is
your best reward down here for all your earthly toil.
—*Ecclesiastes* 9:9

Chapter 1

"Ms. Williams, Mr. Teagan Elliott is here to see you."

Renee Williams took a deep breath, slipped off her reading glasses and pushed aside the medical report on Karen Elliott, bracing herself to deal with the woman's son, who from what Renee had heard was causing problems.

Since learning of his mother's breast cancer, and trying to assist Karen in dealing with all the paperwork for her upcoming surgery, Teagan Elliott was going about it the wrong way by putting unnecessary pressure on the hospital staff just because his last name was Elliott.

She pressed down the respond button on her phone and said, "Please send him in, Vicki."

Renee silently prayed that her confrontation with him would go well. She didn't want to remember the last time she had taken a stand against a man who thought his last name was the key to open any and all doors.

Her job as a social worker at Manhattan University Hospital meant helping everyone and making sure they were treated fairly, regardless of their economic, educational and cultural backgrounds.

A knock on the door brought Renee's thoughts back to the business at hand. "Come in."

She stood and placed a smile on her face when the man she knew to be Teagan Elliott, of Elliott Publication Holdings, one of the largest magazine conglomerates in the world, walked into her office dressed as if he had just posed for a photo shoot in *GQ* magazine. Renee had to concede he was a handsome man with all the sure-sign characteristics, which included expressive eyes, a symmetrical face, a straight nose and a chiseled jawline.

Moving from around her desk, she met him halfway and offered him her hand in a firm handshake. He automatically took it. "Mr. Elliott?"

"Yes, and you're Ms. Williams, I presume."

His northern accent was polished, refined and spoke of old money and lots of it. "Yes, I am. Would you like to have a seat so we can discuss the matter concerning your mother?"

He frowned. "No, I don't want to sit to discuss anything. I want you to tell me just what will be done for her."

Renee lifted a brow as she stared into the icy blue eyes that were holding hers. So he wanted to be difficult, did he? Well, he would soon discover that when it came to handling difficult people, she could be a force to reckon with. She crossed her arms over her chest. "Suit yourself if you prefer standing, but I've had a rather long and taxing day and I don't intend to stand."

With that, she resumed her seat. The glare he gave her was priceless, and if it weren't for the seriousness of the situation at hand, she would have quirked her lips into a smile. Evidently, not too many people sat down and left him standing.

"Now, about your mother," Renee said after taking a sip of her coffee, which had turned cold. "I see that her surgery is scheduled for—"

"I think I need to apologize."

Renee glanced up, put down her mug and gave him a look. The eyes staring back at her were no longer icy but were now a beautiful shade of clear blue. "Do you?"

"Yes." A smile touched his lips. They were lips that Renee thought were beautifully shaped.

"Normally I'm a likeable guy, but knowing what my mother is going through right now is a little hard to deal with. It wasn't my intent to come across as an arrogant ass. I just want to make sure she's getting the best of everything," he said, coming to take the seat across from Renee.

A part of Renee wondered if there was ever a time an Elliott hadn't gotten the best of everything. "That's what I'm here for, Mr. Elliott. My job is to make sure that not only your mother, but anyone faced with emotional concerns that can impede their recovery is given help to deal with those issues."

He nodded and his smile widened. "Have you met my mother?"

Renee returned his smile. For some reason she was drawn to it. "Yes, I had a chance to talk to her a few days ago. I found her to be a very beautiful person, both inside and out."

He chuckled. "She is that."

Renee could tell Teagan loved his mother very much. In talking with Karen Elliott, Renee had discovered the woman had three sons and a daughter. Teagan, at twenty-nine, was the third child, youngest of the sons, and a news editor at one of the family magazines, *Pulse*. Renee had also discovered during her talk with Karen that of all her children, she and Teagan had the closest relationship.

"So tell me, what are we up against, Ms. Williams?"

Teagan's question broke into Renee's thoughts. "Now that the doctor has given your mother the diagnosis and a decision has been made for surgery, what Karen needs from her family more than anything is support. I understand some of you don't comprehend her reasons for having a double mastectomy when a tumor was found in only one breast. She wants to have both removed as a precaution. Doing so is her choice and should be accepted as such.

"Karen also will need all of your love and support when the surgery is over and during her period of recuperation before she starts her chemotherapy treatments. Again, although there is no sign the cancer has spread to the lymph nodes, she has decided to undergo chemo as a precaution. The outlook at this point is still guarded, but I truly believe everything will work out in your mother's favor since the lump was found early."

Renee leaned back in her chair. Now that it was pretty obvious that Teagan Elliott was just trying to help his mother, although he had approached it in the wrong way, her heart went out to him. It was admirable for a son to care so much for his mother the way he did.

"Do you have any idea when the surgery will take place?" he asked.

"Right now, it's scheduled for next Tuesday."

Teagan sighed as he stood. "I really appreciate you taking the time to explain what the family needs to do. And again I apologize for my earlier attitude."

Renee smiled as she also got to her feet. "You are forgiven. I completely understand how an unexpected medical condition can cause havoc to even the mildest-mannered individual."

He laughed. "I said I'm normally a likeable guy. I never said anything about being mild-mannered."

Renee grinned. Nobody had said anything about him being a handsome hunk, either, but the proof was standing before her. With his six-foot athletic build, jet-black hair and blue eyes, she couldn't help wondering if anyone had ever told him that he bore a marked resemblance to what she perceived would be a younger-looking Pierce Brosnan. He was definitely worth taking a second look at. But she knew a look was all she'd ever take. Men with the kind of money the Elliotts had didn't bother dating people out of their social class. Besides, he was white and she was black.

"Here's my business card, Mr. Elliott. As your mother's social worker, I'm here whenever you need me. Just give me a call."

Teagan accepted the card and placed it in the pocket of his jacket. "I appreciate that. I'll get the family together tonight and we'll talk about what you and I have discussed. Right now my mother's health, as well as her peace of mind, is the most important thing. Thanks for everything."

Renee watched as he turned and walked out of her office.

Teagan, better known to family and friends as Tag, stepped into the elevator, glad he was alone. He released a deep sigh that came all the way from his gut. What the hell had happened to him while in Renee Williams's office? The woman was definitely a beauty, and radiated an almost palpable feminine presence that nearly knocked him to his knees. Nothing like that had ever happened to him before while sharing space with a woman.

When she'd spoken, the silkiness of her voice was enough to stroke everything male inside of him. It had been like a physical caress on his senses. And when their hands had touched in that handshake, it had taken everything he had to control the urge to pull her closer to him. He figured she was about five feet five inches without the pumps, and the outfit she'd been wearing, a tangerine-colored business suit, had definitely defined her curvy figure.

Then there was the coloring of her skin, a creamy color that reminded him of rich caramel. Combined with long, black hair that flowed around her shoulders, and dark brown eyes that had stared at him, she reflected, in addition to striking good looks, compassion, intelligence and spunk.

He actually had to chuckle when he thought of what she had told him when he had initially refused to sit down. Yes, she had spunk, all right, and he would give anything to have the opportunity to get to know her better. But he knew that would be impossible. A romantic involvement with anyone was the last thing he had time for. Since his father had decided, and rightly so, that spending time with Tag's mother was more important than what was going on at the office, Tag was more involved with the magazine than ever. And then there was that blasted challenge his grandfather, Patrick Elliott, had issued that had sparked a rivalry between EPH's top four magazines.

Each of the four magazines was run by one of Patrick's children. There was *Pulse,* the one run by Tag's father, Michael, which was a world-class news magazine; *Snap,* a celebrity magazine run by Tag's uncle Daniel; *Buzz,* which focused on showbiz gossip and was headed by Tag's uncle Shane; and *Charisma,* a fashion magazine run by Tag's aunt Finola.

Last month, Patrick had decreed he was ready to retire and whoever made his or her magazine the biggest success by the end of the year would be given the position of CEO of the entire Elliott Publication Holdings.

When the elevator came to a stop on the bottom floor, Tag couldn't help but look forward to the day his and Renee Williams's paths would cross again.

"So, there you have it, the gist of what the social worker said today," Tag said to his siblings at dinner that evening. The four of them had met at a restaurant in Manhattan, not far from the building that housed the Elliott publications. Gannon, at thirty-three, was second in command to his father at *Pulse*; Liam, at thirty-one, was currently working in the corporate financial department and Bridget, who was twenty-eight, was the photo editor for *Charisma*.

"And you're sure this social worker knows what she's talking about?" Bridget asked, taking a sip of her wine. There was a worried expression on her face. "The decisions Mom has made lately are so unlike her. It's as if she's going to the extreme."

Tag nodded, knowing where his sister was coming from, especially their mother's decision to have a double mastectomy. But all he had to do was recall his meeting earlier that day with Renee Williams to know the woman did know what she was talking about. She seemed very competent and professional...as well as beautiful. The latter seemed to stick out in his mind and he couldn't let go of it. Even now, he couldn't help but remember the smiles he had coaxed out of her after apologizing for his behavior.

"Yes, she knows what she's talking about," he finally said,

responding to Bridget's question. "But as I was reminded to-day, it was Mom's decision to make and what she needs from all of us is our love and support."

Tag felt that he and his siblings always had a rather close relationship, and a crisis such as this was making them that much closer. After thanking the waitress who handed them menus, he turned to his older brother Gannon. Gannon had recently become engaged and Tag, like everyone else, was happy for him. Erika was just what Gannon needed, not to mention, as an editor, an asset to *Pulse*.

"How is Dad holding out?" Tag asked Gannon.

Gannon, who had been studying the menu, glanced up at his youngest brother. "He's doing all right. Today he cancelled an important meeting with a representative from St. John's Distributors to fly with Mom to Syracuse to check on one of her charities there."

"It's hard to believe he's actually putting all work aside," Liam said, shaking his head. All of them knew what a work-aholic Michael Elliott was, but even so, they also knew what a strong marriage their parents had.

"That just goes to show how much Mom means to him," Bridget said smiling, touched by the way their father was de-voting his time to his wife during her medical crisis.

Bridget glanced over at Tag. "This social worker you met with today. What can you tell us about her?"

Tag leaned back in his chair and smiled. "Her name is Renee Williams. She's African-American, probably about your age. She's very professional and definitely seems to know her business. There is also a calming quality about her that can make anyone feel comforted and reassured."

Liam nodded. "She sounds like just the person Mom needs.

This illness has made her spirits decline, and that bothers me more than anything."

That was bothering Tag as well, but he believed Renee could help his mother get through this particular emotional stage. "Ms. Williams is also very beautiful." The moment the statement left Tag's lips he knew it was a mistake, because it immediately captured the attention of his siblings.

Gannon raised a dark brow at Tag. "Oh, you happened to notice that, did you?"

Bridget and Liam chuckled. Everyone knew how it was with Tag when it came to his interest in women. His mind was spent more on business than romantic pursuits.

Tag knew where his siblings were coming from and smiled. "Yes, I noticed." The last thing he needed was to be thinking about a woman, especially one as good-looking as Renee Williams, but he couldn't help himself. There was just something about her that had touched him on a level that no woman had done before.

"Mmm, the salmon looks good tonight."

Tag glanced over at his sister who was studying her menu. However, his brothers were still staring at him with curious gazes. Uncomfortable with being the center of their attention, he frowned. "Hell, it was just an observation. Don't try and make anything of it."

Gannon laughed. "If you say so, kiddo."

Chapter 2

"Ms. Williams? This is a pleasant surprise."

Renee glanced up from the novel she was reading to gaze into the friendly blue eyes of Teagan Elliott. "Mr. Elliott, how are you?" she said, smiling and adjusting her reading glasses on her nose. "And how is your mother doing?"

She watched his lips thin and a worried look appear in his eyes. "She's not her usual vibrant self and isn't saying a lot about her upcoming surgery to any of us. I talked to Dad and he says it's the same with him."

Renee nodded. "How she's handling things is understand-able. Just give her time to come to grips with everything. She has a lot to deal with right now."

Tag shook his head. "I know you're right, but I'm still con-cerned about her."

"That's understandable. All of you will get through this and so will your mother."

Tag couldn't help but return her smile. Just as he'd told his siblings, Renee Williams had such a calming nature about her. From the first time he had met her a few days ago, he had quickly concluded that she was the perfect advocate for her patients. He knew his mother liked her and spoke highly of her often.

"So, what brings you to Greenwich Village? Do you live close by?" he asked. He had been walking down the street checking out paintings by various artists when he'd happened to spot her in the window seat of the café. At first he hadn't been certain it was she, but then, from the way his body had responded, he'd known for sure. Whether he liked it or not, he was definitely attracted to this woman, and seeing her today wasn't helping matters.

In her office there had been this professional demeanor surrounding her, but here on a Saturday morning, sitting at a window-seat table at a small café and wearing a wool skirt and a blue sweater, she made him even more aware of just how beautiful she was. Even her ponytail didn't detract from that beauty. The temperature was in the upper fifties, one of those inexplicable, rare heat waves that warmed New York in February.

"No, I live in Morningside Heights. I was supposed to meet someone here this morning, but they called at the last minute to cancel. I decided to come here, anyway."

"Oh, I see." Tag couldn't help wondering if the person she'd planned on meeting was a man, then wanted to kick himself for even caring. He quickly decided the blame wasn't all his. He was someone who appreciated beauty and Renee Williams was one of those women whose sultry good looks rang out loud and clear.

"Well, I'll let you get back to your reading. I didn't mean to interrupt you."

She tilted her head to the side, her eyes holding his captive. And when she took her tongue to moisten her lips, he found his gaze glued to her mouth. "You didn't interrupt me. In fact, I'm glad I ran into you," she said, giving him a throaty chuckle that did something to his insides.

He gave her a crooked smile. "In that case, do you mind if I join you?"

He could tell she was surprised by his question, but without missing a beat, she said, "No, I don't mind."

As soon as he pulled out a chair, a waiter came to take his order. "Can I get you anything, Mr. Elliott?"

"The usual, Maurice." The man nodded and quickly walked off. Tag looked across the table to find Renee watching him with open curiosity. "Is there anything wrong, Ms. Williams?"

She shook her head, grinning. "No, but I take it that you're a regular here."

His mouth curved into a smile. "Yes, I have a condo in Tribeca and come here often, usually every Saturday morning. I love art and there's nothing like seeing an artist at work." He watched her smile again and wondered if she had any idea how seductive it looked.

"I like art, too. I even dabble in it every now and then."

"Really?"

She laughed. "Yes, really, and when I say *dabble* I mean *dabble*. I've never taken any art classes or anything. I think I just have a knack for it. I believe it was something I inherited from my mother. She was an art major and taught the class at a high school in Ohio."

"Ohio? Is that where you're from?"

"Yes. I even went to college there. Ohio State."

Tag leaned back in his chair. "What brought you to New York?"

Renee sighed deeply. She didn't want to think about Dionne Moore, the man who had broken her heart. After graduating from college she had taken a job at a hospital in Atlanta where she had met Dionne, a cardiologist. She'd thought their relationship was special, solid, until she'd found out that Dionne was having an affair with a nurse behind her back.

What was sad was that while she hadn't known about the other woman, several of the other doctors—friends of Dionne—had known and had been taking bets as to when she would find out. Once she did, it had caused quite a scandal that had had everyone talking for days.

Embarrassed, she had promised to never allow herself to be the hot topic over anyone's breakfast, lunch or dinner table. To repair her heart and put distance between her and Dionne, she had jumped at the chance to relocate to New York when Debbie Massey, her best friend from college, had told her about an opening at Manhattan University Hospital. That had been almost two years ago, and since then she had pretty much kept to herself and had refrained from dating altogether.

"It was a job offer I couldn't refuse and don't regret taking," she finally said. "I love New York."

"So do I."

At that moment they were interrupted when the waiter returned with a tall bottle of beer for Tag. Tag tipped the bottle to his lips, then setting it down on the table looked over at Renee. "So, Ms. Williams, how do you—"

"It would make me feel better if you called me Renee."

"Okay," he said slowly. "And I'd like it if you called me Tag, which is what everyone calls me."

"All right, then, Tag it is."

He glanced at her glass. It was almost empty. "Would you like another drink?"

"No, thank you. The fruit punch here is delicious, but too rich. I'm going to have to do a lot of walking to burn off the calories."

"I'm sorry your date didn't show up."

Renee laughed. "Don't be. It's not the first time Debbie has gotten called away at the last minute. When duty calls, you have to go. She's a friend of mine who works at *Time* magazine."

"Ouch, they're *Pulse*'s strongest competitor."

Renee chuckled. "Yes, that's what I hear."

"But we're definitely better."

Renee reared her head back and laughed. "And of course, I would expect you to make that claim."

Tag took another long pull of his beer. The sound of Renee's laughter was breathy and intimate and he immediately felt a jolt of desire in the pit of his stomach.

He couldn't remember the last time he had allowed himself to unwind, certainly not since his grandfather had challenged the family, sparking everyone's competitive nature. But for once his mind was on something else besides work. It was on a woman. This particular woman. If she could have this sort of effect on him just by being in his presence, he didn't want to think what would happen if he were to touch her. Kiss her. Or better yet, make love to her.

The image slammed into him, sizzling his brain cells and making slow heat flow through every part of his body.

"I guess it's time for me to get up and start browsing the shops."

He glanced over at her, not ready to part ways. "Would you

mind if I browse with you? There are a couple of places that are giving private showings today that you might be interested in."

Renee met his gaze. What he hadn't said was that the only way she could attend those showings was with him. The Elliott name carried a lot of weight. She sighed and chewed the inside of her cheek. She had heard about those private art showings and knew that now was her chance to go to one. So why was she hesitating? Browsing the shops and attending a private show or two with Tag wouldn't be so bad as long as she kept things in perspective. She was his mother's social worker and he was being kind. End of story.

She drained the last of her drink before saying, "Are you sure you don't mind me attending those showings with you?"

He placed his beer bottle down. "Yes, I'm sure. I'd like to spend some time with you, anyway."

She licked her lips. "Why?"

He tried not concentrating on her mouth. Instead, he gazed directly into her eyes. "Because I've been working a lot of hours lately and this is the first opportunity I've had to grab time for myself. And because I really enjoy your company."

Her smile was slow but he knew it was also sincere. "Thanks, I'm enjoying your company as well, Tag."

"Then," he said calmly, "that pretty much settles it."

There was a moment of silence, and Renee quickly wondered if anything between them was settled, or just about to get pretty stirred up.

"Oh my goodness, this is simply beautiful."

Tag glanced at the painting Renee was referring to and had to agree. The piece, titled *Colors,* depicted an

African-American child standing beneath a rainbow. The artist had been able to vibrantly capture all the colors, including the child's skin tone, as well as the blue-green ocean that served as a backdrop. The happiness that shone on the toddler's face was priceless, and the way the painting was encased in a black wooden frame made all the vivacious colors stand out. "Yes, it is, isn't it."

He picked up the tag attached to the painting and glanced at it. "It's a Malone and the price isn't bad, considering he's making a name for himself now. I was able to purchase several of his paintings at a private art show when he first got started."

Renee could envision the paintings adorning the walls of Tag's condo. Alton Malone, who was of mixed Caucasian and African-American heritage, had a wide range, but she personally liked his contemporary ethnic paintings the best.

It was obvious Tag liked fine art. But then, so did she. The only difference was that money to buy it came more easily to him than to her.

At the moment, the difference in their incomes wasn't the only thing on her mind. So was the difference in their skin colors. Although New York was one of the most diverse cities on earth, some people's opinions about interracial dating just didn't change. More than once, as they strolled along the sidewalk together, darting in and out of various shops, Renee had felt people's curious eyes on her. Whether accepting or disapproving, she wasn't sure. But the stares had been obvious, as were a few frowns. There was no way Tag hadn't noticed. However, he didn't seem bothered that people were erroneously assuming they were a couple.

"It's four o'clock already," he said. "What about grabbing something to eat before I take you home?"

Renee glanced over at Tag. Earlier, he had asked how she had gotten to Greenwich Village and she had told him that she had ridden the subway. He had offered to drive her home, saying his car wasn't parked too far away. She had graciously declined the offer. Hanging out with him on a lazy Saturday was one thing, but she didn't intend for him to go out of his way to take her home.

"Tag, thanks for the offer, but I'm used to taking the subway wherever I need to go."

"I'm sure you are, but I don't have anything else to do. Besides, it will be late evening by the time we finish eating."

Renee shook her head as a smile touched her lips. "I wonder when it will dawn on you that I didn't agree to eat with you."

He grinned. "Sure you did. That was our deal, remember?"

Renee lifted a brow as they continued to stroll along the sidewalk. "What deal?"

"Don't you remember?"

She eyed him suspiciously. "No, I do not."

"Then you must be having a senior moment."

"No, I don't think so," Renee said, enjoying this camaraderie with him. "I'm twenty-eight and way too young to have senior moments."

"Not so," he said, teasing Renee. "I'm twenty-nine, but I used to have—"

"Hey, Tag! Wait up!"

Tag and Renee stopped walking when the person called out to him. They turned to see a man—who appeared to be about

Tag's age, dressed in a jogging suit and running shoes—trot over to them.

"Hey, man, where have you been keeping yourself?" the man asked Tag when he finally reached them and the two men shook hands. "It's been ages since I've seen you at the club."

"Work has been keeping me busy," Tag said. He then glanced at Renee. "Renee, I want you to meet a friend of mine from college, Thomas Bonner. Thomas, this is Renee Williams."

Renee accepted the man's hand. "It's nice meeting you, Thomas." She could immediately feel the unfriendliness in the handshake and watched as he plastered a phony smile on his face.

"Uh, yes, nice meeting you, too." Then, as if she was of little importance, he dismissed her and glanced up at Tag through disapproving eyes. "Evidently, you're not too busy to carve out some colorful playtime."

Renee immediately picked up the censorship in his expression. Evidently, Thomas Bonner thought that she wasn't the type or the color of woman that Tag should be seen with. But his insinuation that she was nothing more than an object of Tag's amusement really got next to her. Breathing deep, she held back her anger, deciding this man wasn't worth it. However, Tag evidently disagreed. He placed his hand on the small of her back and eased her closer to him.

She could hear the iciness in his voice when he said, "You should know I'm too serious a guy to ever indulge in playtime. Besides, when a man meets someone this beautiful he doesn't waste his time by acting a fool. If he's smart, he uses it wisely to impress her. And what I'm doing, Thomas, is trying to impress. Wish me luck."

Renee could tell Tag's comments left the man at a loss for words. "Uh, well, I'd better continue my run. Give my best to your family," Thomas finally stumbled out before jogging off without looking back. Renee could just imagine the rumors that would be flying around in Tag's social circle tomorrow. Maybe he could handle a scandal, but she could not. She had been there, done that. And she didn't want to ever live through it again.

She glanced up at Tag. "Why did you give him the impression that we're romantically involved?"

The corners of his lips turned up and she hated admitting how much she liked the way his smile seemed to touch his eyes. "Does it bother you that I did?"

She shrugged. "I could handle his comment. He's not the first prejudiced person I've met in my lifetime and he won't be the last. Over the years, I've experienced my fair share of bigotry," she said softly.

"Well, that's one thing I won't tolerate."

She believed him.

They began walking, and neither said anything for a few moments, then Renee decided to break the silence. She glanced over at him. "You never did say why you did it."

Tag sighed. There was no way he was going to tell her that for a moment he hadn't been able to help himself. He had refused to let Thomas think that his intentions toward her—if there had been any—were anything less than honorable. To insinuate that she wasn't someone he could possibly take seriously had hit his last nerve because it was so far from the truth. And that, he quickly concluded, was the crux of his problem. Renee was someone he could take seriously if he was free to engage in a serious relationship. But he wasn't. The situation with his mother was bad enough. Add to that what was happening at Elliott Publication Holdings and it was enough to make a nondrinker order a bottle of gin and guzzle the entire thing.

Knowing that she was waiting for an answer, he decided to give her one. "Thomas was going to think whatever he wanted without any help from me. You're a beautiful woman and I don't consider myself a bad-looking guy, so quite naturally people will assume we're a couple."

"And that doesn't bother you?"

"No, but it evidently bothers you. I learned early in life, Renee, not to care what other people think."

Renee ceased walking and placed a hand firmly on Tag's arm. "And that's probably just one of the many differences in our upbringings. I was raised to care what others think."

Tag nodded. "In this case, with us, now, today, why should it matter?"

She raised her eyes heavenward. Did she have to spell it out for him? It wouldn't matter if it were today or tomorrow. The circumstances would still be the same. "Because I'm black and you're white, Tag."

He smiled, and his eyes sparkled as if he'd just been told something scandalous, simply incredulous. "You're joking," he said in mock surprise. He took her hand, held it up to his, denoting the obvious contrast of their skin coloring. "Really? I hadn't noticed."

She couldn't help but chuckle. And she couldn't help but decide at that moment that she liked him. "Get real."

"I am. And what's real is that I like you and I enjoy your company. This is the most relaxed I've been in a long time, especially since finding out about my mother's cancer and taking on added responsibilities at work. And I'm not about to let a bunch of prejudiced fools decide

whom I should or should not date. As for my caring what
others think, I've had to deal with people's misconceptions
all my life. They think just because my name is Elliott that
I've had it easy."

She hated admitting that she'd assumed the same thing.
"And you haven't?"

"Far from it. There's no such word as easy with a grandfather like Patrick Elliott."

Renee glanced over at Tag. "Tell me about him."

They had reached the café where Tag had mentioned earlier
would be a good place to eat. They sat down right away, the
crowd from earlier that day having thinned out.

"Patrick Elliott is one tough old man. He was raised by
Irish immigrants who instilled in him a strong work ethic.
He worked to put himself through school and because of his
keen mind and street smarts, he went to work at a magazine
company and eventually founded his own empire."

He paused when the waitress delivered their waters and
gave them menus. Renee, who'd evidently been thirsty, took a
deep gulp and licked the excess from around her lips. At that
moment, a surge of desire hit Tag. It was so overwhelming,
he had to briefly look away.

"And?"

He blinked at her single word. "And what?"

She smiled. "You were telling me about your grandfather,
but I don't think you were finished."

He chuckled, thinking of how he'd gotten sidetracked. "Oh,
yes, where was I?" he said, leaning back in his chair after taking a sip of his own water. "While in Ireland visiting family,
he met and fell in love with a young seamstress named Maeve
O'Grady. They eventually married and raised many children
together. My grandparents have a very loving relationship.

However, it's my belief that my grandfather's fear of poverty is what has made him devoted to his business."

Tag paused for a moment, reflecting on what his next words would be. "Although my grandfather dotes a lot on my grandmother, he hasn't always spent a lot of time with his children and grandchildren and isn't very demonstrative, although we all know he loves us. Over the years we've accepted that his true love is his empire, Elliott Publication Holdings, or EPH for short. All of his children are working for the company and he runs a strict ship. He also insists that all family members, including his grandchildren, must earn their way to the top by working their butts off within various levels of the business. No exceptions."

Renee took another sip of water before asking, "How old were you when you began working at the company?"

He smiled, remembering those days. "I was sixteen and started out in the mail room without any special treatment because my last name was Elliott. I later got a degree in journalism from Columbia University."

At that moment, the waitress returned to take their order. They ordered hamburgers, milkshakes and fries. After the woman left, Tag turned to Renee and said, "I don't remember the last time I ate junk food. I'm usually too busy."

Renee looked surprised. "You're kidding. Most people eat junk food because they don't have time for the real thing. So what do you eat?"

"Too much nourishing food. The guy who lives next door to me is a chef and he keeps my refrigerator loaded."

"Jeez, life must be good," Renee said as a smile touched her lips. "Especially since you could call me the microwave queen. I don't have time to cook. I'm so busy, I barely have time to change my clothes after work before tackling some project or another. It's easier for me to just pop a meal in the microwave."

Tag swallowed. Heaven help him, but he could picture her rushing through her house after a long, taxing day at work and taking her clothes off. He wondered how many or how few underthings she wore. He then wanted to kick himself for even letting that speculation rule his thoughts. It wasn't like he was ever going to get involved with her, and needed to know.

"I meant what I said earlier, Tag. You don't have to take me home."

Tag glanced over at her. So they were back to that again, but he was determined to dig in his heels. There was no way he would put her on a subway when it wouldn't be any trouble giving her a ride. "You did say you've met my mother, right?" he asked, looking deep into Renee's eyes.

The blue gaze almost held her spellbound. "Yes. Why?"

"There is one trait she has that you may not have picked up on yet, and of all her children I'm the one who inherited it the most."

Interested, Renee couldn't help but ask, "And what trait is that?"

"Stubbornness."

"Ah," she said, nodding. "And what if I told you that I can probably be just as stubborn as you?"

He studied her a moment before a smile touched his lips. "The only thing I can say is that a standoff between the two of us ought to be very interesting."

Chapter 3

"Okay, I concede, Teagan Elliott. You won this round."

She might have to concede on that issue, Tag reasoned, but he personally had to concede that she looked good sitting in his car. "Now come on, Renee. Did you really think the gentleman in me would have you roaming all over New York in the dark?"

She gazed at him in obvious frustration when he brought his vehicle, a Lexus SUV, to a stop at the traffic light. "I don't see why not, since I do it all the time. And riding the subway isn't roaming. It's getting from point A to point B."

Tag couldn't help but shake his head and silently admitted that he had totally enjoyed the time he had spent with her today. It had been clean, honest, wholesome fun. Although he would be the first to admit that developing a relationship with her would be high on any man's agenda, it wasn't on his. Not that he wasn't interested, because he definitely was.

He just didn't have the time. *Pulse* was the only thing he was romancing these days. *Pulse,* and his family.

"I live in the next block."

Her voice reined his thoughts back in. "Nice neighborhood. I used to jog a lot in the park while attending Columbia."

She smiled over at him. "I jog there a lot now. I'm a member of the Morningside Park Coalition. We work with the city to preserve and improve the park."

When he came to a stop in front of her apartment building, she said, "You don't have to walk me to the door."

A part of Tag couldn't help wondering if the reason was that she didn't want to be seen with him. For some reason the thought bothered him. He leaned toward her and touched her cheek. "Sorry, there's no way I can deliver you home halfway. My task wouldn't be completed until I walked you to the door and made sure you got into your place okay."

"Thanks. I didn't want to put you out." She smiled and he immediately felt her warmth. Relief ran through him that she wasn't uncomfortable being seen with him. Still, he sensed her nervousness. Was she worried that he would try to kiss her goodbye? What if he did? Would she reciprocate? There was only one way to find out.

Renee watched as Tag came around the front of his vehicle to open the door for her. She couldn't help but think about how much difference there was between him and Dionne. Other than the obvious skin coloring, there was the way they regarded women. Because Dionne had been raised by a single mother who'd evidently been a superwoman, he had expected a woman to be able to do just about anything for herself, including opening her own car door and seeing herself into the house. The only time he'd walked her to the door was when he had expected to spend the night.

"Thanks," she said when Tag opened the door and offered his hand to help her out of the vehicle. Her heart fluttered at the feel of their hands touching, and she couldn't help wondering if the reaction was one-sided. Evidently it wasn't since he continued to hold her hand while walking her up the steps to her apartment.

He stepped aside while she unlocked the door. She wondered if he was waiting for her to invite him in. All day they had enjoyed being together without any type of flirtation, or promises of getting to know each other better. So why was her heart beating a thousand beats a minute, and why was she feeling heated from the way he was looking at her?

She cleared her throat. "Thanks again, Tag. I really enjoyed today."

"So did I. And bundle up good tonight. I understand the temperature will begin dropping around midnight."

"Okay." She thought of her huge bed where she would be sleeping alone, and for the first time in two years the thought actually bothered her. It also made her realize that Dionne had been the last man she'd been serious about. Once she moved to New York she had spent more time developing her career than seeking out any worthwhile relationships with the opposite sex. She had kept telling herself she was only twenty-eight and there was no rush. Now she suddenly felt… rushed.

"Will you have dinner with me tomorrow night?"

She blinked, then gazed into Tag's piercing blue eyes. She swallowed the thickness in her throat. "Dinner?"

"Yes, dinner. Tomorrow night."

Renee sighed. Okay, he had asked the million-dollar question, so how would she respond? She had to be honest with herself. If he had been an African-

American male she would probably not have hesitated, but there were issues she needed to consider with him being white. The difference in their race was a major factor, but then so was the difference in their social backgrounds. His family owned a magazine publishing company whose headquarters took up an entire Manhattan block, for crying out loud. He lived in Tribeca of all places. An area known for its high-rise condos, quiet streets, good schools and wealthy lifestyles. It was a haven for the well-to-do. For people like the Elliotts.

"Renee?"

She glanced over at him. "Yes?"

"Can we step into your apartment to finish this conversation? I think we're drawing unwanted attention."

Renee glanced around, noting his statement was true. A couple of people in her apartment building were openly staring at them. She returned her gaze to his. "Yes, let's go inside."

She opened the door, and the moment they stepped over the threshold, heat filled her insides in a way it hadn't ever before. "Can I get you something to drink?"

He leaned back against her closed door, placing his hands in the pockets of his jeans. "No, I'm fine, but what you can do is give me an answer to my question about dinner tomorrow night."

Renee nervously licked her lips.

"Don't do that."

"Do what?"

"Lick your lips like that. You've done it several times today and each time I've wanted to replace your tongue with my own. Even now I'm standing here fighting the urge not to."

His words fanned an already heated spot deep within her. Her heart suddenly began beating faster. Out of habit she automatically licked her lips again and when she realized what she'd done, she quickly said, "Oops. I didn't mean to do that."

His eyes stayed glued to her face. "Too late. It's been done."

He slowly moved away from the door, removing the distance separating them. When he came to a stop in front of her he studied her with an intensity that she felt all the way to her toes.

"This is crazy," he said in a deep, husky voice, "but I'm dying to kiss you."

Yes, it *was* crazy, she silently agreed. Because she was dying for him to kiss her. Earlier, she had listed in her mind all the reasons they couldn't become involved, but at that very moment, the only thing she could concentrate on was the way he was looking at her, the heat that seemed to take over her body and the desire that was flowing through her veins. No man had ever made her feel this way before.

He was watching her as carefully as she was watching him. They both knew their next move would be one they wouldn't forget in a long time—if ever. Tag studied her lips, saw them quiver nervously and knew the exact moment she would lick them with her tongue.

He was ready.

His tongue captured hers outside of her mouth, tangled with it as he thoroughly explored all of her, taking this intimate pleasure to a level he had never taken it before. Kissing was a special way to communicate without words, and what they weren't saying was turning him on even more, stirring emotions he had denied himself for so long. Affection, passion and even lust ruled his thoughts, his mind and his body.

He thought her lips were beautifully shaped and her response to him had been spontaneous. He liked her taste, he was drowning in her fragrance and he was taking the kiss to a level he hadn't known was possible.

Renee was literally panting for breath, but the thought of their mouths disconnecting was something she didn't want to think about. She had never been kissed like this before. Tag was taking the art of French kissing to a whole other level. He wasn't just keeping her tongue busy, he was intimately mating with it, leaving her breathless, weak in the knees, moaning out loud. He seemed to be lapping up each and every sound she made.

A part of her brain wanted to shut down everything she was feeling. It tried reminding her that what they were doing wasn't good. He was white, he was rich, his mother was her patient…and so on and so forth. But at that very moment, the only thing that was getting through to her was the tingling she felt all the way to her toes as well as the pool of heat that had settled right smack between her legs. And there was also the hardness of him that she felt against her thighs, and the sensitive feel of her nipples pressed against his solid chest.

Slowly, he pulled away, drawing in a deep breath. The sound filtered through her like a soft caress. The blue eyes staring at her held such intensity it made her pulse race even faster.

"That," he said softly, "was my first."

She held his gaze, had been drawn into it, was locked into it. "Your first what?" she somehow managed to ask in a tone that sounded like a whisper.

"My first real kiss." His brow furrowed as if he was somewhat troubled at the thought. "I've never given so much of myself to a woman before."

His words touched her in a way she had never been touched before. They were just as deep and profound as his kiss had been. He reached out and lifted her chin with the tip of his finger. "You are simply beautiful." He then shook his head as if amazed. "No, I take that back. You are beautiful. There is nothing simple about it."

He leaned forward and kissed her lips again. "Now to repeat my earlier question, will you have dinner with me tomorrow night?"

Renee released a long, drawn breath. Her mind, thanks to Tag, was jumbled in mass confusion, but the one thing that rang clear was the fact that they shouldn't see each other again this way for a number of reasons on which she didn't want to dwell at the moment. "I don't think having dinner with you is a good idea."

He lifted a dark brow, angled his head and asked, "Why not?"

She sighed deeply. He was making this difficult. What was obvious to her evidently wasn't to him. That kiss had revealed too much. Too many more of those and she would be falling hard and heavy for him, not caring about the differences between them.

Knowing he was waiting on an answer, she decided to take the easy way out. "Your mother is my patient so we shouldn't be getting involved."

Tag opened his mouth to say having dinner with him was not getting involved, but that wouldn't be completely honest. If he were to take her to dinner, he would want to kiss her good-night, and another kiss like the one they'd shared just might have him begging for a taste of something else. When they had kissed, and he had stroked her tongue with his own, her lips had been so soft, her tongue welcoming and her flavor so sweet....

"For how long?" he asked, leaning back against the closed door.

Renee blinked. "How long what?"

"How long will my mother be your patient?"

Renee nervously shoved her hands into the pockets of her skirt. "Officially, until after her surgery and she is released from the hospital. But I'll still be there for her if she needs me once she begins her chemotherapy."

He nodded. "And this rule about not getting involved with your patient's family is yours or thes hospital's?"

Renee swallowed. The blue gaze that had her within the intensity of its scope seemed to burn fire wherever it touched. Right now it was on her lips and her mouth was feeling the heat. She nervously licked her lips and saw the moment his stomach clenched and remembered his reaction whenever she did that. "It's mine, but I think it's for the best."

"Do you?" The smile that suddenly appeared at his lips was challenging, sexy and brazen. "Then I guess I'm just going to have to prove it's not for the best, won't I?"

He reached out, gently pulled her close, gave her a hug and then whispered close to her ear, "Stay warm tonight and think about me." And with that he turned and left.

"So how's your weekend going, Tag?"

Tag glanced up from pouring wine into two glasses and met his brother's gaze. Liam had dropped by for a visit but Tag could tell how he'd spent his Saturday was the last thing on his brother's mind; however, he answered anyway. "It was rather nice. I decided to take some time away from work and attended a couple of art shows in the Village."

Liam rubbed his hand down his face. Tired. Frustrated.

Agitated. All three. "It's good to know someone can put work on hold for a while to enjoy himself."

"So can you," Tag said, leaning back against the counter. Liam, financial operating officer at EPH, was known as a financial wizard. "Taking time off to rest and relax won't put the company in the red, Liam. Besides, you deserve it."

Liam sighed deeply. "Speaking of putting the company in the red," he said, after taking a sip of his wine, "I'm worried about Granddad's challenge. Personally, I don't see it helping the company. In fact, I see it hurting us in the long run. What on earth could he have been thinking to pit us against each other like this? Yesterday I was walking down the hall and as soon as I turned the corner whatever conversation Aunt Finola and Scarlet were having practically died on their lips when they saw me. It was as if they considered me a spy or something."

Tag nodded at what Liam was saying. He'd encountered a similar situation last week when he'd walked in on a conversation between his uncle Daniel and his cousin Summer. It was weird how everyone had begun acting all secretive because of his grandfather's challenge.

"Granddad is a smart man," Tag said. "Although I don't understand why he would do such a thing, I have to believe he'd never do anything that would eventually hurt the company. You know how he feels about it. It's his baby."

Liam, grudgingly, had to agree. "So, are you ready for Tuesday?" he asked, taking another sip of wine.

Tag shook his head. Tuesday was the day their mother was scheduled for surgery. "No, but the sooner Mom gets it over with, the sooner she can get better."

Liam closed his eyes for a moment in sheer exhaustion. "Yes, you're right." He then checked his watch and stood. "I think I'm going to stop by the office and finish up a couple of things before going home."

After Liam left, with nothing else to do, Tag showered and got ready for bed. The moment he crawled under the covers he thought about Renee. He hadn't meant to kiss her but he had and that had been the beginning of his problem.

He hadn't expected to develop a taste for her, but he'd done that as well. He had wanted to keep on kissing her, tasting her, mating their mouths. To keep indulging. Her lips had felt warm beneath his. Warm and heated with a surrender she hadn't wanted to make but he had coaxed out of her anyway, each and every time he had lowered his mouth to hers.

And earlier today, while with her in Greenwich Village, they had talked about a number of things. She had shared with him that her parents were both deceased. When she was ten years old her father had died of a work-related injury, and her mother had died of colon cancer when Renee was in her last year of high school. She had remembered how kind the social workers and hospital staff had been to her and her mother, and eventually followed in their footsteps, obtaining a degree in social work, with a specialty in health services.

During the time they had spent together today, he had watched her and had been touched at how the smallest thing could make her smile. He'd watched how she interacted with people in general; always respectful, courteous, polite and considerate. Even when she hadn't needed to be...like with Thomas Bonner.

The man had seen something in Renee that Tag hadn't. Color. To Tag, Renee was a beautiful woman. He didn't see her as a woman of a particular skin tone but as a desirable woman he wanted. But he had a feeling it hadn't been the same with her. He had seen the same frowns, stares and censored expressions that she had today. However, while he'd merely chalked them up to ignorance, he could tell they had bothered Renee. All day with her he'd assumed they were developing a friendship. But after kissing her, tasting her, he wanted more. He wanted something he hadn't thought about sharing in a long time with a woman. He wanted a relationship.

Damn.

How could he decide something like that after spending one day with her? Sharing one kiss? He wasn't sure just how deep he wanted the relationship to go but he did know that he wanted one. He wanted to take her out to dinner, the movies, and the theater…just to name a few places. He wanted to show up at her apartment some afternoons and discuss how his day had gone and hear how hers had gone as well. He wanted to invite her over to his place and cook for her…or have Lewis, his friendly chef next door, do the cooking. And he would love taking her to Une Nuit, his cousin Bryan's restaurant, and introducing her to his entire family.

He shook his head and sighed deeply. He'd never thought about introducing any woman to his family before, but he wanted to do it with Renee. He wanted to share all things with her.

He ran his hand down his face, frustrated, because she didn't want any of that. He knew he had to give her time, space and not rush her. Not only would they be engaging in an affair, but it would be an interracial one. At least that was probably how she would see it. He saw it as simply a man and woman who were attracted to each other deciding to take it to the next level.

But that had to wait. Right now, he had to be content to see her on Tuesday at the hospital. Somehow, though, that wasn't good enough.

Chapter 4

"Your wife's surgery was a success, Mr. Elliott."

Tag could see profound relief on his father's face as well as on the faces of his siblings gathered in the waiting room. "And you think that you got it all?" Michael Elliott asked.

Dr. Chaney nodded. "Yes, although her condition will still be guarded for a while, I believe we got all the cancer. She will remain here for a few days, and then I'll release her to you for convalescent care."

"How soon can we see her?" Gannon asked with his fiancée by his side.

"Not for a while yet, possibly an hour or so. She was put under heavy sedation and is still in the recovery room. I suggest all of you go grab a bite to eat. When you come back, she should be awake."

After the doctor left, Michael met his offsprings' intense

gazes. "Your mother is going to be fine now. When she's released I'm taking her to The Tides to recuperate."

Tag nodded. The Tides was the Elliott family's five-acre estate on Long Island. His grandfather had purchased the estate forty years ago when he became successful and had moved his young family out to the island because the area had reminded Tag's grandmother of her Irish homeland. It sat on a bluff like a fortress and overlooked the Atlantic Ocean. Tag agreed it would be the perfect place for his mother to rest, relax and heal.

"I like your mother's social worker," Michael Elliott said. "It was nice of her to drop by and check on us earlier."

Tag's head snapped up. "Renee was here?" He noticed the way his father looked at him, probably surprised with his use of the woman's first name, indicating some personal familiarity.

"Yes, she dropped by an hour or so ago, when you, Gannon and Liam had left to go downstairs for coffee."

Tag nodded, absorbing that statement silently. He wished he had been there when she'd shown up. He checked his watch, making a quick decision. "Since Dr. Chaney said it will be at least another hour before any of us can see Mom, I think I'm going to walk around a bit." He glanced over at his brothers and their expressions clearly said, *Walk around? Yeah, right*.

Ignoring them, Tag excused himself and headed for the nearest elevator.

"Is it true that you're Karen Elliott's social worker?"

Renee glanced up from her sandwich and met Diane Carter's curious gaze. Diane was a trauma nurse and one of the hospital's worse gossips. She was quick to get upset if someone got into her business yet she made it a point to get into everyone else's. Usually Renee avoided the woman at all cost but every once in a while she would join Diane for lunch when no one else would.

Renee had to concede that with Diane's blond hair and blue eyes she was a natural-born beauty. But rumor had it that besides having a problem with loose lips, she also had a tendency to be too clingy, which turned off a lot of the men in whom she'd shown interest.

"Yes, I'm Karen Elliott's social worker," Renee finally said after taking a sip of her lemonade.

"Boy, aren't you the lucky one," Diane said with a smirk. "Have you met her sons?"

Renee thought about Tag. "I've met only one. Teagan Elliott."

"And what do you think of him?"

The last thing Renee would do was tell Diane what she really thought of Tag. "He's okay."

Diane leaned back and looked at her like she definitely had a few screws loose. "Just okay? I've seen photographs of him in the society section of the newspaper a few times and he's so handsome he makes your eyes ache."

No sooner had Diane's words left her lips than Renee's hand froze on the glass of lemonade she was about to bring to her lips when Tag walked into the hospital's café. He glanced around as if he was looking for someone, then his eyes lit onto her.

The connection of their gazes did funny things to Renee's insides. It didn't take much to remember the kiss they had shared three days ago; a kiss that still heated her all over whenever she thought about it.

"Renee, are you all right?"

She quickly looked at Diane. No, she wasn't all right, but Diane would be the last person she would tell why. "Yes, I'm fine." And with as much effort as she could muster, she took a sip of her lemonade then bit into her sandwich, trying not to notice that Tag was standing across the room staring at her.

Tag sucked in a deep breath the moment his gaze slammed into Renee's. He wanted her. How could he not? Why had he thought for one moment that he'd convinced himself he could not get involved with her or anyone because he didn't have the time? Who was he kidding? He definitely wanted to get involved when the object of his attraction was Renee.

He drew in a deep breath of air as he began making his way across the room. He had gone to her office and was told by her secretary that she was at lunch and chances were he would find her in the cafeteria. He had hoped she would be alone but it seemed she was dining with someone. But that didn't stop him from wanting to see her, talk to her.

Renee hadn't realized that Tag had crossed the room until he was standing right next to her table. She glanced up and felt the sensuous undercurrents automatically radiating between them and wondered if Diane noticed them too.

Immediately putting her professional facade in place Renee leaned back in her chair, cleared her throat and in her best businesslike voice, said, "Mr. Elliott, how are you? And how is your mother?"

Tag sensed her nervousness, saw the guarded look in her eyes and watched how she caught her bottom lip between her teeth. He gave her companion no more than a cursory glance, but quickly registered how she eyed him with keen interest. He knew what Renee was silently asking him.

"My mother is fine, Ms. Williams," he said in his own businesslike voice. "Her doctor indicates the surgery was a success. However, that's what I want to talk to you about and I hate to intrude on your lunchtime, but I was wondering if I could speak with you privately for a moment."

Renee felt Diane's eyes on them, taking it all in, and was glad Tag had picked up on her silent warning. The last thing she needed was for the nurse to start rumors floating around the hospital. "Yes, I was finished here anyway. We can go back to my office."

Feeling a gentle kick to her leg under the table, Renee realized Diane was eager for her to make introductions. "Mr. Elliott, I would like for you to meet Diane Carter. She's one of our trauma nurses."

Diane was beaming when she presented Tag her hand. "Mr. Elliott, it's so nice meeting you."

"The same here, Ms. Carter. I hate to take her away from you, but there is this pressing matter I need to discuss with her."

Diane waved off his apology. "Hey, there's no reason to apologize. Trust me, I understand."

Renee doubted that Diane really did when she herself didn't.

Warmth spread through Renee's veins the moment she and Tag stepped into the elevator together. Alone. Neither of them said anything and as they rode up to the sixth floor, she tried to remind herself of all the reasons they could not become involved.

"I'm sorry I missed you earlier when you came to see how my family was holding up."

"It's part of my job to check on the family of my patients during surgery, to see if there's anything I can do for them."

Tag leaned against the paneled wall. "That's good to know, since there is definitely something you can do for me."

"And what can I do for you, Mr. Elliott?"

"For starters, since we're alone now, you can stop pretending Saturday night never happened. That we never kissed. Touched. Lost our heads and minds to passion."

He heard the air when it suddenly rushed from her lungs. He saw the shiver that passed through her body, but before he could make another comment, the elevator came to a stop.

When the door slid open, Tag stood back to let Renee step out. Neither said anything as they crossed the lobby to her office, walking side by side. Her secretary looked up and smiled before returning her attention to her computer. Renee appreciated the fifty-something woman who had been her secretary for the nearly two years Renee had worked there. Vicki was efficient, trustworthy and someone who respected Renee's need for privacy.

Renee opened the door and stepped into her office. Tag followed and closed the door behind them. He watched as she quickly crossed the room, and couldn't help but admire how she looked in her chocolate-brown business suit. The skirt hit her just above her knees, and his first thought was that she definitely had a great pair of legs.

"I'm glad you mother's surgery was successful."

Tag's gaze moved from her legs to her face. She was standing in the middle of her office, eyeing him nervously. "So am I."

She cleared her throat again. "In the cafeteria you said you needed to talk to me about her."

He shrugged, deciding to be completely honest with her. "It was something I said to get you alone."

He watched her eyes narrow. Okay, so she wasn't happy

hearing the truth, but seeing her standing here, alone in the room with him, made him realize the lie had been worth it. He smiled.

Renee wished she could somehow banish the sight of Tag standing there dressed in a tailored suit, like he was the epitome of every woman's fancy. But then she had to quickly concede that he could have been dressed in a T-shirt and a pair of tattered jeans and he still would have looked good.

And then there was the way his mouth could curve into a smile. The way it just did. She swallowed. "Mr. Elliott, I'm going to have to treat this strictly as a business meeting."

"If you'd like."

Renee was becoming frustrated and Tag wasn't helping matters. "I have a job to do."

He leaned back against the door and chuckled. "You don't have to remind me since your job is what brought us together."

"We aren't together."

"It depends on your definition of the word," he said easily.

Deciding enough words had been said, he moved forward, closing the distance between them, and came to a stop in front of her. "I need to get back. My mother should be coming around and I want to be there when she does." He paused briefly and then added, "But I wanted to see you, just to assure myself that Saturday had been real and not a pleasant figment of my imagination."

Renee crossed her arms over her chest and lifted her chin. "So what if it was real? That was then and now is now. I should not have let things get out of hand like that."

"You sure about that?" Tag asked. He wanted to kiss that

lie right off her mouth. There was no way she could convince him that she regretted what they'd shared Saturday.

"Yes, I'm sure."

"And you don't want me to kiss you again?"

"Absolutely not! I wish you'd never kissed me in the first place!" Renee glared at him and noticed his eyes seemed more intense than ever. She sucked in a deep breath when he leaned down and brought his mouth close to hers, mere inches away.

"Now tell me again that you wish we'd never kissed," he whispered hotly against her lips.

Renee opened her mouth to say the words and had planned to come up with a comeback that would set him back a notch. But she couldn't make the words come out and quickly closed her mouth. She gazed at the face so close to hers and knew frustration, want, desire as she felt herself being pulled in, falling helplessly into the depths of his bottomless sea-blue eyes.

"Tell me," he whispered against her lips.

She inhaled deeply as a throbbing sensation took over her body that seemed to start in the nipples of her breasts and was slowly moving down past her waist to land right in the middle between her thighs.

This was not supposed to be happening to her. She'd never been drawn to a man this way. And she had always stayed within what she'd considered her comfort zone while dating. Although she'd accumulated a number of white male friends over the years, she'd never given thought to developing a serious relationship with any of them. But there was something about Tag that defied logic. Her logic anyway. He seemed to find her as sexually appealing as she found him.

And she wanted to kiss him again.

Knowing that she would regret her decision, she tilted her chin which brought their mouths closer. But he didn't move. Instead he stood there, cool as you please, his gaze holding hers while sending delectable shivers down her body. The shivers, combined with the racing of her heart, were having one hell of an effect on her. But still he stood there, immobile, letting her know that if she wanted the kiss she was going to have to be the one to take it. With a moan she hadn't known she was about to make, against her better judgment she leaned closer and captured his mouth with hers.

She grabbed his shoulders and welcomed his tongue when it entered her mouth, mating it with hers, stroking it and sending tremors of pleasure through her body.

Then the tempo of the kiss changed when he took it over. It went from soft and gentle to hot and possessive. And she responded automatically, feeling her abdominal muscles clench. Intense heat pooled between her legs and the scent of all male teased her nostrils.

The ringing of the phone intruded and Renee pulled back, breaking off the kiss. Inhaling deeply, she reached across her desk and pushed the respond button on her phone. "Yes, Vicki?" she managed to say while heat continued flowing around in her stomach. She glanced over at Tag. The eyes staring at her were smoldering with desire and he was standing there waiting, as if he hadn't finished with her yet.

"Your one o'clock appointment is here, Ms. Williams."

Renee moistened her lips nervously. Kissing Tag had made her forget everything, including the fact that this was her office and she was standing in the middle of it, kissing him. What if someone had walked in on them? She could imagine the scandal that would have started. "Thanks, Vicki. Give me a few minutes to wind things up with Mr. Elliott."

Renee then turned her attention back to Tag. He was still standing in the same spot, staring at her. Okay, so she had been the one to initiate the kiss this time. Call them even. It didn't change the fact that they couldn't become involved and she needed to make him understand that. She had more to lose than he did. "A relationship between us won't work, Tag," she said slowly, distinctively stating each word.

"You don't think so?"

"No."

"Because my mother is your patient?"

"Among other reasons that are just as important," she said, deciding to spell it all out for him since he was acting like he didn't have a clue. Surely he could see the obstacles they faced as a couple as well as she could.

He crossed his arms over his chest. "And what are these other reasons?"

"I don't believe in casual affairs, which includes involving myself in relationships that I know upfront won't be going anywhere. You're white and I'm black. You're a wealthy businessman and I'm a social worker whose income won't come close to yours in a million years."

He continued to stare at her. "And your point?"

Renee narrowed her gaze. *Her point?* How could he ask her that when it was so clear? But if he wanted her to break it down even more, then she would. "My point is that I've never dated outside my race. I prefer staying in my comfort zone, and I'm not a woman who ever dreamed of marrying rich."

He laughed, but she could tell he wasn't amused but was

rather pissed off. "Are you saying you're basing your decision on my skin color and my finances?"

Hearing him say it made her feel no better than Thomas Bonner. Immediately, she put her defenses up. "Why would you want to become involved with me, Tag? Come on, let's get real here. Am I a woman your family would expect you to bring to dinner?"

His eyes darkened in anger and he quickly closed the distance between them. "First of all," he said in a low, angry tone, "I don't recall asking you to have a relationship with my family, just with me. Second, my family has never, nor will it ever, dictate how I live my life and with whom. Of course I would be lying if I said I wasn't raised with a certain set of values, but one of the things my grandparents and parents instilled in me more than anything was to judge a person on his character and not his outside appearance. And it's obvious that you're not doing that. If you're judging me by the way I look and by the size of my bank account, then we have nothing left to say."

He turned and walked out the door.

This was one of those days Renee was glad she didn't have any more appointments scheduled after her one o'clock. She needed to leave work as soon as she could to clear her mind of any lingering doubts she had regarding Tag. The words he'd spoken, the accusation, were still hanging there in her mind, refusing to move on. Why had he made things so complicated? Why didn't he understand her decision had been to spare them undue heartache and pain and unnecessary gossip?

Oh, she was sure there were a lot of interracial couples out there falling in love and making things work despite the odds. But it was those odds that bothered her more than anything. He wasn't living on another planet. He knew the rules that society dictated and the problems you could encounter if you decided to go against them.

She remembered all too well Cheryl Hollis and how she had sneaked behind her parents' backs and dated a white guy while they were in high school. Cheryl had gotten pregnant and both sets of parents had been up in arms. The guy's parents had money and threatened to cut him off if he so much as claimed the child as his. So he had done exactly as his parents had dictated, leaving Cheryl alone, pregnant and brokenhearted.

Granted, Tag wasn't a high school senior dependent upon his parents' income, but he was still an Elliott. His family's influence and wealth ranked right up there with the Kennedys and Bushes. Heck, his grandmother could probably call Oprah directly and invite her to dinner. Renee ran a frustrated hand down her face. She refused to let Tag lay a guilt trip on her. She wasn't prejudiced, just cautious.

But still, as she shut down her computer for the day, she couldn't erase from her mind that Tag Elliott had done something no other man had been capable of doing since Dionne. He had reminded her she was a woman—a woman with emotions, wants, physical needs and desires. She just wasn't used to a man making her lose control. Even now her palms were sweating just from her thinking about the kiss they had shared earlier here in this office.

She drew in a frustrated breath. No matter what, she had to believe that she had done the right thing letting Tag know where she stood and how she felt. But if that was the case, why was doing the right thing making her feel so bad?

Chapter 5

"I don't understand what you're saying, Dad. What do you mean Mom doesn't want to see us?" Tag asked, completely baffled.

Michael Elliott met the confused looks of his four offspring. He'd known this conversation would be difficult but somehow he needed to get them to understand how things were with their mother.

"As you know your mother is being released from the hospital today and I'm taking her to The Tides to recuperate. She has requested that when we get there she be left alone for a while. She doesn't want to see anyone. Not even the four of you."

"What?" Tag, Liam, Gannon and Bridget exclaimed simultaneously in shocked voices.

"Are you sure that's what she said, Dad?" Gannon asked,

shaking his head, finding his mother's request hard to believe, totally unacceptable.

Michael nodded sadly. "Yes, and I hope all of you can understand how Karen is feeling right now. She's been through a lot, both emotionally and physically. She needs this time alone."

"What she needs is time with her family," Bridget said, her eyes huge, dark and hurt. "We need to do something if she feels that way. Can't we call her social worker since it's obvious Mom's going through a deep state of depression?"

"I agree with Bridget," Liam said. "There has to be something we can do to lift her spirits."

"I agree as well," Tag chimed in. "I'll visit with Renee Williams to see what can be done." Just saying Renee's name caused pain to ripple through him. It had been almost a week since that day he had angrily walked out of her office. He knew she had visited with his mother a couple of times in the hospital but she'd done so when he hadn't been around to run into her.

"How soon can you meet with Ms. Williams?" Gannon asked, regarding Tag thoughtfully.

"I'll go and see her today."

It was one of those days when Renee had needed to stay at the office after closing hours to get a few things done. She glanced over at the clock as she shut down her computer. It was close to seven o'clock. Normally, she would have left hours ago. Vicki, bless her heart, had hung around to assist Renee in finishing a report.

"I'm out of here," Vicki said smiling, sticking her blond head in the doorway.

Renee returned the older woman's smile. "Thanks for your

help. I'm glad we've gotten everything finished for tomorrow's meeting."

"Me, too. I'll see you in the morning. Don't stay too late."

Renee grinned. "Don't worry. I won't be too far behind you."

Minutes later Renee had put everything she needed into her briefcase and glanced up when she heard the knock at the door. Thinking it was the maintenance crew to clean the office, she didn't look up when she said, "Come on in, I'm just about finished and—"

She lifted her head and the rest of the words died on her lips when she saw that the person standing in her doorway was Tag. Suddenly, heat flowed through her body and blood rushed through her veins. He didn't say anything. Neither did she. The silence between them stretched, weaving around them like a silken thread.

Renee breathed in a deep, shuddering breath. She hadn't seen him since that day they'd had words and couldn't help wondering why he was here. They had said everything that could be said and would never see eye to eye on things, so why bother?

Sighing deeply, she closed her briefcase with a click. Instinctively, she squared her shoulders, putting her protection gear in place since it appeared his entire expression was an unreadable mask. But even with that he was a very handsome man. She would always give him that.

"Tag, what are you doing here?"

He stepped into the room and closed the door. "I saw your secretary downstairs and she said you were still here. I need to talk to you."

Renee shook her head. "I don't think there's anything else we need to say."

"I don't want to talk to you about us, Renee. I want to talk to you about my mother." At her raised brow he added, "And that's no lie this time."

It was then that Renee noticed a couple of things about him. His rigid shoulders, the lack of spark in his eyes, the strain of controlled emotions in his features. She quickly crossed the room to him. "What is it, Tag? Has something happened to Karen?"

"No," he said calmly, attempting a faint smile. "Nothing has happened to Mom."

"Then what's wrong?"

He cleared his throat, finding it still hard to believe and even harder to get the words out. "She told Dad that she doesn't want to see any of us while she's recuperating at my grandparents' home."

Renee slowly nodded, understanding. The last time she had met with his mother she could tell that Karen had begun slipping into a state of depression. It had been the same day the doctor had unwrapped her chest to show Karen how to go about caring for her stitches after leaving the hospital, although Renee knew that Michael Elliott had hired a private nurse for his wife.

"None of you should take your mother's request personally, Tag."

Tag's eyebrows snapped together in anger. "What do you mean we shouldn't take it personally? She's our mother and—"

"She's also a woman with a lot to deal with at the moment. Having both breasts removed isn't some-thing any female would take lightly. For a while, when her chest was bandaged, she was going through denial. But now since she's gotten a chance to see the surgeon's handiwork, reality has set in and she's combating it the only way she knows how, which is with anger, fear and withdrawal. I was with her the day she became angry. Dr. Chaney and I were prepared for it. We were also prepared for the days when she went through stark fear, thinking that perhaps the doctor didn't get all the cancer and it would return to other parts of her body and that she would eventually lose those parts as well."

Renee sighed deeply, knowing she had to get Tag to accept his mother's present state of mind. Accept it as well as understand it. "Now she's going through withdrawal. She doesn't want to deal with anything or anyone, even those whom she loves. If she could, she would block your father out as well but he won't let her do so, although trust me she has tried."

Tag closed his eyes, not wanting to believe what he was hearing. His mother had always been the strong one in the family. Like his grandmother, she was the one who could always hold things together in a crisis. Now she was going through her own personal crisis and he was finding it hard to conjure up even a little bit of the strength his mother always seemed to have had.

He leaned back against the closed door, suddenly feeling exhausted. "So what are we supposed to do? Let her continue to wallow in self-pity and do nothing?"

Renee shook her head. "No. To start with, you should all honor her request and give her the space she needs right now, while working together behind the scenes and doing something that can and will lift her spirits."

"Like what?"

Renee shrugged. "Anything that will make her appreciate

the fact that she's alive. I understand she enjoys working with her charities. You can arrange for her to continue to do so even while she's convalescing. Remember, she'll be going through both physical and emotional healing. The most important thing is helping her to get beyond her ordeal and concentrate on something else."

Renee studied Tag's expression and knew he had absorbed her words. His next question, however, surprised her. "Will you help, Renee?"

She shook her head. The last thing she needed was complications, and Tag was nothing if not that. "No, I don't think that's—"

"Please."

Renee nervously gnawed the insides of her mouth. Could she handle doing what he was asking? She let out a small breath. Yes, she could handle it if it meant helping Karen. Over the past few weeks she and Tag's mother had developed a relationship that had gone beyond social worker and patient. She admired Karen for all the good things she did for others, especially all her charitable work.

"Will you do it, Renee?"

She glanced into Tag's face and saw the heartfelt plea in his eyes. And then she knew what her answer would be. "Yes, Tag, I'll help out with your mother any way I can."

Both relief and appreciation shone on his face. "Thank you, Renee. Are you willing to meet with my sister and brothers and explain everything to them as well? Tomorrow night we're having dinner together at Une Nuit, a restaurant owned by my cousin Bryan. Is there any way you can join us there?"

Anyone living in New York had heard of Une Nuit, the restaurant whose patrons oftentimes included a number of celebrities. Now that she had agreed to help him lift Karen's spirits, Renee knew she had to move forward. At least she and Tag wouldn't be dining at the restaurant alone. She wasn't sure how many times she could be alone with him without wanting to comfort him and assure him that everything with his mother would be all right. But she knew to comfort him meant she would also want to kiss him, take his pain away, touch him….

A sexual awareness she only encountered when she was around Tag tried taking over her mind, but she fought it. "Yes, I'll be glad to meet with you and your siblings tomorrow night."

Tag nodded. "I'll pick you up around seven."

"You don't have to do—"

"Yes, I do. I don't want you taking the subway to meet with us. Okay?"

She sighed, knowing his stubbornness was coming out and to argue with him would be pointless. "Fine."

He smiled. "Good. And do you need a ride home now?"

"No, I'm meeting Debbie at a restaurant not far from here. She's leaving in the morning for an assignment in London so we decided to make it a girls' night out. I'll be fine."

"Are you certain?"

"Yes." She'd never met a man who was so concerned for her well-being. Tag was so thoughtful, caring and attentive.

"Then the least I can do is walk you there."

She knew telling him that wasn't necessary would only be a waste of her time. Clutching her briefcase, she walked out with him, stopping to turn out the lights. Moments later they stepped into the elevator and as the car descended she couldn't help hoping that busybody Diane Carter had left for the day. The last thing Renee needed was to run into her in the lobby. No doubt she'd get the wrong idea about her and Tag.

When the elevator came to a stop and the doors slid open, Tag stood back to let her step out. "You really don't have to walk me to the restaurant, Tag. It's only a few blocks from here," she said, stepping into the hospital lobby. "I'm sure you have more important things to do."

"No," he said, slanting her a sideways glance. "There's nothing more important."

Darkness enfolded them as they stepped outside and began walking. The sidewalks were congested and more than once he gently pulled her closer to him to avoid her getting trampled by someone hurrying past.

When they reached her destination, she turned to him. "Thanks."

"And thank you, Renee, for everything. I'll see you tomorrow night at seven."

"All right."

She quickly entered the restaurant and when she glanced over her shoulder through the window he was still standing there, looking at her.

Tag leaned forward on the conference table with his palms down as he stared at the man and woman sitting at it. "I want anything and everything you can find on Senator Vince Denton, especially his activities over the past year. No one walks away from politics after thirty years without a good reason, especially someone that close to the present administration."

"He gave us his reason. He's been in politics long enough and wants to return to his farm in South Carolina and live the rest of his days in peace and harmony. Sounds like a damn good plan to me," Peter Weston, *Pulse*'s special edition editor,

said, carelessly throwing out a paper clip. Peter was responsible for *Pulse*'s campaigns, opinion polls and surveys.

Tag met the man's nonchalant expression. "I don't care how
good it sounds, I'm not buying it and I suggest you don't either." He sighed. It was time Tag and his father had a serious
talk about Peter's lack of interest in his job. Peter had worked
for *Pulse* for over fifteen years, starting out as an investigative
reporter—one of the magazine's best—and working his way
up through the ranks. Lately, it had been noticed by a number
of co-workers that he lacked the hunger, instinct and drive he
used to have. Peter had been placed on paid administrative leave
on two occasions when his work habits had begun declining
and it appeared things were beginning to go downhill again.

Rumor had it that Peter was involved in an affair with a
Radio City Rockette and was sacrificing everything, including
a good marriage, to be at the woman's beck and call. It was
Tag's opinion that what Peter did on his free time was one
thing. What he did on *Pulse*'s time was another.

Peter's interest in *Pulse* had started waning a few years
ago when Gannon had gotten a position that Peter evidently
thought should have been his. He was of the mind that Gannon's name and not his hard work had gotten him where he
was, which was not true.

"I thought his resignation was rather strange, too,"
Marlene Kingston said, scanning the notes she'd taken
from an earlier meeting. At twenty-seven, she had been
working for *Pulse* since college and always had a good
eye for the news. Currently she edited the analysis
pages and wrote editorials. "I find it odd that he would resign
right before next week's vote on that big oil bill," she added.

Tag liked the woman's sharpness. However, he could tell
by the glare Peter had given her that he did not. "That's a good

point, Marlene, and one we should look into. Just make sure whatever you have to report is accurate and from a reliable source." He sighed deeply then added, "Pull out all stops and let's dig to see what we can find. Make plans for us to meet in a few days, same time, same place, with some answers."

Half an hour later Tag was poking his head in the room where the smell of ink teased his nostrils. Making his way past old issues of *Charisma*, canisters of ink and reams of paper, not to mention numerous pictures of Elizabeth Taylor plastered on the wall, he made it to the workstation of Edgar Rosewood and sat down in the chair next to it.

The man sitting at the desk looked up at him beneath bushy eyebrows. Edgar, who would be celebrating his seventieth birthday in a few months, had been hired by Patrick within a month of EPH opening its doors, and to this day refused to call it quits by retiring. That was fine with Tag since Edgar had been Tag's father's mentor as well as mentor to Gannon, Liam and himself when they'd come through the ranks. Tag always had and always would consider the man someone special and an asset to *Pulse*. To this day, one thing Edgar retained was a sharp eye for headlines that were so well buried that even a hunting dog couldn't find them.

"What's bothering you, kid?" Edgar asked, his tone rough, his frown deep. "Personal or business?"

Another thing Tag liked about the old man was that he knew how to cut to the chase. Not wanting to delve into his personal problems, not even with Edgar, Tag said, "Business. I think there's more to Senator Denton's resignation than meets the eye."

Edgar swung around from his computer. "So do I."

Tag lifted a paperweight off the pages of last month's magazine. He felt good knowing Edgar was also on to something. "I just hope we can find out what it is before *Time* does."

"We will, as long as you let Marlene Kingston do the digging. She has a nose like a bloodhound. If Denton's not clean, she'll find out just what's dirty. Personally, I like her."

Tag couldn't help but smile. "Why? Because she reminds you of a young Elizabeth Taylor?"

The old man smiled. "Yeah, that's one of the reasons. The other is that she's a good newswoman. The best thing you can do is get her from under Peter and have her work with Wayne Barnes. Peter has been taking credit for Marlene's hard work long enough. The only interest he seems to have these days is a pair of breasts pouring out of a Rockette costume. He's doing nothing but stifling Marlene's growth."

Tag had to agree, which was something else he needed to talk to Gannon about.

Edgar looked at him, studied him. "You sure there's nothing else bothering you?"

Tag shrugged. "Of course this thing with Mom is constantly on my mind."

"That's understandable but I think you might have another problem."

"What?"

Edgar gave him a pointed look. "The absence of a good woman in your life."

Tag smiled. Edgar had given him and Liam that same speech after Gannon had announced his engagement to Erika last month. "Still trying to marry me off, are you?"

"There's nothing wrong with settling down. I've been with my Martha for over fifty years and have been involved in a secret love affair with Elizabeth for forty of those fifty."

Tag chuckled and raised his eyes to the ceiling. "In your

dreams." He stood and checked his watch. A part of him couldn't wait to see Renee later. He had been thinking about her all day. Gannon, Liam and Bridget were anxious to meet with her tonight as well, to hear what she had to say.

"Time for me to get back to work," Tag said, walking toward the door. He paused in the doorway and stared at the huge poster of Elizabeth Taylor on the wall next to it. "What do you think about when you look at her?" Tag asked Edgar over his shoulder.

He could hear the old man chuckle softly. "Passion and desire."

Tag turned around. "And what do you think about when you look at Martha?"

Edgar stretched out his legs, leaned back in his chair and locked his fingers behind his head. "Same thing, but added to those two is love. And that's the key, kid. Find a woman who can ignite you with passion and desire and who can also fill your heart with love."

Tag grunted. He doubted there was a woman in existence who could fill his heart with love, but when it came to passion and desire there was one face that readily came to mind.

Renee's.

"Thanks for picking me up," Renee said as she eased into the leather seat of Tag's SUV.

"You don't have to thank me, Renee." He closed the door and came around the other side and slid into the driver's seat.

He glanced over at her. "You look nice. But then you always do."

His compliment made her smile. "Thank you."

"You're welcome." He pulled out into traffic.

She was silent, her gaze skimming the buildings and people as they drove by. Although she had never eaten at Une Nuit, she had heard a lot of nice things about the restaurant. According to what Tag had told her earlier, his cousin Bryan had gotten out of the family business a few years ago to try his hand in the restaurant business. The change in careers had proved successful. Tag had also mentioned that Bryan traveled quite a bit and when he did, the restaurant was managed by a capable Frenchman by the name of Stash Martin.

"My sister and brothers are looking forward to meeting you tonight. They appreciate all you did for our mother while she was in the hospital."

To say what she'd done was merely her job would sound rather cold, Renee thought, especially when she considered the time she'd spent with Karen more valuable than that. She glanced over at Tag. "I'm looking forward to meeting them as well and look forward to doing what I can to help lift your mother's spirits."

When the vehicle came to a stop at a traffic light, she said gently, "Tell me about them." She inhaled sharply when he turned and met her gaze. The depths of his blue eyes shone darkly under a flashing street sign. He did something to her each and every time he looked at her, whether she wanted the reaction or not.

"Gannon, who is thirty-three, is my oldest brother and the second in command to my father at *Pulse*. He always loved his carefree bachelor lifestyle but last month he became engaged to a woman he'd had an affair with over a year ago by the name of Erika Layven. You'll also get to meet her tonight."

Tag hit the brakes when a yellow cab carelessly darted out in front of his Lexus. "Liam," he continued, "is thirty-one and is EPH's financial operating officer." He chuckled.

"We tease him about being my grandfather's favorite grandchild because he's the one who keeps tabs on the money, and trust me, he does a damn good job of it. He's sharp when it comes to numbers.

"Last but not least, there's Bridget, who is your age. She's a photo editor for *Charisma* and according to what she tells me, she's still trying to find herself."

He glanced over at Renee. "And there you have it." And with that timely ending, the car came to a stop in front of Une Nuit.

Chapter 6

If Renee had felt strange and uncomfortable when she'd first walked into Une Nuit with Tag, then those feelings were definitely behind her now. His siblings had a way of making her feel relaxed, and she could easily tell that the four of them shared a rather close relationship.

The inside of the restaurant looked sensational and the place was filled to capacity, with a number of celebrities in the house. She and Tag bypassed the long line of patrons waiting to be seated and were escorted to the "Elliott Table" where Gannon, Liam and Bridget were waiting for them. Gannon's fiancée, Erika, joined the group a few minutes later.

Tag was quick to explain that with so many family members frequenting the restaurant, Bryan had designated a rear table as the "Elliott Table."

Renee had blinked twice when she'd met the restaurateur. With his jet black hair and blue eyes, she could easily tell that he and Tag were related. And he was so laid-back and friendly.

"Are you sure you don't prefer wine, Renee?" Gannon asked, smiling.

Renee liked Tag's brothers and his sister, as well as Erika. She thought there wasn't a pretentious bone in Erika's body, and like the others, she went out of her way to make her feel comfortable. "No thank you," Renee said. "I better stick with this coffee since there's work tomorrow."

"Yes, there is that. And we want to thank you for your willingness to help with Mom," Gannon said, acting as spokesman for the group. The others nodded in full agreement.

Renee's smile spread to each corner of her lips. "None of you has to thank me. Your mother is a wonderful person and I'm happy to do anything that I can to help her." She had explained earlier exactly what Karen needed. All of them had listened attentively and had thrown out several good ideas and suggestions, but it was Gannon and Erika's suggestion that everyone decided was the best.

In light of Karen's breast cancer, the couple had decided to fly to Vegas and marry at the end of the month instead of having a traditional wedding. However, if planning a wedding would give Karen something to do and lift her spirits, they would certainly change their plans. It was decided that Erika would contact Karen and ask her assistance in planning a small wedding. The family had already made plans to gather at Patrick and Maeve's Hampton estate at the end of the month to celebrate the older couple's anniversary, and Gannon and Erika thought it would be special to exchange their vows on the same exact date Gannon's grandparents had fifty-seven years ago. Since everyone knew how much Karen loved planning special events, they hoped assisting Erika with her wedding would lift Karen's spirits.

While Renee sipped her coffee she couldn't help but notice when Gannon leaned over to Erika and whispered something into her ear. Whatever he said brought a smile to Erika's face, and she tilted her head for him to kiss her on the lips. Renee was touched by the romantic gesture, just one of several that had passed between the couple that night. She'd been surprised by how open they had been in admitting their love for each other and their desire to get married and start a family right away.

"Ready to leave?"

Renee nearly jumped when Tag leaned over and whispered into her ear. She lifted her gaze but she didn't dare move her head. Doing so would have their lips practically touching. Yet, they were so close there was no way their breath wouldn't mingle when she did speak. "Yes, I'm ready."

She regretted having to say good-night to everyone and was surprised when Bridget slipped her business card into her hand and told her to call her one day soon so the two of them could do lunch. Erika did the same thing.

"I enjoyed myself tonight," Renee said to Tag when they were in the SUV and on their way back to her place. "You have special siblings, and after meeting your parents I can see why. They did a great job in raising all of you."

Tag glanced over at her and smiled. "Thanks." Although she had given him a compliment, he couldn't forget it had just been a few days since she had stood in her office and practically said she could not have a relationship with him because of their different races and his family's wealth.

"What's this joke about the family feud?"

Renee's question interrupted Tag's thoughts. He glanced

over at her. "It's no joke, it's the truth. My grandfather is re-tiring at the end of the year and has decreed that whoever makes their magazine the biggest success by the end of the year will be given the position of CEO of EPH."

Renee glanced at him with widened eyes. "You're kidding, right?"

Tag chuckled. "No, I wish I was but I'm dead serious. And what's so crazy is that although the four magazines are run by a different offspring, the staff is mixed. For example, Bridget doesn't work with me, Gannon and my father at *Pulse*. She works with Aunt Finola at *Charisma*. So in essence, in trying to put *Charisma* on top, she won't be rallying to our father's side in his bid for the CEO position."

"Uh-oh, that can be a pretty sticky position to be placed in," Renee said, wondering why Tag's grandfather would do such a thing in pitting his family against each other that way.

"It already is and personally, I don't like it. The feud be-tween the different magazines is making things tense at the office."

Renee turned her head and recognized the deli on the cor-ner. They were within a block of her place. She shifted in her seat, suddenly feeling nervous. When Tag had picked her up earlier she had been dressed and ready to go and had walked out of the apartment before he'd had a chance to knock. She couldn't help wondering, considering their argument in her office over a week ago, if he would just drop her off at the curb and keep going. She had to be realistic enough to know that the only reason he had shown up at her office last night was to ask for her help with his mother.

When his car turned the corner and came to a stop in front of her apartment building, she began unbuckling her seat belt. In a way, she was sorry the ride had ended. "Thanks again for tonight."

"I should be thanking you, and I do," he said huskily, seconds before opening his door and quickly walking in front of the car to open the car door for her. He offered her his hand.

She took it and immediately felt flushed from the top of her head all the way to her toes. All it took was a look in his eyes to know he'd felt it, too. Tingles of awareness were electrifying the space between them. A yearning sensation was spreading all through her limbs and she suddenly longed for the feel of his lips on hers. She blinked, forcing those thoughts away, and knew she had to take control of what was happening to her. Put a stop to it immediately.

They didn't say anything as he walked her to her apartment, and when they reached her door he stood silently by while she took the key from her purse and unlocked it. She turned to him. "Thanks for walking me to the door, Tag."

"You don't have to thank me, Renee."

If she had been focused more on her surroundings than on Tag, Renee would not have noticed the deep timbre of his voice or the intensity that filled his blue eyes. But she did notice those things although she wished she hadn't, because in doing so she felt more heat spread through her.

She remembered their conversation that day in her office. She knew every single word she had told him, could probably recite it in her sleep. But now, at this very moment, none of it mattered. She was dealing with an emotion she'd never dealt with before and she knew, whether she wanted it to happen or not, she had fallen in love with Tag.

Forbidden love.

She sucked in a deep breath at the realization and wondered

how she could have let such a thing happen. The big question was not how he had gotten through her defenses so quickly, but how he had managed to get through them at all. They were completely wrong for each other, on different ends of a spectrum, worlds apart. They could never share a happy life together without stares and frowns. There was no reason to think about a future with him, but there was something they could share tonight that would be theirs and theirs alone.

"Good-night, Renee." Tag leaned down and kissed her cheek before turning to leave. He took a few steps, stopped, and then, as if he was compelled to look at her just one more time, he turned back around.

The moment their gazes reconnected she knew she was doomed. She loved him and she wanted him. It was as simple as that. At least for tonight it would be simple. "Would you like to come in for a drink or something?" she asked softly, unable to hold her silence any longer.

With a smile that would have endeared him to her for life if he hadn't already been so, he recovered the distance separating them and whispered, "Are you sure you want to be alone with me tonight, Renee?"

Emotions clogged her throat. She knew what he was asking.

He had tried walking away but couldn't. Like her, he had reached the end of his rope. Desire had thickened their minds, taken control of their thoughts, and, God forbid, pushed them over the edge. Once they stepped into her apartment there would be no turning back and they both knew it.

"Yes, I'm sure," she said, her mind completely made up. They would have this night together. With that decision made, an unexpected rush of relief and pleasure washed over her, forcing any and all opposition from her mind. He was man.

She was woman. And at this moment, he was the man she loved and wanted.

"If you're sure," he said, slowly opening the door.

"And I am," she said as an assured smile touched the corners of her lips.

"In that case, I think we should take this inside."

He held the door open to let her go in first and then he followed, closing and locking the door behind him.

There was definitely something sexual and elemental about being alone with the woman you desperately wanted, Tag thought as he leaned against the closed door.

He watched as Renee went to stand in the middle of the room. She was nervous. He could tell. But then he was aroused and he knew that she could tell that as well. There was no way his body could keep something like that a secret. He suddenly felt like holding her in his embrace, needing to feel the heat of her body against his.

He held his hand out to her. "Come here, Renee," he said in a voice that wanted to retain control but was slowly losing it.

She placed her purse on a table and crossed the room to stand in front of him. His hands automatically slid around her waist. "I want to hold you for a little while," he said, bringing her body closer to the fit of him. Renee's head automatically rested upon his chest.

Tag knew there were still unresolved issues between them but at this very moment, while she was in his arms, nothing mattered but them being together this way. What was important was that when it came to passion and desire they were in accord.

Passion and desire.

Edgar's words rang loudly in Tag's ears. He thought of all the other women he'd ever dated, some as stunning as a woman could get, but there was something about Renee that was different. She was as beautiful as the rest but there was this ingrained, unadulterated sense of kindness and decency that pulled him to her each and every time.

"Tag?" she whispered moments later, the warmth of her breath splaying against his cheek.

"Mmm?"

"Are we going to stand here like this all night?"

His lips parted in a smile. Only Renee could ask such a question at a time like this. Instead of answering her, he bent and swept her into his arms at the exact moment his mouth settled hungrily over hers. It was by no means a gentle kiss and was intended to let her know just how much he desired her.

She moaned and the sound intensified the deep-rooted longing within him. He pulled his mouth away briefly to ask, "Which way to the bedroom?"

"Down the hall then to your right."

Holding her tight against him, he moved in that direction. When they reached the bedroom doorway he resumed kissing her, letting his tongue explore and devour every inch of her mouth. Somehow, with their lips locked, they made it to the bed. He was grateful she had left a lamp on in the room.

She gave a nervous laugh and pulled him down on the soft mattress with her. He tilted his head back and looked at her, thinking that he'd never wanted a woman as much as he wanted Renee. Anticipation filled his entire being as he slipped off the bed to remove his clothes.

He watched her watch him remove his shirt then he reached his hand out and pulled her off the bed to him. After removing her shoes he turned her around to work at the zipper on her dress. He liked her dress, a silky-looking A-line blue dress that showed off her shapely figure. He had definitely liked seeing her in it, but would enjoy seeing her out of it even more.

"I've wanted you from that first day I walked into your office," he whispered, placing a wet kiss on her shoulder. He felt a shudder race through her body and gloried in the fact that he had been the one to make it happen.

"You did?"

"Yes, and it shook me up some because I've never wanted a woman that much before."

He slid the zipper down and then pushed the garment off her shoulders. All it took was for Renee to do one sensuous shimmy of her hips and the dress fell in a heap at her feet. Next, on one bended knee, he removed her panty hose, leaving her clad in the sexiest bra and panty set he'd ever seen. Simply seeing the baby-blue lace against her dark skin made his loins tighten. Added to that were her gorgeous legs and bright red painted toenails that matched the color of her fingernails. He was of the opinion that for all intents and purposes, she took the word *sexy* to a whole new level. She was the epitome of every male fantasy, definitely his own. His mind began spinning, blood pumped hot and heavy through his veins as he unbuckled his belt and began removing his pants.

From their first kiss he had been fighting the need to make love to her. She was constantly in his thoughts, even when he hadn't wanted her there. Fantasizing about her had become his favorite pastime.

He tossed his pants aside and stood before her wearing only his briefs, and suddenly felt a jolt of desire when she reached out and slid her hand down his chest, letting her fingers slowly work their way beneath the waistband of his underwear to curl around his rock-hard erection. And when she began stroking him, he thought he was going to lose it. He *knew* he was going to lose it if she didn't stop.

"Renee…"

"Yes?"

Her response was as innocent as it could get and he quickly decided that two could definitely play her game. And in this case, two definitely would. He sat down on the edge of the bed and gently pulled her to him to straddle his hips. His hands spanned her waist just before they began kneading her buttocks. He liked the feel of her soft skin and the scent of her as well. Damn, she smelled good.

And when she leaned forward and began nuzzling his jaw with her lips and running her hands over his shoulder and chest, he inhaled sharply, gripping her hips and pushing upward, wanting her to feel just what she was doing to him, how deeply aroused he was.

His mouth captured hers as he lay back, bringing her atop him in the process, the softness of her flesh sinking into him. Moments later she lifted her mouth and stared down at him. "We still have some clothes on," she whispered in the silence of the room.

He shifted his body, placed her beneath him and then leaned up and began removing her bra. The moment he uncovered her breasts, his senses jolted and desire slammed into him. They were high, sensuously shaped with protruding dark-tipped nipples that seemed to beg for his tongue. There was no way he could resist.

He cupped a breast in his hand as his mouth greedily latched onto it and began devouring it with deep male appreciation and far-reaching primitive hunger, trying to pull all the sweetness out of it. A rapturous gasp tore from deep within her throat, and moments later, when she shuddered and cried out his name, he was amazed that she had climaxed just from him kissing her breasts.

Good. It would make what he intended to do next even more enjoyable for the both of them. He pulled back slightly, ran his hands down her thighs, fingering the edge of her lace panties. He touched her there in the center and found the fabric damp. He was definitely grateful for that.

Without wasting any time, he removed her panties and then just as quickly he leaned back and removed his own underwear. He looked at her and immediately thought of a chocolate sundae, his favorite treat. He leaned forward and began nuzzling the soft skin of her flat stomach, licking the area around her navel. Her feminine scent surrounded him, making his body harden even more.

"Tag, what are you doing?" she asked, barely able to get the words out.

He lifted his mouth long enough to say, "I'm about to eat you alive, sweetheart. You look beautiful, sexy and delicious." As soon as those words left his mouth he eased his head between her open legs and captured her with his mouth, kissing her there.

"Tag!"

He didn't let up and when she began squirming beneath his mouth, he gripped her hips to keep her still as his tongue continued to devour her in this very intimate way. The succulent taste of her pushed him over the edge and made him even greedier, as desire rocketed through his veins, making him growl low in his throat.

He felt her feminine muscles suddenly clench beneath his mouth and then she came and his tongue savored each and every orgasmic vibration that filled him with more of her taste. She rocked her pelvis upward at the same time as she screamed out his name again.

Before she could catch her next breath, he quickly put on a condom and then eased his body over hers, positioning his erection right smack against her satiny flesh, settling his hips in the cradle between her thighs.

"Open your eyes and look at me, Renee."

Their eyes met and the glaze of stark passion he saw there filled him with male satisfaction. "Don't see color when you look at me," he whispered huskily as he began easing inside of her. "Don't think of social status when you feel me inside of you," he continued, his voice rough and low. "Think of passion, desire. Think of me…the man who wants you."

He continued going deeper into her, holding her gaze. "Say my name, baby."

Renee bit her lip, trying to stop the fears of the future from overtaking her mind. She knew if she said his name now, when they were like this, it would become embedded in her soul forever. He had already found a way into her heart, but to take part of her soul…

"Say it."

Tag tilted his head up and stared down at her. He was buried deeply inside of her, to the hilt. He hadn't wanted to hurt her but she had been so tight and entering her hadn't been easy. He held still, refusing to move his hips until she acknowledged that what they were sharing was passion between a man and a woman, and color and social status had nothing to do with it. On this point he was determined to be of one accord with her. In a voice that was lower still, he whispered, "Speak my name."

Renee dug her fingers into his back, unable to fight it any longer. He was so intensely male that she knew who he was and what he was to her, whether she wanted to admit it or not. She would admit it but on her own terms. "Speak mine," she countered.

He stared at her and smiled and brushed his fingertips against her cheek. "Renee," he said huskily.

The caress was so tender that she fell deeper in love with him at that precise moment. "Tag." And as every cell in her body vibrated in response to his touch, she said his name again. "Tag."

He leaned down and buried his face in the curve of her neck, holding her close to him. Now that they had put things into perspective, at least for the time being, Tag began moving inside of her, mating with her in a way he'd never done with another woman. He felt the quivering deep in her womb with each and every push and pull. He feasted on her mouth, on her breasts while he increased the pressure, multiplied the thrusts and enhanced their bodies' rhythm.

Moments later when she flew apart, he was flying right along with her. A release, of a magnitude he had never before experienced, ripped from him, shattering him to a degree that made his thighs quake. The low, guttural sound from his throat was necessary to keep the veins from popping in his neck when he threw his head back. He was worshipping her body, claiming her as his.

And he knew when another climax suddenly rammed through him, to piggyback with the first, that no matter what protests Renee might continue to make about them pursuing a relationship, there was no way he could ever let her go.

"I don't want to leave you tonight," Tag's dark-velvet voice murmured softly against Renee's ear, bringing her awake.

She opened her eyes and gazed up into his deep-blue ones and gave him a sleepy smile as she thought of all they had done together for the past few hours. "Then don't."

"Is that an invitation?" he asked, leaning down and kissing her jaw, savoring the line around her lips with his tongue.

Renee's senses immediately responded. "Yes," she purred against his lips. "That's an invitation."

She wrapped her arms around his neck and parted her mouth to welcome his strong, hot tongue that started seducing her all over again, sucking her very breath. At the same time his hand traveled down her naked body to the apex of her thighs. Within minutes he had her writhing and moaning into his mouth.

He slowly lifted his lips from hers and his gaze roamed over her face as he pulled a shuddering breath into his lungs. "I can't get enough of you, Renee. It's like you're entrenched within every pore in my body."

She watched as he stood to pull another condom from his wallet and swiftly roll it into place. When he returned to the bed she held his gaze as he slid his body over hers once more, her thighs automatically opening for him. Like dry tinder, her body ignited when joined to his, and she could feel the tension building inside of her as she raced forward, fast and furious, toward the release he was driving her to.

Moments later she screamed his name, as she felt herself shattering into a thousand pieces. He continued his intimate strokes, withholding his release with iron-clad control while pushing deeper and deeper still. Ecstasy seized her once again and a sensuous cry tore from her lips at the same time she felt him buck and call out her name.

Tag continued to murmur her name repeatedly and it sounded like music to her ears. She slid her hands up over the tense muscles of his back, kneading them as she savored the slow aftermath of what they were sharing. A part of her knew it was time to start pulling back. She was falling in love with him even more and was beginning to need him too desperately.

She knew if she didn't start thinking straight that she would find herself in deep trouble, but at that moment the only thing she wanted to think about was Teagan Elliott, what he meant to her and how he was making her feel.

Chapter 7

Tag slowly began waking just as the first light of morning shone into the room. He breathed in deeply as Renee's sensuous, womanly scent was drawn into his nostrils.

Shifting his body, he glanced over at the empty spot in the bed but relaxed at the sound of the shower. He looked at the clock. It was a little past six. He sprawled on his back and threw one arm across his face to ward off the daylight that was coming through the window blinds. Instinctively, he ran a tongue over his top lip and discovered the taste of Renee was still there, and without any control he released a groan of pleasure at the memory.

Last night had been special to him in many ways and even now his body was exhausted, drained from spent passion. But if she were to walk out of the bathroom, he would be revived and want her all over again.

But by no means, regardless of how sexually compatible

they were, did he think what they were sharing was all about sex and nothing more. He had been there with other women, but this thing with Renee was different. He sighed as an un-explainable sensation began developing deep within his chest and a breath he hadn't realized he'd been holding forced its way from his lungs. He wasn't sure what any of this meant but he did know that no matter what problems she thought they had, they would work them out because he had never wanted a woman like he wanted Renee.

With that thought in mind he shifted back on his stomach, buried his head into the pillow and slowly drifted off to sleep again.

Renee adjusted the shower cap on her head as she stood beneath the spray of water. The soreness in her thighs and the area between her legs were a blatant reminder of how long it had been since she had made love to a man, and never with the intensity of what she had shared with Tag.

She had lost count of the number of times they had come together during the night, but each time the pleasure had in-tensified even more. She had slept with only two other men in her lifetime, a guy she'd dated in college and Dionne. Neither had had the time or the inclination to prolong their lovemak-ing, and would never have considered withholding their own pleasure to make sure that she soared to the highest peak.

But Tag had.

He had proven there wasn't a selfish bone in his body when it had come to pleasuring her, and no woman could ask for more than that. The thought of everything he'd done made her quiver, deep down in her womb.

She sighed deeply. It was a new day and with it came all the insecurities of yesterday. Nothing had changed. He was white and she was black; he was rich and she was a work-ing girl. But none of that could stop her from thinking about how right he had looked in her bed when she'd slipped out of it, being careful not to wake him. Although it was Friday, it was a busy workday for her, but Tag had a position within his family's company where he could make his own hours, and since he hadn't gotten much sleep last night, there was no telling when he would wake up.

Turning off the water, she stepped out of the shower. She had meetings most of the day and couldn't afford to be late. She would be as quiet as she could while dressing for work. She wasn't used to having a houseguest, especially one like Tag.

Tag awoke with a jolt at the sound of a car backfiring. He sat up and glanced at the empty spot in the bed beside him and saw the note pinned to the pillow.

> I had to leave for work. Thanks for everything last night. Renee.

A smile touched his lips. She was always thanking him whether he wanted her to or not. But in this case it should be him thanking her. Everything they had shared had been special and he had gotten the best sleep he had in a long time, ever since that outrageous feud between the magazines and his mother's bout with cancer.

Last night he and Renee had shared a night of passion but he wondered what her thoughts were today. Would she allow their relationship to move to the next level without making a big deal out of things? Maybe it was pure possessiveness on his part, but he didn't intend to wait around for her to call the shots. He wanted to be with her, to continue to share this special relationship with her and he refused to let her end things between them before they got started. Somehow he had to show her that with them, color and social status didn't matter. And he intended to start doing so today.

Getting out of bed, he crossed the room to dig his cell phone out of his pants pocket. Within minutes he had his secretary on the line. "Joanne, clear my calendar of any appointments and meetings this morning. I won't be coming in before noon. And tell Gannon to call me the minute he gets back from his meeting with Rick Howard."

He then placed a call to his father to check on his mother. The news wasn't too uplifting. His mother was still withdrawn, not very talkative and still wasn't ready to see her children.

Sighing deeply, he then placed a call to a florist and ordered a dozen red roses to be delivered to Renee. And last but not least, he dialed the phone number for his good friend Alton Malone.

"Hey, Al, this is Tag. That painting you had displayed at Hollis on Saturday, I want it."

He smiled when his friend joked about Tag having enough of his paintings already. "It's not for me but for someone I've met. Someone special."

Tag laughed when he heard Alton pretend to be gasping for breath. Like Tag's siblings, Alton knew how limited his time was when it came to indulging in affairs. "Okay, knock it off, and yes, I think she's special. I think she's very special."

Renee leaned back in her chair and stared at the vase of flowers that had arrived that day. To say they were beautiful would be an understatement, and it didn't take long for word to get around the office that Renee Williams, the quiet, keeps-to-herself social worker who never dated, must have finally found a boyfriend since she had gotten flowers—and a dozen long-stem red roses at that.

She was glad she had taken off the card and inserted it into her desk drawer before Diane had breezed into her office to see the flowers that everyone was whispering about. Diane had looked high and low for the card, evidently feeling she had every right to read it.

But as far as Renee was concerned, it was a card meant for her to read in private, and since she had a few moments alone now, she pulled it out of her desk and reread Tag's words.

Last night meant more to me than you'll ever know. Have dinner with me tonight so I can thank you properly. Tag.

Renee sighed. According to Vicki, Tag had called twice while she had been in meetings. More than likely he wanted to confirm that she would be free to go out to dinner with him tonight.

She stood and went to the window. Although there was no way she would regret what she shared with Tag last night, a part of her knew it may have sent him the wrong message. Her thoughts and feelings on them dating hadn't changed. She wished things could be different but they weren't and she had accepted that. If only he would.

She turned when the phone rang on her desk and quickly crossed the room to pick it up. "Yes, Vicki?"

"Mr. Teagan Elliott is on the line for you."

Renee briefly closed her eyes, inhaled deeply. "All right,

please put him through." Her legs felt weak as she eased into the chair behind her desk.

"Renee."

She swallowed upon hearing the sound of her name from Tag's lips, those same lips he had used to make love to her. His skill and virility in the bedroom surpassed anything she'd ever known. "Yes, Tag, it's Renee."

"How are you feeling?"

She knew why he was asking. No woman made love as many times as they had last night without feeling some discomfort. But then a part of her didn't mind the discomfort. The pleasure she had received had made any discomfort well worth it. "I'm feeling okay, and you?"

"I feel better than I've felt in a long time and you're the reason."

She nervously licked her lips as she glanced across the room at the flowers. "Thanks for the roses. They're beautiful."

"And so are you. I don't think there's an inch on your body that isn't beautiful."

Abruptly she flushed and moved her gaze away from the flowers, remembering just how much of her body he had seen, touched, tasted. Red-hot embers swiftly flickered to life within her, forcing her to remember every moment, every intimate detail. "Tag, I don't think…" Her voice trailed off. The fact of the matter was that at the moment she couldn't think. She could only remember, and the memories were overwhelming her.

"Have dinner with me tonight, Renee. I want to take you someplace special."

She leaned back in the chair and closed her eyes. "Tag, I don't think that's a good idea."

"And I happen to think it's a wonderful idea, unless…"

Involuntarily, she reopened her eyes. "Unless what?"

"Unless you're ashamed to be seen with me."

She sat straight up in her chair. "That's not it and you know it," she defended stubbornly. "I have been seen with you. I was with you last Saturday and again last night."

"But I don't consider those real dates. I want to take you out to dinner and dancing."

"But I've told you that I don't think it's a good idea for us to take things further," she implored, desperately needing for him to understand. Why couldn't he get it that they were from two different worlds in more ways than one?

"Too late, sweetheart. We've already taken things further. In my book they can't get any further then they got last night. You might chalk it up to merely a night of passion, a night we lost our heads to lust, but I consider it something more solid and substantial. If you don't think so, then I need to convince you otherwise. Don't try to make what we shared last night nothing more than casual and fun. It *was* more and you know it."

Renee bowed her head. Yes, she knew it. She also knew something else that he didn't know. She loved him.

"Have dinner with me tonight, Renee. Please."

Renee lifted her head. What would it hurt if she had dinner with him? Maybe she could use that time to convince him there were too many issues facing them in a relationship. And then there was the fact that she did want to be with him, share time with him, make love to him again, even though she shouldn't.

"All right. I'll have dinner with you."

"Great! I'll make reservations on board the Harbor."

Renee swallowed. The Harbor wasn't just any dinner cruise

ship. It was one that sailed down the Hudson River while catering to the affluent. She'd heard that you had to be a member of the private club to even step on deck, and that the prices were so high she'd never go there in her lifetime and definitely not on her budget. "The Harbor? It's still running, even in February?"

"As long as the weather cooperates, it sails. And I'd like you and I to be on it. What do you say?"

Renee exhaled. How could she possibly tell him no? "Okay."

"And I'll pick you up around seven. Is that time all right?"

"Yes, seven is fine."

"Good. I'll see you then."

Moments after hanging up the phone, Renee couldn't help wondering if she had gotten in deeper than she should have. After all, the deeper she got, the harder it would be to eventually walk away.

Tag glanced first at Gannon then back at Marlene Kingston, not knowing exactly what to say. He'd had a hunch that Senator Denton's resignation hadn't been as benign as it seemed. "And you're sure about this, Marlene? Can we trust our sources?" Tag was well aware how the use of anonymous sources by news organizations had been under heightened scrutiny over the past year.

"Yes, more than you can guess. Here's the name," she said, handing him a sheet of paper.

Tag took the paper and glanced at it, then raised a brow before passing it on to Gannon. After reading it, Gannon whistled. The name on the paper was that of the senator's niece. "This is definitely a strictly confidential source. How did you manage it?"

Marlene smiled. "Jeanette and I attended classes together at Georgetown. Once I started asking questions she broke down and told me everything. She's a highly ethical person and over the years found anomalies in the Senator's behavior that she didn't approve of. She's always felt compelled to keep quiet, but this last thing was the final straw. As you can see, we have a reliable story here, Tag. And what's even more special is that it seems *Time* doesn't even have a clue, which gives us an advantage."

Tag sighed. Marlene's source indicated that Senator Denton had participated in a cover-up in the worst possible way and it was up to *Pulse* to report it. Not only did the American people have a right to know but Tag knew what being the first to print the article would do for sales. It would definitely put *Pulse* ahead in his grandfather's competition game. Big headlines brought in readers, and readers drove the profits up.

Gannon stood and rubbed a hand down his face. "We're going to have to have all our ducks in a row for this one. Senator Denton is well-liked and highly respected, and a cover-up of this magnitude will cause one hell of a scandal. But I want *Pulse* to be the one to expose it."

Tag smiled, feeling the adrenaline rush he'd always experienced when they were on the verge of breaking a story. Top that off with his dinner date tonight with Renee and he felt like a man riding high above the clouds.

"I'll finalize my report and have it on Peter's desk by Monday," Marlene said, interrupting his thoughts.

Tag shook his head. "No. This is going to be **your**

story. You're doing all the digging and the Senator's niece is your contact. You write the article."

Gannon nodded in agreement. "Where the hell is Peter, anyway?"

"He's still at lunch," Marlene said, gathering up all her papers to put in her briefcase.

After Marlene had left, Tag looked over at Gannon and said, "We're going to have to do something about Peter. He knew about this meeting."

Gannon was about to respond when the phone on his desk rang. He quickly picked it up when he saw it was his private line. Tag, who figured the caller was probably Erika and didn't want to intrude on his brother's private conversation, strolled across the room to look out the window. It was a beautiful day, and seeing all the red paper hearts being displayed in the store window across the street reminded him that Tuesday was Valentine's Day.

"That was Dad."

Tag turned and met his brother's smiling face. Evidently their father had called with good news. "And?"

Gannon grinned. "He called to say that Erika talked to Mom and she agreed to help out with the wedding." Gannon's smile widened even more when he added, "Dad also wanted me to tell you, Liam and Bridget that Mom wants to see us on Sunday for dinner."

A smile broke on Tag's face. Although Renee had explained to him what his mother was going through, it hadn't been easy to be shut out by her. "Hey, that's great!"

Gannon chuckled. "Yes, it is, and we have Renee to thank for helping us come up with a plan to boost Mom's spirit. Thank her when you see her again."

Tag lifted a curious brow. "And what makes you think I'll see her again?"

Gannon met Tag's stare and grinned. "You will. I saw the way you were looking at her at dinner the other night. You are definitely interested in her. I like her and you're right, she's beautiful."

Tag absently picked up a paper clip on his brother's desk and said, "I'm taking her out tonight. To the Harbor." He was excited about his and Renee's official date and didn't mind sharing it with his brother.

Gannon raised a brow as he leaned back in his chair. "The Harbor? So, I'm right in assuming you're interested in her."

Tag moved toward the door and slid his brother a parting glance. "Yes, I'm definitely interested."

From where Renee was standing at her bedroom window she could see a silver-gray Mercedes sports car stop in front of her apartment building. The way her heart began beating she knew it was a different vehicle but the same man.

Tag.

She couldn't help standing there, watching as he exited from the vehicle. He said he would be by to pick her up at seven but for some reason she'd known he would arrive a few minutes early.

She couldn't help but study him as he made his way to her apartment door, his stride long, his steps hurried, unusual for a man who wasn't late getting to where he was going. He wore a black suit and even from where Renee stood she could tell it was made from the highest quality fabric and probably had a designer name attached to it. Tag had Hollywood good looks and watching him was forcing her to participate in one hell of a mind exercise.

Suddenly, as if sensing that he was being watched, Tag glanced up and their eyes connected and Renee felt it, just as surely as if he had been able to defy logic and actually reach up and touch her. He smiled and goose bumps began to rise on her arms, her heart literally skipped a beat, and when he waved up at her, she couldn't do anything but lift her hand and wave back. Turning away from the window, she braced herself for the man who was doing a good job of rocking her world.

Moments later she stood in front of the door, her stomach knotting, her breasts becoming sensitive, a tender ache in certain muscles. Forcing herself to get a grip, she opened the door.

Whatever Renee had expected, it hadn't been Tag sweeping her into his arms and closing the door behind him with the heel of his shoe and then hungrily capturing her mouth, locking it with his as if joining them with some kind of magnetic force, immediately driving her mad with desire. She wrapped her arms around him and whimpered, the sound quickly drowned out by their heavy breathing.

Renee quickly came to the conclusion that she could go without dinner if she could remain here and feast on Tag. When he finally released her mouth and placed her back on her feet, she pressed her face into his chest, thinking that no one had ever kissed her hello quite that way before.

She looked up at him when she felt his hand glide through her hair, and then he was lifting her chin up and leaning down for yet another kiss. There was no way she could not respond to this. To him. Whether she wanted it to or not, loving him was taking her beyond any boundaries she wanted to set.

When it came to Tag there were no limitations, but she had a feeling there was unchartered territory that he planned for them to explore. Together.

"I thought of you a lot today," he said, his voice strained. As he whispered against her ear, his tongue flicked out to taste her skin there.

"And I thought of you a lot today, too," she replied honestly. She hated herself for admitting such a thing but knew she had to admit it anyway.

Slowly, he took a step back and looked at her and then he captured her hand in his, held it above her head and twirled her around, letting the ruffles at the hem of her black dress swirl about her ankles. "You look gorgeous tonight, Renee."

She knew he meant every word and was glad that she had left the office early to do a little shopping. "Thanks."

He took a step closer to her and leaned down and kissed her slowly, thoroughly. Moments later, Renee slipped from his arms. "If we don't leave now we might be late," she said, her pulse racing fast and furiously.

Tag smiled. "You're right. But then I'll have something to look forward to after dinner, won't I?"

Renee swallowed as she nodded. She would have something to look forward to after dinner as well.

The Harbor was a beautiful dinner cruise ship and the moment they stepped on deck via a heated tented walkway, a uniformed waiter escorted them to their table in the Tropicana Room.

Renee glanced around, tempted to pinch herself. This was a new ship and everything looked elegant and expensive, including the marble floors and crown molding. Tag squeezed her hand and smiled down at her. "I hope you like the setting."

She gave him an assuring grin. "Trust me, I do."

They were shown to a white-linen-covered table with a huge glass window that provided a panoramic view of the Hudson. After handing them menus, the waiter left them alone just as the ship began moving. Soft music was playing and not far away a dance floor was set up for dancing later. Muted conversation filled the rooms as hosts and hostesses escorted other arrivals to their tables.

Renee had never been on a cruise before and when she felt the movement of the ship she planted her feet firmly on the floor. "I can't believe we're actually moving," she said nervously.

Tag chuckled. "We are. We'll be out on the Hudson for a couple of hours or so."

She nodded. "You come here often?"

He smiled at her. "I've dined here a number of times with various members of my family." And then, because he wanted her to know just how special tonight was to him, Tag added, "But this is the first time I've ever brought a date here."

Renee opened her mouth, then immediately closed it when nothing came out. The thought that she was the first made her entire body tingle in appreciation, blatantly ignoring the warning signs of what doing so could mean. "Thank you," she said politely.

His smile widened. "You're always thanking me."

"Because you're always doing something nice."

He leaned forward in his chair and whispered, "Can't help it with you. You bring out the best in me."

"And I'm supposed to believe that?" she asked, chuckling.

"I hope you do because it's the truth."

At that moment the waiter returned with a bottle of wine.

"I asked for a bottle to be brought out before our meal so we can toast my good news," Tag told her.

Renee lifted a brow. "And what good news is that?" She could tell he'd been in a rather good mood but he hadn't shared the reason for it her during the car ride from her apartment. Instead he had told her how his day had gone at work and she shared tidbits about hers.

"Good news about Mom. Dad called to tell us that she has agreed to help Erika with her wedding and that she also wants to see all of us on Sunday for dinner."

Renee's face beamed with happiness. She knew how much his mother's depression had bothered Tag. "Oh, Tag, that's wonderful! It will take her concentration off her condition and put it on something else. I told you that planning Erika's wedding would do wonders for her."

"Yes, you did tell us, didn't you? And Gannon asked me to thank you for all the advice you gave to us last night. We will be forever in your debt."

For some reason the thought of Tag thinking he owed her something didn't sit well with Renee. "Neither you nor your family owes me anything, Tag. Like I told all of you that night, I like your mother, I think she's a special person and I empathized with all of you. I just wanted to help."

That was exactly what he found so special about Renee. She had such a sweet spirit about her and a passionate spirit as well, judging from last night. The memory of them coming apart in each other's arms was etched deep into his brain.

He had a lot going on in his life with his mother and work, but he couldn't imagine not carving out this time to spend with Renee. "Let's make a toast," he said, lifting his glass. "To my mother's continued good health."

Renee held up her glass to his. "Yes, to Karen's continued good health."

Renee thought that everything about tonight was perfect. The man, the cruise down the Hudson River and the cozy atmosphere. Over dinner they talked more about his mother, his grandfather's outlandish proposal and he provided tidbits on his other family members, especially all the cousins he was close to. It was the information on his grandfather that intrigued her the most.

"Things will work out, Tag, I'm sure of it. From everything you've told me, family means a lot to your grandfather. I can't imagine him doing anything to intentionally destroy that. There must be a reason for what you and your family see as his madness. I've discovered in life that things aren't always as they seem to be."

Tag wondered if she felt that way about them. He clearly remembered what she'd told him that day in her office. Still, she had agreed to go out with him tonight, and he hoped that last night meant as much to her as it did to him. Was she willing for them to give things a try? He was convinced they should continue to see each other, but knew convincing her of that wouldn't be easy. But he would not give up.

"Would you like dessert?" he asked, after the waiter had returned to clear their table. The river was beautiful and the cruise was setting the mood for romance. During several lulls in their conversation, heat and desire had surrounded them. He had felt it and knew that she had felt it, too.

Renee smiled. "No. I doubt that I could eat a single thing more. Everything was delicious, Tag. Thanks for bringing me here."

"It was my pleasure. Would you like to dance?"

Renee heard the soft, slow music and had been noticing several couples move on the dance floor during different times all night. She'd always liked dancing but couldn't remember the last time she'd done so. Dionne had never taken her out dancing. His idea of a good date was her preparing him dinner at her place. Since their breakup she had analyzed their relationship and knew exactly where they had gone wrong. In Dionne's mind he had been the king and she had been his queen who was supposed to cater to his every whim.

"Renee?"

Tag's voice pulled her thoughts from the past. She smiled. "Yes, Tag, I'll dance with you."

Moments later Tag led her out on the dance floor among all the other couples. She could feel a lot of eyes on them but at the moment she didn't care. All she wanted to think about was Tag, and being surrounded by his kindness, his strength and his warmth. And when he gathered her in his arms, every reason she thought they couldn't be together like this floated from her mind. When he pulled her even closer she seemed to melt against him and an involuntary shudder passed through her body.

"You're cold?" he asked, leaning down and whispering the question in her ear.

She shook her head. "No, I'm not cold." There was no way she could tell him that she was just the opposite. Her insides were burning up with a heat that she'd recently discovered only he could generate.

Renee shifted her attention away from Tag to the dining area filled with smartly dressed couples enjoying their meals. Her gaze lit on one couple in particular when the woman leaned over and whispered something in her husband's ear before turning back and staring at Renee and Tag, frowning deeply. She could only imagine what the woman said since her husband was now staring at them with an equally fierce and disapproving look. Evidently they didn't approve of interracial dating.

Not wanting to see their scornful glares anymore, Renee turned and buried her face in Tag's chest and he pulled her tighter to him as the music swirled around them. She refused to let anyone put a damper on things. Tonight was her and Tag's night and she intended to enjoy it.

She sighed contentedly when she felt his warm and tender hands move from around her waist to the center of her back. He leaned down and began humming the tune that the band was playing. She thought he had one hell of a sexy voice.

The ship made its way to shore and after a couple more dances he took her hand in his. He brought it to his lips. "I hope you enjoyed your evening, Renee."

A quiver passed through her. "I did. Everything was perfect."

He smiled. His gaze was intent when he said, "You were the most perfect thing here tonight and I'm proud that you were with me and no one else."

Renee couldn't help but smile. If he was using all his skill at that moment to set her up for seduction later, he was doing a good job of it. "And I'm glad I'm here tonight with you, as well."

His gaze held hers for a long moment before he took her hand and led her through the crowd. "I want us to be the first ones off this ship," he said, leading her back to the table. "Our night is far from over yet and with tomorrow being Saturday, just imagine all the possibilities."

She did imagine them and doing so only made her fall in love with him that much more.

Chapter 8

Renee sank into the soft leather cushions of Tag's sofa and focused her gaze on him. He was standing across the room in front of a wall-to-wall entertainment system, and the moment he'd pressed a button, soft jazz music filled the air surrounding them.

She glanced around and saw a number of Alton Malone paintings on his wall as well as paintings from other artists. All beautiful. All expensive. But then his condo, being in Tribeca, had to be up there in the high price range. The wine oak furniture was tasteful and blended well with the modern contemporary decor.

Besides the framed Malone paintings, the living room was decorated with several Asian figurines. Tag had indicated they had been gifts from the Watari Museum in Tokyo after he had done an article about it in *Pulse* a few years ago.

Tag had given her a brief tour of the downstairs but hadn't

bothered showing her where his bedroom was. She was rather anxious to see it but when the time was right tonight, there was no doubt in her mind that she would.

Given the heat that had generated off them, between them and with them all evening, a visit to his bedroom was inevitable. After what they had shared last night, she was looking forward to it.

When he had whisked her away from the docks and into his car he had asked if she would like to spend a little time over at his place. She had come close to refusing, remembering the cold, disapproving look the couple had given them on board the ship, but then had decided that tonight she wanted to spend as much time with Tag as possible, and when he took her home later she would explain to him why they couldn't see each other again.

"Would you like something to drink?"

He reclaimed her attention and she met his gaze. Her breath caught. The lamp's light seemed to enhance the vividness of his eyes and the blue was so deep that for a moment it seemed like she was drowning in the ocean. "No, I don't want anything to drink."

"And what do you want?"

Renee was silent. There wasn't an answer she felt comfortable in saying out loud. The silence that drifted between them was tangible, as potent and hot as the very air they were breathing. It didn't take much to recall last night and the way his body had taken hers, had gone deep inside of her, thrusting in and out. Then there was his mouth that had acquainted her with a warm, succulent sweetness that would have her licking her lips for days, nights. And last but not least was the memory of his hands and the way they had glided over her skin, touching places that made ripples of sensation start deep in her abdomen and spread to other parts of her body.

"Renee?"

She continued to hold his gaze, hearing the sound of his voice, strained, husky and filled with something else. Urgency. Need. "Why don't you find out what I want," she said softly, invitingly. She then deliberately took the tip of her tongue and traced her lips, knowing what watching her was doing to him.

She licked steadily as she stared into his tense face. Blatant need shone in the depths of his eyes. Her gaze moved lower, past his tightly muscled stomach to the crotch of his pants, and she saw the erection that strained against the zipper. She suddenly felt hot, and the ventilation from the air conditioning was doing nothing to cool off her heated flesh.

"I think I will."

She shifted her gaze back up to his face as he slowly moved toward her with a smile that sent her pulse racing. "You will what? Find out what I want?"

"No, seduce you into telling me."

Instead of joining her on the sofa he pulled her up and settled her body against his, to feel his hardness. Eyes locked to hers, he whispered huskily, "I want you, Renee."

"And I want you, too, Tag."

As if her words were the go-ahead he had been waiting for, he leaned down and his mouth covered hers in a hungry, desperate, ravenous kiss that had Renee moaning in need when he abruptly ended it.

Questioning eyes met his and he smiled and reached out and tenderly caressed her cheek. "I want you to tell me what you want, sweetheart. Your wish will be my command."

Renee drew in a ragged breath, not being able to

imagine such a thing. She'd never had anyone cater exclusively to her needs while they made love. She'd never met anyone like Tag before. Telling him what she wanted and him actually carrying out each and every fantasy she had was an incredibly erotic thought.

"Tell me," he repeated.

She met his gaze and said, "For starters, take me to your bedroom and undress me."

Renee saw his blue eyes go hot just seconds before he bent and gathered her into his arms to carry her up the stairs. Her stomach quivered with the excitement of what would happen when they got to his bedroom. Even now, while they were in motion, she caught his scent. Masculine. Robust. Sexy.

When they entered his bedroom she glanced around. His bed, king-sized with a black platinum steel frame, sat in the center of the room with matching nightstands on each side. A dresser and chest were on the other side of the room. The bedroom reminded her of Tag. Neat, manly and with everything in order.

"Now to remove this dress."

He lowered her down his body and immediately went to work at removing her dress, easing down the zipper as his fingers grazed the warm flesh of her bare back. She wasn't wearing a bra. He moved the soft fabric down her shoulders to drop in a heap at her feet, his gaze locked on the breasts he had grown quite fond of the night before.

"Taste them again, Tag."

She didn't have to ask twice. His tongue flicked out and captured a budding nipple into his mouth. When he heard her moan and felt her knees weaken, he reached out and caught her by the waist. He remembered the orgasm she had the last time he had made love to her breasts, but this time he wanted to prolong her enjoyment, make her want him as much as he wanted her.

He gathered her into his arms and carried her over to the bed and placed her on her back, then lifted her hips to slide the panty hose and thong off of her. Driven by a desire whose depth he couldn't understand, he felt compelled to touch her and instinctively his fingers went to the damp curls between her legs.

She closed her eyes as he focused his concentration on pleasuring her with fingers that stroked her mercilessly. He watched as her lips parted slightly and she moaned out her gratification, while her heavy breathing pleaded with him to quench her desire.

"Too soon, sweetheart," he said, pulling back to remove his own clothes.

When she opened her eyes to watch him they were hot, dark and dilated. He didn't waste time as he tore off his shirt and eased his pants down his legs. With his gaze still locked with hers, he began removing his briefs and once he stood naked in front of the bed, her concentration shifted from his face down to his erection.

"Tell me what you want now," he said, his control almost shot to hell. Anticipation was killing him but he was determined to give her everything she wanted.

"I want you inside of me," she whispered before lying back on his thick bedspread.

The darkness of her skin was a stark contrast to the beige coverlet and he thought it was a breathtaking sight. Not wanting to waste any more time, he quickly pulled a condom out of his nightstand drawer. He kept them there although he'd never used them since Renee was the first woman he'd ever brought home with him. Before, it had been his companion's place or no place. He always considered his condo private and never wanted the memory of a woman's presence there. But with Renee he felt differently. He wanted her memory. He wanted her presence. Point-blank, he wanted her.

He knelt beside her on the bed, eager to join their bodies. He took her mouth again in a deep, hungry kiss, the only kind he shared with her. He knew he had to make love to her right then and pulled back to position his body over hers, and just like the contrast of her skin with his bedspread, he noted the same distinction with his skin. The only word he could think to describe the difference in their coloring was *beautiful*.

He broke off the kiss and looked down into her dark brown eyes. "Ready, sweetheart?"

She smiled up at him. "Only for you."

Her words, whispered seductively, released a surge of heat within him, and clenching his teeth he entered her in one smooth thrust. He breathed in deeply, inhaling her body's sensuous scent, and she arched her back, taking him deeper still, clutching him tightly with her womanly muscles, just as she'd done the last time. And just as before, he could only take so much of her agonizing torture.

Tag felt himself on the brink of tumbling over the edge and knew he had to move. He began setting a rhythm, first by starting a slow rocking motion and then thrusting in and out of her, glorying in the perfect fit they made. With each surge into her body he stoked the fires blazing between them and with each retreat he rekindled them all over again. All he could concentrate on was the woman beneath him, how they seemed made for each other. He called out her name each and every time her muscles clenched pleasure out of him, demanding he give more.

And he did.

An orgasm so intense that it shook his entire body tore through him the exact moment she screamed his name and her body bucked beneath him. He suddenly lost awareness of everything except Renee.

With one last hard thrust, he groaned as he felt her shudder beneath him.

As ecstasy slowly gave way to sweet contentment, he shifted his body, but remained buried deep inside of her, not ready to sever their intimate connection. They faced each other, gazed into each other's eyes as each of their limbs slowly became warm, heavy, pleasured.

Tag looked at her in amazement, thinking that Renee Williams was definitely what dreams were made of. He leaned closer and gently kissed her, needing to taste her, to absorb her, to appreciate her. And to thank the powers that had brought this beautiful woman into his life.

After Tag finished getting dressed he turned to watch Renee slip back into her dress. He stared at her for a long, thoughtful moment and a feeling he had never experienced before tugged at his heart, kicking his pulse into high gear.

The passion between them was fiery, breathtaking, but he didn't just want her sexually. He also enjoyed doing things with her, spending time with her, taking her places and sharing his thoughts with her. Tonight over dinner he had told her about his work and the challenges he, his father and brother at *Pulse* were facing trying to compete against the other three magazines. She had listened, hung on to his every word and then she had made several comments that had made him think.

Renee had pointed out that if his grandfather's challenge was making them tense, then imagine what it was doing to the people who worked for them. Were they worried about what would happen to their jobs if the magazine they worked for didn't make a good enough profit? And what changes in the corporate structure would the new CEO make? Changes in corporate dynamics could send workers into a panic and could result in a serious employer-employee relationship problem.

He knew her comments had only been the result of her innate concern for people. She was a person who cared about how people were treated, how a person felt and what a person thought. The latter, he sighed deeply, was the root of their problem, and the very reason she continued to put a roadblock in the way of a developing relationship between them. Tension rippled off him in acknowledging how far apart they still were on the issue of them getting together. They needed to talk.

He leaned against his dresser and watched as she struggled with the zipper on her dress. He liked her outfit. The sexy black dress fit her as if it had been made for her body alone, and the ruffles at the hem showed off a pair of truly gorgeous legs. He felt as though he could stand there and stare at her forever. "Need help?" he finally asked when her attempts at the zipper proved futile.

She shot him a look over her shoulder and smiled. "Only if you'll help me get it up."

He chuckled as he crossed the room to her. "Oh, I think that can be arranged." He easily slid up her zipper then reached around and wrapped his arms around her waist, pulling her back to him, liking the feel of her butt resting against his groin.

"Are you sure I can't convince you to spend the night?" he leaned down and prodded softly in her ear. "I promise to make it worth your while."

Renee sighed deeply and leaned back farther against Tag, luxuriating in the feel of his arms around her. More than anything she wanted to spend the night, to wake up beside him in the morning, like they had the previous night. But she knew that doing so would only make it that much harder to walk away and not look back.

"No, Tag, I don't think my spending the night here will be wise," she said with a shake of her head.

"Why?" he asked, turning her around to face him, although he already knew her argument. But tonight he was ready for it. His gaze locked with hers. "Explain to me why you won't spend the night."

She raised her eyes to the ceiling. "What will your neighbors think when they see me?"

"That I'm one hell of a lucky man."

Renee sighed. Everything about tonight had been beautiful and she didn't want to shatter the enchanted moments, but she had to make him understand. "Not everyone will think that, Tag. There will be some who will not like the fact we're dating."

He frowned and crossed his arms over his chest. "Then I'd say it's their problem and not ours."

Renee shook her head. "What about your family?"

He remembered she had brought up his family before. "I thought I had made things perfectly clear about my family. They don't and won't dictate who I see."

Renee crossed her arms over her own chest and lifted her chin. "No, but they would be concerned. I can't see the public-conscious Elliotts welcoming an African-American into their fold. You even said tonight how your grandfather has always drilled into all of your heads never to do anything unsavory regarding your family name."

Tag's frown deepened. "And you see our dating as unsavory?"

"I don't but there are others who would." She could clearly remember what had happened the last time her name was linked to gossip. It hadn't been a good feeling knowing she was the hot topic of everyone's conversations.

Frustrated, Tag rubbed his hand against the back of his neck. "Don't you think you're blowing this out of proportion, Renee? Almost everywhere you go these days you encounter mixed-race couples. This is New York, for heaven's sake. How about stepping back into the real world and looking around you? Notice the social trend that's evolving. The mainstream of American society isn't concerned about mixed couples anymore. They have a lot more to worry about, like the economy, making sure our country is kept safe, healthy and free. That's what's on their minds, Renee, and not who's crossing racial lines."

"For your information, Teagan Elliott, there are many people in the real world who do care about who's crossing racial lines."

"And you want to give in to them?"

Renee drew her head back and glared up at Tag. "It's not giving in to them."

"Then what do you call it? I like you. You like me. Yet you don't want to date me because of what people might think or say? I call that giving in to a segment of society who can't move on and accept people as people and not attach a color to them."

"Maybe one day things will be different but—"

"I don't want to wait for one day, Renee. The only thing I want is today, this moment. I don't give a damn that your skin is darker than mine. What's important is that I care for you. I want to be with you, get to know you better, spend time with you. And I want you to get to know me. And the more you get to know me the more you'll see that I am my own man. I make my own decisions. I choose my own woman."

He reached out his hand to her. "Will you give me a chance? Will you give *us* a chance?" A smile touched the corners of his lips. "You're a very beautiful woman and personally, I don't think I'm such a bad catch. What do you think?"

At that moment Renee thought her heart would swell over with the love she felt for this man standing before her. She stared into his blue eyes and saw the sincerity shining in their depths. "I think," she said in a somewhat shaky voice as she took the hand he offered, "that you've presented a very good argument."

"And?" he asked, drawing her closer to him. She came to him willingly, which to Tag was a good sign. She smiled while placing her palms against his chest, which, in his book, was another good sign. His heart rate increased and he felt his blood thicken in his veins.

"And," she said, taking another step closer to him, molding her body against his and igniting an inferno within him, "I think that we'll try things your way and see what happens."

"I can tell you what's going to happen," he said in a quiet voice, lowering his head toward hers.

"And just what do you predict?" she asked, rising on tiptoes to meet him.

"I predict that one day we're going to wonder why we even had this argument."

Renee opened her mouth to disagree, but his mouth came down on hers, effectively kissing away any words she was about to say. Sensation ripped through her when he parted her lips with his tongue and claimed the depths of what awaited him inside.

Moments later he tore his mouth free of hers just long enough to whisper, "Will you stay the night with me?"

"Yes," she murmured through kiss-swollen lips. "I'll stay."

He smiled and kissed her again as his hands eased around to her back and slowly began unzipping the dress that he had zipped up earlier.

Chapter 9

Gannon snapped his fingers in front of Tag's face. "Hey, Tag, are you with us?"

Tag snapped out of his reverie and blinked. He looked first at Gannon and then at Erika, Liam and Bridget. All four had silly grins on their faces at having caught the ever-alert Teagan Elliott daydreaming.

They were sitting in the living room in The Tides, his grandparents' primary place of residence, and where his mother was currently convalescing. As a child he'd loved visiting his grandparents here. Situated on five acres on a bluff above the Atlantic Ocean, the Elliotts' compound had its own private, guarded road. On the estate was the house, a large pool, the pool house, a beautiful English rose garden and a helicopter landing pad. The feature he loved the most was the hand-carved stone staircase that led down the bluff to a private beach with a boat dock. It was from that dock that his father and grandfather had taught him how to sail.

"Tag?"

Hearing his brother speak to him a second time, Tag thought he'd better respond. "Yes, I'm with you guys, although I'm getting bored to tears," he said, smiling. "Talk about something that won't put me to sleep, will you?"

Bridget made a face. "Um, how about if we discuss the fact that you were seen at a Broadway play on Saturday night," she said, tipping a glass of wine to her lips.

Tag rolled his eyes, knowing his sister had gotten her information from Caroline Dutton, a high school friend of hers who was known for her loose lips. Everyone knew Caroline was a chip off the old block since her mother, Lila Dutton, was one of the worst gossips anyone could have the misfortune of knowing. He had run into Caroline at the play on Saturday, and if Bridget knew he had gone to the play then she also knew the person he had taken with him.

"Don't hold your breath for that one." Tag leaned back in his chair and smiled. Waking up beside Renee had been a wonderful experience on Saturday morning. After making love again, they had showered together and then he had taken her home to change clothes.

He had talked her into going to see the *Lion King* and they both enjoyed it immensely. Afterwards, he had taken her back to her place and he had spent the night.

"Your smile is downright sickening, Tag."

His smile widened as he glanced over at Liam. "Is it? Sorry." He knew everyone was curious but he had no intention of sharing the reason for his blissful contentment with anyone.

"Dinner is ready to be served."

Tag stood, grateful for Olive's timely announcement. Olive and her husband, Benjamin, had worked for his grandparents for years as The Tides' main caretakers. Olive, at fifty-five, was the housekeeper and Ben, at fifty-seven, was the groundskeeper. Both ran their own staffs and kept things orderly.

"When will Mother be coming down?" he hung back and asked when the others had left the room.

"She's on her way now," Olive said, smiling brightly. "Whoever's idea it was for her to help with Gannon and Erika's wedding definitely had the right idea. Her mood has improved dramatically."

Tag was glad to hear that. He had been worried that at some point she might start withdrawing again. "I'm anxious to see her." He hadn't seen her since before she'd been released from the hospital.

"And I know she's anxious to see all of you as well. The last few weeks have been difficult for her."

Tag shook his head. "When do you expect my grandparents to return?" He knew they had taken a pleasure trip to Florida to meet with other couples that belonged to the Irish American Historical Society.

"By the end of next week, in time for Gannon's wedding and to get things ready for their anniversary dinner. They call every day to check how your mom is doing and be sure she gets all the rest she needs before she begins her chemotherapy treatments."

Tag sighed and traced his hand down his face. He tried not to think about that additional phase in his mother's recovery. When he heard voices he walked out into the foyer and glanced in the direction of the staircase. His parents were standing together on the top stair and whatever his father had told his mother had made her smile.

Although she looked somewhat pale and exhausted, there was a part of her fighting for the sparkle and glow to come through. He'd noticed more than once that his father had the ability to bring out that sparkle by coaxing her into a smile with whatever private words he would tell her.

A part of Tag admired what his parents had shared for over thirty years and for the first time in his life he knew that one day he wanted that same thing for himself. The chance to share his life with someone who would not only be his spouse, but his lover and best friend, as well.

"Come on to the kitchen and leave them alone for a little while longer," Olive whispered in his ear.

Tag nodded and followed Olive into the kitchen.

Tag could only be grateful that his mother was doing as well as she was. In a way, dinner was just like old times when they would all share a meal together. But the one thing that was different was that his father hadn't rushed out in the middle of it, thinking there was something at the office he just had to do. Another thing was that after dinner everyone lingered, not in a hurry to leave, and most importantly, his mother was the center of all their attention and concern.

"So how are things going with you, Tag?" his mother asked, sending him a fond smile as they walked together outside on the grounds, her hand firmly anchored to his sleeve, her steps slower than usual.

He looked down at her and smiled. "I'm doing better now that I see that you're doing well." His siblings had left moments earlier and he had remained, needing this time alone with his mother. The two of them had always had a rather close relationship. As a child he'd thought she was beautiful. He still did. And he'd also been convinced that she was the smartest person in the world since any advice she'd always given him had been timely and needed—whether he'd wanted to receive it or not.

"How are things at the office?" she inquired, evidently feeling the need to break her question down further.

Tag let his lips curve, recognizing her strategy. "Work is kind of crazy right now and a part of me is angry at Granddad because of the way things are. Over the years I've felt more than once that some of the decisions he has made were based more on keeping up appearances than putting his family first, but I think this recent antic of his is a real doozy. I can't imagine what he was thinking. Dad is the eldest, so when Granddad retires, he should rightfully become CEO. Everyone expected it, so I just don't get it."

Karen nodded in understanding. "At the moment none of us do, Tag. I think Patrick's decision hurt Michael somewhat, but you know your father. He will abide by your grandfather's wishes."

Karen stopped walking for a moment and looked up at Tag, fixing her dark eyes on his. "So now, tell me, how are things going in your personal life?"

Tag was acutely aware that his mother, in her own way, was probing. And although she'd always been curious about his personal life, she'd kept the pointed questions to a minimum. For some reason he felt she was asking out of more than polite curiosity and quickly wondered if someone had mentioned something to her. One of his siblings? His father?

He couldn't help but recall that day in the hospital waiting room when he had referred to Renee by her first name and his father had given him that surprised look. One thing Tag had discovered while growing up was that Michael Elliott was not slow. He caught on quickly. Dismissing the thought that the informant was one of his siblings, Tag concluded his father had said something.

He met his mother's gaze and smiled, deciding to be completely honest, the only way he could be with her. "My personal life is going great, although I was having problems with this certain young lady not taking me seriously, but I've finally convinced her otherwise."

"Is it Renee?"

Tag lifted a brow, knowing it was as he'd suspected. His father *had* told her. His smile widened as he answered, deciding not to question how she knew. It was enough that she did. "Yes, it's Renee. We're seeing each other."

Karen smiled. "She's a beautiful girl and I know firsthand how genuinely caring she is. She helped me through a difficult time and for that I'm most grateful. There's something so uniquely elegant about her and I can't help but notice how she goes out of her way to help someone. I think she's good for you and that the two of you would make a beautiful couple."

After a brief moment of silence, she said, "Earlier, you mentioned something about Renee not taking you seriously. Does that mean she's not fully accepting of sharing a relationship with you?"

Tag chuckled, thinking that was one way to put it. "She was pretty reluctant at first but she's slowly beginning to thaw. I've gotten her to at least agree to give us a chance to see where things will go. Because we're an interracial couple she's concerned about what people will say."

"The family?"

"Yes, among others. We've garnered our share of frowns

and stares whenever we're seen together. I can ignore them a lot better than she can."

Karen nodded. "As far as the family's acceptance, I don't think you'll have any problems, however, you know your grandfather. He can take protecting the family's name to uncompromising heights."

Tag frowned, controlling the quick surge of anger that consumed him at the mere thought. "Yes, and when the time comes I will deal with him about this if I have to. Under no circumstances will I let him, or anyone, dictate how I spend my life and with whom."

Karen looked at her son, feeling his resentment. "I'd like to offer some words of advice, if I may."

"Certainly." Although she had asked, Tag knew she would give her advice anyway.

"Since finding out about my cancer I've discovered just how little time we have on this earth to do the things we want to do, to be with the person or people we want to be with. It's made me realize one very important thing and that is nothing, and I mean nothing—not prestige, power or pride—is worth sacrificing the things that you truly want, the things that you truly love.

"Don't be afraid to take time and smell the roses. Don't hesitate in seeking out those things you hold dear. Seeking them out and holding on to them. And don't ever cease standing up for what you believe in, and fighting for those things that you want. Life is too short. Do what makes you happy, regardless of how others might feel. Do what makes Tag happy."

Tag sighed deeply. He smiled, thinking his mother was still the smart woman he'd always thought her to be. He lifted her hand to his lips. "Thanks for the advice. I intend to take it."

* * *

"So, how was your mom?" Renee asked as she sank onto the edge of her sofa. As soon as the phone rang she had gotten this excited feeling in the pit of her stomach. For some reason she had known it would be Tag.

"Considering all she's been through I think her spirits are rather high. Her health seems to be improving each day and she's getting around a lot better."

"That's good."

"And she's excited about the plans for Gannon and Erika's wedding, although she understands they want it to be a small affair with just family. Dad says Mom has been busy on the phone with caterers and florists, and I can tell just from talking to her that she's really enjoying it."

There was a pause, and then he said, "Mom and I got a chance to spend some time alone and I told her that you and I were seeing each other."

An uneasy shiver crept up Renee's spine. "You did?"

"Yes."

"And what did she say?" she asked, trying to keep her voice even.

"She smiled and said she thought we made a nice couple."

Renee arched her brow. "Was that the only thing she said?"

"No. She also told me how much she liked you and how much you had helped her through a difficult time. She actually thinks you're good for me."

A jitter of happiness shot through Renee. She couldn't help but smile. "Did she really say that?"

"Yes, and those were her exact words."

Renee sighed. "Thanks for sharing that with me."

"I'd like to share a whole lot more."

She shook her head, grinning as she thought of all they'd shared that weekend, especially the intensity with which he had made love to her. "Haven't you shared enough?"

"You haven't seen anything yet. I'd like to make plans for us for this Tuesday night. Would you go out with me?"

"Tuesday?"

"Yes, it's Valentine's Day."

"Oh." She hadn't had a reason to celebrate Valentine's Day in so long that she'd forgotten. "And you want to take me out?"

"Of course. I want to plan a special evening just for you."

Renee shifted her body on the cushions of her sofa. "Are you sure?"

Tag laughed. "Of course I'm sure. There's no one else I'd rather spend such a special day with. Will it be okay to pick you up around seven?"

She sighed deeply, remembering the decision they had made. "Yes, seven will be fine. Any particular way I should dress?"

"It's a semiformal affair. One of my mother's favorite charities, the Heart Association, is holding its annual Heart to Heart Ball."

Renee swallowed. That meant a lot of people would be attending. She was just coming to terms with her decision that she and Tag give things a try. She wasn't sure if she was ready to handle something of this magnitude. Panic rose within her. The last thing she wanted to do was to give people something to talk about. "Tag?"

"Yes, sweetheart?"

His endearment caused a sudden calming effect to settle over her. She would do as she promised and give them a chance. "Nothing. I'll see you on Tuesday."

"I can't wait."

She smiled. "Neither can I. Good-night."

As soon as she ended their call she placed her arms across her stomach when it began to feel tense. No, she wouldn't give in to any panic attacks. For now she would follow her heart and see where it led.

"So what do you think, Erika?" Tag asked.

Erika pursed her lips and sighed. She glanced across the *Pulse* conference room at Gannon, Tag and Marlene Kingston, then leaned back in her chair and smiled. "I think an excellent job was done with this article and that we should definitely make it our cover story."

Gannon lifted a brow. "In next month's issue?"

Erika shook her head. "No. I suggest we go to a special edition. If we sit on this story we run the risk of *Time* doing it first. You can't convince me that sooner or later someone won't get suspicious about Senator Denton's resignation like we did and start digging."

Tag nodded. "Okay then, we're in agreement," he said excitedly. He turned to Marlene. "And I'll add my kudos to Erika's for a well-written story."

"Thanks," Marlene said beaming. "I appreciate you giving me the opportunity to do it."

After Marlene left, Erika lifted an eyebrow and asked, "Where's Peter?"

Gannon sighed. "I don't know. This is another important meeting that he's missed." No one said anything, but Tag knew his brother was being forced to deal with an issue that he'd been avoiding. Peter Weston was simply not pulling his weight.

Tag stood. "All right then, it's all settled," he said excitedly. "Let the presses roll and let's watch the sales flow in."

Later that evening Tag joined Liam, Bridget and his cousin Scarlet at Une Nuit. Despite everyone's smiles he could feel tension at the table the moment he sat down. "What's going on?"

Releasing an affronted sigh his sister said, "Nothing, other than that earlier today I saw Cullen at the office and asked him how things were going at *Snap* and he almost bit my head off. You would have thought I was asking him for some deep, dark secret."

"Personally, I think Grandfather's challenge has got all of you on guard," Bryan said, in defense of his younger brother as he pulled up a chair and joined them. "That's why I'm glad I got out of the family business and started this place. Even then there was too much pressure at EPH. I don't want to think how crazy things are now."

Tag nodded. "Bryan is right. Granddad's challenge has all of us tense. We've always worked together for the good of the company as a whole and have never been pitted against each other like this before. But we can't lose sight that no matter what, we're family."

Liam took a sip of his drink. "I agree with Tag."

Scarlet rolled her eyes, grinning. "You would, since your job as financial operating officer doesn't align you with any particular magazine."

Liam frowned. "Yes, but it doesn't make my job

easier when I have to do damage control with all four. Try doing my job."

"No, brother dear, you can keep your job," Bridget said. "I don't know of anyone who could do it better. It's just that things are getting crazy already, just like Bryan said, and it's only the second month. I don't want to think what the summer will bring when things really begin to heat up."

Bridget then glanced over at Scarlet. "And speaking of Summer…where is she?" she asked Scarlet regarding the whereabouts of her identical twin.

Scarlet took a sip of her drink before saying, "Summer's excited about John returning to town in time for the ball tomorrow night and decided to go shopping for something to wear."

Bridget smiled. "I'm glad that I'm not the only one who's looking forward to the ball tomorrow night."

Tag leaned back in his chair and thought of the evening he had planned with Renee and said, "I'm looking forward to the ball tomorrow night, as well."

Renee looked in the full-length mirror that was on the back of her bathroom door, not believing the transformation a visit to the hair salon and an exclusive dress boutique could make. But she wanted to look as special as Tag had promised the night would be.

The day had started off promisingly when a prettily wrapped cookie bouquet was delivered to her at work. She had gotten a curious stare from Vicki, but as usual, her secretary had respected her privacy by not asking any questions. Tag's card had simply said, *Be My Valentine.*

Then when she'd gotten home there had been the delivery

of the Malone painting she had fallen in love with that Saturday she and Tag had spent together in Greenwich Village. She didn't want to think how much Tag had paid for the painting and her first reaction was that there was no way she could accept it. But when she'd finally reached him on his cell he'd told her there was no way she could return the painting; it was hers to keep. He then bid her goodbye, promising to see her at seven.

She chuckled as she tossed her hair from her face. Instead of the straight strands she usually wore, her hair was a silken mass of curls that framed her face and tumbled around her shoulders.

She stepped back to study the effect of the semi-formal dress she had purchased to wear. Made of red velvet, it looked sophisticated, chic, tailored to fit. Matte sequins dotted the v-neck that emphasized her high, full breasts, accentuated even more by delicate spaghetti straps. The soft fluttery hemline stopped just above her knees.

The way the dress flowed over her body elegantly displayed every feminine curve she possessed, and the glamorous matching red velvet cape, lined with white satin, was a plus to keep the tonight's chill at bay. She wished that her friend Debbie were here to give her a thumbs-up, but Debbie wouldn't be back in New York until Saturday.

When the doorbell sounded, Renee's pulse jumped before she took a quick glance at her watch. It was precisely seven o'clock.

The lady in red...

Tag's gaze moved with deep male appreciation over Renee's stunning features. In the gorgeous gown she was wearing, she was definitely making a statement tonight, and he was glad he was the man whose arm she would be on.

"You are beautiful," he said, stepping inside her apartment and handing her a single red rose.

"Thank you." Renee brought the rose to her nose and inhaled softly. She then took in the man standing in front of her. There was just something about a good-looking man in formal attire. Tag was elegantly dressed in a black tux that fit his tall, muscular frame as if it had been specifically tailored just for him. She smiled thinking that it probably had been. The white shirt and formal black bow tie added the finishing touches. "I think you are beautiful, too," she said, meaning every word of it.

A slow smile spread across his features. "I don't think I've ever been told that I'm beautiful."

"Well, I'm telling you," she said, bringing the rose to her nose once again. The blue eyes holding hers were igniting a slow burn inside of her. She had a feeling if they didn't leave now they would arrive at the ball inappropriately late.

"Ready to leave?" she decided to ask.

A grin touched the corners of his mouth and she had a feeling he had read her every thought. "Yes, I think we'd better."

The first thing Renee noted when they arrived at the Rockefeller Center was that the main entrance was surrounded by the media. Television cameras, newspaper reporters and photographers were positioned close to the main entrance, which was lined with red carpet.

"Because of the importance of this event, a number of celebrities will be in attendance," Tag whispered in her ear just moments before she saw John Travolta and his wife entering the establishment as flashbulbs exploded everywhere.

Renee nodded, already feeling nervous. She had never been to a ball before, nor could she recall ever having been in a limo. Tag had surprised her when he'd shown up at her apartment in a limousine, giving her neighbors a reason to raise their blinds in the evening.

When the limo came to a stop in front of Rockefeller Center, a uniformed doorman stepped forward and opened the door for them. The moment they exited the vehicle, flashbulbs went off. Evidently, someone had assumed they were celebrities. Renee felt good knowing that once it was discovered they weren't anyone famous, the photos would be disposed of. She smiled up at Tag when he took her arm, and together they walked into the building.

The first people she recognized upon entering the ballroom were Gannon and Erika. For some reason, the couple didn't appear surprised that she was Tag's date tonight.

"Doesn't this place look fabulous?" Erika said. "Whoever was responsible for the decorating did a wonderful job."

Renee nodded. She had to agree. With Valentine colors of red and white, everything was reminiscent of love and romance. It was there in the red and white carnations that seemed to be practically everywhere and in the red heart-shaped ceramic centerpieces that adorned the tables that were draped in red and white linen tablecloths. Then there were the bright chandeliers overhead as well as the love song being played by the live orchestra. There was no doubt in her mind there would be dancing later, and a part of her was looking forward to dancing with Tag.

For the next hour or so Renee and Tag walked around, socializing. He kept a hand on her arm, keeping her close by his side as they moved around the room, while introducing her to people he knew. And it seemed that just about everyone knew him as an Elliott and immediately inquired about his mother's health and his grandparents' whereabouts. He answered by saying his mother was recuperating nicely and his grandparents hadn't returned yet from their trip to South Florida.

Dinner was extravagant as well as delicious and Renee was extremely grateful they had been seated at the table with Gannon and Erika as well as with Tag's cousin Cullen and his date. When they had spent the weekend together, Tag had told her a little bit about each of his siblings and cousins and she distinctively remembered him saying that Cullen, at twenty-seven, was the playboy in the family. With his dark, good looks she could tell why. But then, she thought, glancing over at her date, no one was more handsome than Tag.

"Dance with me," Tag whispered in her ear once the dance floor opened. She nodded, and without any hesitation she let him lead her to the dance floor.

He slid his arms around her waist, bringing her closer to the fit of him, and she went willingly, deciding that so far tonight everything had been perfect. There were even enough celebrities in attendance to take everyone's attention off her and Tag.

"Thanks for coming with me tonight," he said softly, leaning down as his warm lips gently touched her ear.

His amorous caress sent chills of desire escalating through her body. "Thank you for inviting me."

He chuckled quietly. "There we go again, thanking each

other like broken records. If we were alone I would take the time to thank you properly."

She glanced up at him and gave him a jaunty grin. "And which way is that?"

He leaned closer and whispered, telling her of his fondest desire for later. Renee chuckled softly and said, "It's a good thing I don't embarrass easily."

"Yes, it is a good thing."

After the dance was over he was leading her back to their table when someone called out his name.

They turned just in time for a woman to fling herself into Tag's arms and kiss him on the mouth with a familiarity that made Renee blink. "Where on earth have you been keeping yourself, Tag? I haven't seen you for months."

"Hello, Pamela," he said with a dry smile. Reaching out, he pulled Renee closer to his side. "Renee, I'd like you to meet Pamela Hoover, an old friend," Tag said as a way of introduction.

"Hello," the woman said coldly, then turned her full attention back to Tag. Dismissing Renee completely, she said, "What are you doing Friday night? I have tickets to—"

Tag interrupted her. "Sorry, but Renee and I have plans for Friday night."

Although Renee knew that she and Tag really didn't have a date Friday night, she decided not to mention that fact.

"Oh." The woman then gave Renee an unfriendly glance before turning back to Tag. "Then perhaps we can get together another day, for old times' sake. You know my number." She then walked off.

Evidently, Tag felt the need to explain. "Pamela and I dated over a year ago. When she didn't like competing against my work, we decided things weren't working out and went our separate ways."

"Oh, I see." Renee decided not to tell him that what she saw was someone very much interested in rekindling what they once had.

"There're a few people I know over there. Let's go over and say hello," Tag said, leading her across the room.

Moments later Renee found herself surrounded by a number of famous people, most of whose movies she enjoyed watching on the big screen. And Tag was on a first-name basis with each and every one of them. She ignored the feeling of being way out of her league since everyone appeared to be genuinely friendly.

"I figured I would see you here tonight," said a man who walked up behind Tag.

Tag turned at the sound of the voice and smiled. "And I was hoping I'd see you." He pulled Renee closer to his side to make introductions. "Renee, this is a good friend of mine, Alton Malone."

Renee smiled as she presented the man her hand. "Mr. Malone, Tag never mentioned that you were a good friend of his."

Alton laughed, shaking his head. "Then I will definitely take him to task for that, Renee. I understand you like my work."

"Yes, I do, and I was happy to receive a special painting of yours today as a gift."

"Then I hope you can come to the private art exhibit I have planned this Friday night at a museum in Harlem."

Renee glanced over at Tag, wondering if this was the date he'd earlier insinuated they had. His mischievous smile let her know it was. She nodded her head, grinning. "Thanks, Alton, and I think I will."

A half hour later Renee excused herself from Tag's side to go to the ladies' room. She was about to enter when a very distinct voice from the inside stopped her.

"Can you believe the nerve of Tag coming here with her?" Pamela asked her unseen companion. "What on earth could he be thinking?"

Another woman laughed. "Yes, I saw them the moment they walked in together. I couldn't believe it."

"Me neither," Pamela tacked on. "I looked for Tag's grandfather to see his reaction and someone mentioned that he's out of town. He's going to croak when he finds out that Tag is dating a black woman. Just think of the talk it's going to cause. The one thing Patrick Elliott detests is his family name being connected to any type of scandal."

Renee stiffened and backed slowly away from the door. Deciding she didn't have an urgent need to use the bathroom after all, she returned to the ballroom.

It didn't take long to find Tag. His tall, elegantly attired form was standing across the room talking to his brother and his cousin, Cullen. And then, as if he were in tune with her very presence, he glanced up and met her eyes.

He made the mistake of letting his gaze linger on her too long. The longer he looked at her, the more she could feel the wanting and desire radiating from the very depths of him. Love for him took over her mind, erasing Pamela Hoover's cutting and spiteful words, and filling Renee's mind with one thought: just how much she loved him.

She watched as he excused himself from the group and without looking around and making conversation with anyone, he strolled over to her as if she was the only person who had his complete attention. She wondered if he was aware of how he stood out—tall, dashing, handsome—and she continued to stare at him. Out of breath. Out of her mind.

When he came to a stop in front of her, she wet her lips, knowing the provocative and sensuous gesture would send him a silent message.

It did.

He slid his arms around her waist and leaned closer, and, not caring who was looking, he placed an affectionate kiss on her lips. "Are you ready to leave now?" he whispered.

She liked the feel of being in his arms, being pressed so close to him. She liked having his attention. "Only if you are."

"I am."

And without any more words, he took her hand and led her toward the coat check to get her cape.

Renee remembered very little of the limo ride back to her apartment. Nor could she recall the moments she and Tag shared as they walked hand in hand to her door. But she did remember when that same door closed behind them and he whispered her name just moments before pulling her into his arms.

And she did commit to memory how he had gently carried her to her bedroom, placed her on the bed and tenderly undressed her before turning his attention to himself.

She would never forget how she watched as he shoved his pants to the floor and stepped out of them, confident in his sexuality. And when he got in the bed with her, knelt before her, spread her legs, lowered her head and flicked his tongue across her womanly core, she thought that she had died and gone to heaven.

By the time he had raised his head, she had had not one orgasm but two and he'd given her a look that let her know that before the night was over there would be a third and a fourth.

"Careful," she whispered, after he sheathed a condom in place and moved his body into position over hers. "You're becoming habit-forming."

He smiled down at her. "I'm glad. I want to get into your system, Renee. I want to get into it real bad."

She reached out and caressed the side of his face. "Why?" she asked, desperately needing to know.

"Because," he said, as he slowly entered her, "you're already in mine."

"Maybe. But not enough."

At that moment she didn't know what was driving her but she wanted to be the only woman Tag thought about tonight, tomorrow, possibly for the rest of his life. Maybe it had something to do with the words Pamela Hoover had spoken, suggesting that once Patrick Elliott got wind of her and Tag's relationship it would all be over. Renee wouldn't subject him to any sort of rift with his family and she knew what she had to do if that became a possibility. But tonight, tomorrow, just for a little while longer, she wanted this. She needed him.

She wrapped her legs securely around him and then she began trailing her fingers down his chest, initiating a slow, seductive massage before coming to a stop on one taut nipple.

"What are you doing?" he asked, his voice hitched to a feverous pitch from her touch.

"I'm trying to see just how deep into your system I can get," she said, stroking the nipple slowly, sensuously.

"Take my word," he said through clenched teeth. "You're already in there pretty good."

"But I want to make sure."

"You know what they say about payback," he said, sucking in a deep breath.

"No, I don't know what they say, but tonight I've decided that I'm not going to worry about what anyone says. The only thing I want on my mind is us and what we're doing right now."

Laughing, she shifted her body and after a quick maneuver Tag found himself on his back with her straddling him.

He looked up at her through deeply glazed eyes. "Oh, you're asking for it."

"From the feel of things it seems like you're the one asking for it, Mr. Elliott, and I intend to give you everything you want."

And then she began to move on top of him.

It suddenly happened, as soon as she felt his body explode beneath her. With his last hard thrust she screamed his name and shattered into a thousand pieces before collapsing on him, burying her head in the hollow of his shoulder.

Moments later, he kissed her deeply, thoroughly and completely, and at that moment Renee knew that instead of her getting deeper into his system he had gotten totally entrenched into hers.

Contentment surged through every part of Tag's body as he stood at the foot of the bed and drank in the sight of Renee lying there asleep atop the covers. Even now, aftershocks of pleasure rushed through his veins, keeping him hard. The intimacy they always shared was unlike anything he'd ever known. She brought out the sexual hunger in him, his wanting and desire were driven to extreme points, and unleashed within him was something so elemental and profound that it took his breath away just thinking about it.

He started to get dressed as he continued to look at her. The woman was something else—stubborn, proud, beautiful and sexy all rolled into one. She matched him on every level. Surpassed him on some. And pleased him with a magnitude that could leave him gasping.

He sighed deeply as he buttoned his shirt. More than anything he wanted to get back in bed and be there when Renee woke up in the morning, but he couldn't. *Pulse*'s special edition would hit the stands tomorrow morning and there was a lot to do. For the next forty-eight hours the majority of his time would be spent at the office. Once the magazine hit the street he would then have to be on hand to field inquiries from those questioning the story's legitimacy.

Wanting to clear his mind of work, he looked back at Renee and did something he had never done before. He began imagining. How would it feel to have this every day, the chance to sleep with her, wake up with her, spend all the time that he wanted with her?

An emotion he had never felt before suddenly gripped him and the one thing he could not imagine was a life without her. He sucked in a sharp breath when he was filled with a deep longing, a profound sense of need. He'd known that he cared, but until now he hadn't realized how much.

He was in love with Renee.

The thought, the blatant realization didn't make him feel uncomfortable. It sent a warmth through all parts of his body, swelling his heart with love even more. Now he imagined other things. Sharing his entire life with her. Marrying her and making her his wife. The mother of his children.

He wanted to wake her up and tell her how he felt but knew that he couldn't. There were still issues they were working out and although she had agreed to give them a chance, he could still sense her wariness, her uncertainty. The best thing for him to do would be to continue on their present path. He had to prove to her that things between them could work out and there was nothing that existed in this world that could keep them apart.

After getting completely dressed he returned to her, leaned down and nibbled her neck. He couldn't leave without telling her goodbye. "I'm getting ready to leave, sweetheart."

She slowly opened her eyes and drew a long, heavy breath before saying, "How? The limo is—"

"I called for a car." EPH had its own private transportation. "It'll be here in a few moments." As he continued to look at her, he realized this woman held his heart and she didn't even know it. He leaned down and kissed her, tenderly yet thoroughly.

With his lips still locked to hers he slipped his hand beneath her knees and picked her up. He then sat on the edge of the bed with her in his lap. He needed the connection. He needed this. The exquisite sensations that only she could force through his body, an unrestrained surrender that only she had been able to seize.

He reluctantly lifted his mouth sometime later, only after he was thoroughly satisfied that he had given her something to think about for the next few days when he would be so busy with the magazine.

"That special edition comes out tomorrow," he said

hoarsely, placing small kisses around her lips. "I need to be in place."

"I know," she said quietly.

"I'm going to be busy over the next couple of days. I probably won't get a chance to see you until Friday night."

She slid her hand up his shirt, straightened his bow tie and whispered, "I understand."

"I'm going to miss you."

She smiled up at him. "I'm going to miss you, too."

Taking advantage of her parted lips, he slipped his tongue back inside her mouth for one last, sweet, mind-stirring taste. Moments later, with a low groan, he pulled back, stood and placed her back in bed. "If I don't leave now, I won't."

"I know that as well."

He held her gaze for a moment, and then took his cell phone out of the pocket of his pants. Somehow in the midst of his whirling senses he was able to press a few buttons, and when the dispatcher came on the line, he said tensely, "Delay that pickup in Morningside Heights for another couple of hours." He clicked off the phone and placed it aside, then began removing his clothes.

Unrestrained. Uncontrolled. He was a man very much in love and once again he wanted the woman, the object of his desire, the person who held his heart. He wanted to make love to her with the knowledge that love was guiding his thoughts, his actions and his words.

When he was completely naked, he joined Renee in bed, knowing that at that moment, this was where he wanted to be.

Chapter 10

When Renee walked through the doors of Manhattan University Hospital that morning she had the eerie feeling of being watched. It seemed that everyone's eyes were on her, and a number of speculative faces turned to stare at her when she made her usual trek across the lobby before stepping into the elevator.

Hoping that that she was imagining things, she walked out onto her floor moments later only to see Vicki look up from her desk and stare at her as well. "Okay, I give up," Renee said, after hanging up her coat and walking over to Vicki's desk. "What's going on?"

"I take it you haven't seen this morning's paper," her secretary said, easing the tabloid across the desk to her.

Renee lifted a brow before glancing down at the paper. Her heart nearly stopped. There, plastered on the front page, were pictures from the ball, and dead center were two pictures of her and Tag. The first was a photograph of them getting out of the limo together, making all of New York aware of the fact that she had been his date. The other photo was taken when he had leaned down to kiss her—the moment right before they had left the ball. Beneath the pictures the caption asked, Has the Elusive Teagan Elliott Finally Been Caught?

Renee swallowed. She hadn't wanted her relationship with Tag exposed to the world this way, especially while it wasn't yet on solid ground. "With all the other stuff going on in this country, I wouldn't think the ball warranted front page," she said, not knowing at the moment what else to say.

Vicki shrugged. "Yes, you would think not." She then added, "I might as well warn you that Diane Carter has called three times this morning. I told her you were coming in late and I didn't expect you before ten. Brace yourself. I have a feeling she'll be calling back, or better yet, she'll be coming up here the first chance she gets."

"Thanks for the warning."

Renee was about to go into her office when Vicki asked, "Did you enjoy yourself last night?"

Renee met the woman's gaze. She saw genuine concern and interest in the eyes staring back at her. Nothing judgmental and no censorship. "Yes, I had a wonderful time."

Vicki smiled. "I'm glad. You're a beautiful woman, Renee, and a nice person. You should get out more and enjoy yourself."

Renee lifted a brow. "And Teagan Elliott?"

Vicki shrugged. "I don't know him personally, but he seems like a nice young man." She glanced back down at the newspaper that was still spread open on her desk. "And no matter how anyone else might feel, I personally think the two of you look wonderful together."

Renee smiled, not realizing she'd been holding her breath. One thing she knew about Vicki was that she was sincere and forthright. "Thanks, Vicki." She then walked into her office and closed the door.

It was sometime after the lunch hour when Diane burst into Renee's office. "Vicki wasn't out front so I just came on in. This is the first chance I've had to sneak away since seeing today's paper. What on earth were you thinking about by going out with Teagan Elliott? That was definitely not a smart move, Renee."

Renee leaned back in her chair, deciding to give Diane credit. The woman definitely didn't have a problem expressing the way she felt. "And why would you think that?"

Diane frowned. "Surely you're joking. Come on, Renee, walk back into the real world. People like the Elliotts don't become involved with people like us. We're not on their social level and with you it's even more serious. There's the issue of—"

"Race?" She preempted Diane's comment.

"Yes, that's it." Diane smiled apologetically. "Face it. You're probably a novelty to him, something new and different. I hope you aren't taking things seriously because if you are you're setting yourself up to get hurt."

"Thanks for the warning, Diane, but I'm a big girl and I can take care of myself." She reached for a file on her desk, hoping Diane would take the hint.

Diane's smile slipped. "I hope so because you'll need to be strong when he loses interest and drops you like a hot potato. If I were you that would be something I'd definitely be thinking about."

Without saying anything else, Diane turned and walked out of Renee's office.

Renee stood at the window and looked down at the busy streets below. The lunch hour had ended a while ago but the sidewalks were still crowded.

Preferring to have lunch alone in her office, Renee had eaten a sandwich her secretary had brought up from the cafeteria.

She sighed deeply. She hadn't wanted to fall in love with Tag for several reasons, and this was one of them. She hated being the center of attention, detested her name being linked to office gossip. It brought back so many painful memories of when Dionne had humiliated her in the worst possible way.

She tried convincing herself that the talk about her and Tag wasn't the same, but in her mind, talk was talk, and she'd rather not have her name linked to any of it.

She tensed when she heard the phone ring and hoped it wasn't Tag. She hadn't heard from him all day and wondered if he had seen the pictures.

She crossed the room and picked up the phone. "Yes, Vicki?"

"Ms. Elliott is on the line for you."

Renee raised a brow. "Ms. Elliott?"

"Yes, Ms. Bridget Elliott."

Renee swallowed. Tag's siblings had been friendly to her last night but she couldn't help wondering if they saw the photographs in today's paper as damaging to their family name. "Please put her through, Vicki."

For the next minute Renee exchanged pleasantries with

Tag's sister. Then Bridget surprised her by asking, "I was wondering if we could have lunch tomorrow?"

"Lunch?"

"Yes, tomorrow. We could meet somewhere near the hospital. How about Carmine's, that Italian restaurant on Broadway? Say noon?"

Renee took a step around her desk to quickly check her calendar. Finding the time open, she said, "Noon will be fine."

Once Renee ended the call she slumped down in her chair. Was Bridget inviting her to lunch to tell her that she thought Renee seeing Tag was a bad idea? The last thing she needed was another person criticizing her relationship with Tag.

Tag gazed at the special edition of *Pulse*. On the front cover was the silhouette of Senator Denton highlighted by the words—emblazoned in bold, black letters—"Silence is Not Always Golden".

Tag rubbed his hand down his face. *Pulse* had obtained undisputed proof that one of the military guards at Abu Ghraib Prison had written the senator and had sent photographs about the abuse going on, but Senator Denton had failed to do anything about it, and had gone so far as to stage a cover-up by having the informer transferred to a military outfit in the heart of the Iraqi fighting. That same individual had gotten killed within days of being put on the front line.

Although the incident at Abu Ghraib had eventually been brought to light, Senator Denton's actions had not. The plan had been for him to quietly resign from office before anyone could discover the truth. Luckily, his niece had overheard him giving orders to one of his staffers to destroy the letters and photographs, and before anyone could do so, she'd read them. Horrified, she'd decided to expose her uncle for the dishonest person that he was. The loss of that young marine's life couldn't be forgiven.

Tag glanced down at his watch. It was close to 10:00 p.m. He'd been in the office since nine that morning, after finally forcing himself from Renee's bed and going home to shower and change.

Leaning back in his chair, he threw down the magazine and picked up that day's newspaper, a copy of which Gannon had placed on his desk first thing that morning. Tag had smiled when he'd seen the pictures of him and Renee, thinking how good they looked together. He had reached for the phone several times to call her to make sure she'd known about the photographs, but each time he'd gotten interrupted.

It was probably too late to call her now but he'd speak to her tomorrow. In the midst of everything that was going on, he needed to hear her voice and to know that the pictures hadn't bothered her.

He gazed at the photographs and could distinctly remember when they had gotten out of the limo together, as well as the exact moment he had placed a kiss on her lips at the ball. He hadn't been aware that the latter was being captured on film but a part of him didn't care. There was nothing wrong with a man displaying affection for the woman he loved.

The woman he loved.

Thinking it, realizing it and accepting it was easier than he'd ever imagined. He loved her and more than anything he wanted to find a way to make her love him as well, and believe that things between them would work out.

"I can't believe she actually thinks Teagan Elliott is remotely interested in her."

"Hey, isn't that hilarious? I heard that Diane Carter tried

to warn her but she refused to listen. She's going to wish she had when she gets dumped. It won't be anyone's fault but her own."

Renee kept walking, refusing to look over her shoulder to see who was speaking. A part of her wanted to turn around and tell whoever they were just where they could go, but she was too professional. Besides, it would be a waste of time since the remarks were bits and pieces of what she'd heard all day, thanks to Diane's handiwork. She sighed, thinking that the one thing she had hoped would never happen to her again was happening. Once again, she was the topic of everyone's conversations.

She stepped into the elevator, glad she was leaving the building even if it was only for a little while. She hoped she didn't later regret agreeing to meet Tag's sister for lunch. Although Tag had told her that he'd be too tied up at the office to call, a part of her wished he had so she'd know what he thought of the pictures.

She'd contemplated calling him but knew how busy he was. She, like everyone else, had seen the special edition of *Pulse*, and had been shocked to read the article about Senator Denton. It had been the hot topic on the subway that morning.

Her thoughts shifted to her conversation with Diane yesterday. Last night, while lying in bed, she'd been forced to acknowledge that Diane was probably right. Eventually, Tag would lose interest and Renee couldn't help wondering where that would leave her heart. Probably somewhere shattered into a million pieces. Could she handle such heartbreak?

As she stepped outside onto the sidewalk she tightened her coat around her. No, she wasn't a glutton for pain, and if she didn't make decisions about their relationship before Tag eventually did, pain would be just what she got.

* * *

When Renee walked into Carmine's, she was surprised to not only see Bridget but Tag's identical twin cousins, Summer and Scarlet, as well. She had met the two women at the Valentine's Day ball. She nervously gripped the straps of her purse as the host led her across the room to join them.

"Thanks for inviting me to lunch," Renee said with the first real smile she'd managed in a couple of days, after being greeted with genuine friendliness by the three women.

Bridget grinned. "It was supposed to be the two of us, but then I ran into Summer and Scarlet at the office and invited them along. I hope you don't mind, but Summer has a good reason for us to celebrate," Bridget said, picking up her wineglass.

Renee glanced over at Summer and quickly saw the reason. A beautiful engagement ring adorned the fourth finger of her left hand. "Congratulations! It's a beautiful ring."

Summer returned Renee's smile. "Thanks. John proposed to me on Valentine's Day. We only made a brief appearance at the ball since he'd made dinner reservations elsewhere. That's when he popped the question."

"Have you set a date?" Renee asked, lifting her own glass of wine after the waiter came and filled it.

She wondered then if she was the only one who noted how Summer's shoulders had tensed at that question.

"No, a date hasn't been set yet," the bride-to-be replied.

Renee nodded and took a sip of wine, thinking Summer didn't appear to be as pleased with her engagement as a future bride should be. She set down her wineglass, deciding to leave Summer's issue alone since Renee had a huge one of her own. Tag. She wondered how long it would take before Bridget brought him up.

An hour later they had eaten their meal, and still Tag's sister hadn't mentioned him. Instead, she talked about how improved her mother's condition was and had asked questions as to what to expect during Karen's chemotherapy treatment. Tag's name never came up. Instead, Renee spent an enjoyable lunch getting to know his sister and cousins.

It was only when they were leaving the restaurant that Bridget leaned over, smiled and whispered to Renee, "Oh, and by the way, I thought you and Tag looked great together at the ball as well as in yesterday's paper."

Chapter 11

The following day Renee walked into her apartment not in the best of moods. The stares and negative comments at work had been worse than ever today and she wasn't sure tonight would be a good time to go out with Tag. She had spoken to him briefly that day before he'd gotten interrupted by someone coming into his office.

On the subway ride home she had replayed everything she'd had to endure for the past two days. She had been so concerned about what everyone was saying and thinking that she hadn't been able to function at work. That kind of worry and aggravation would definitely put a strain on an already difficult relationship and she was beginning to feel it.

More than ever she was convinced that their differences would always be an issue with them.

She glanced at her watch. Tag was to pick her up at seven, and knowing him, he would be punctual. If she was going to cancel their date, now was the time to do so. She picked up the phone, deciding to call him at the office in case he was still there. The familiar voice of his secretary answered after the first couple of rings. "Teagan Elliott's office."

"Yes, may I speak with Mr. Elliott?"

"He's in a meeting right now. Would you like to leave a message?"

"Yes. Please let him know that Renee Williams called and—"

"Hold on, Ms. Williams. I was given explicit instructions to put you through to Mr. Elliott if you were to call. Just a moment, please."

Renee leaned back against the kitchen counter, waiting to be connected to Tag. A few seconds later, he was on the line. "Renee?"

She sucked in a sharp breath. Just hearing him say her name did things to her. She could vividly remember how he'd woken her a couple of mornings ago, kissing her and whispering her name over and over. Before she'd even opened her eyes, he'd drawn her into his warm embrace, waking her senses up to him and the strong evidence of his desire for her.

Could Diane be right? Was she just a novelty to him? Something different? Someone he would eventually lose interest in when the novelty wore off? And what if she did mean something to him? Would he go against his family's wishes if they decided they didn't want her to be a part of it? Could there ever be a chance of a happy ending for them?

"Renee?"

She breathed in deeply. "Yes, it's me. I called to let you know I don't think it's a good idea for us to go out tonight. And maybe it's a good idea if we cool things between us."

"What are you talking about, Renee? What happened?"

"Nothing happened, Tag. I—I just can't handle the talk, the negativity. Look, I know you're busy so I'll let you go. Goodbye."

She hung up the phone and wrapped her arms around her stomach, swallowing her tears, telling herself that she wouldn't fall apart. But when the tears continued coming nonstop, she knew she was doing that exact thing.

Tag held the phone in his hand as he hung his head, frowning. What the hell had happened? He breathed in deeply, knowing whatever it was had to be connected to the pictures that had appeared in the newspaper a few days ago.

"Is everything all right, Tag?"

He glanced up and met Gannon's concerned gaze. Only then did he hang up the phone. Already, he was moving toward the coatrack for his jacket. "No, everything isn't all right. It's Renee and she's having second thoughts about us again." Last night while the two of them were stuck late at the office, Tag had had a heart-to-heart talk to Gannon about Renee, and had even admitted to his brother that he loved her.

"Maybe it's time for you to erase those thoughts from her mind forever or they're going to just keep coming back."

Tag sighed disgustedly. "And how am I supposed to do that if she keeps letting what people say come between us?"

"Then it's up to you to convince her it doesn't matter. If you love her as much as you say you do, then you'll find a way to convince her."

Tag nodded. "I hate to run out on you like this but I need to go see Renee."

"By all means, go and do whatever it takes to win your lady's heart."

Tag was grateful for his brother's support. "If anything further develops with the Denton story, call me on my cell phone," he said, rushing toward the door while slipping on his jacket. "I'll talk with you later."

Renee should have assumed Tag would show up, and if she'd been in her right frame of mind, she would have. But she wasn't, so when the doorbell sounded she fought to get her tears under control. Wiping the evidence off her cheeks, she took a deep breath before crossing the room to answer the door.

She immediately met Tag's gaze and saw the anger in the depths of his eyes, which she tried meeting with complete serenity in hers, knowing she was failing. There was no way he wouldn't know she'd been crying.

"May I come in?"

Instead of answering, she took a step back and watched as he crossed the threshold then closed the door behind him. "We need to talk, Renee," he said softly, slipping a hand under her chin to stare into her puffy eyes.

The tears she was holding back threatened to fall with his sudden shift from anger to tenderness. "There's nothing to say, Tag," she said simply. "We gave it a try and it didn't work."

"No, you gave up too soon."

Fire suddenly sparked in Renee at his accusation. She stiffened. "I'm sorry you feel that way but people are talking about us and I don't appreciate being the topic of gossip at work. They're probably taking bets like the last time."

"I don't give a damn what people are—" He suddenly stopped talking and lifted a brow. "What do you mean they're probably taking bets like the last time? What last time?"

Renee could have kicked herself for letting that comment slip out. "Nothing."

He gazed at her with intensity. "No, I think it *is* something, so tell me."

Renee looked away from his face. Maybe she needed to do what he was asking and tell him about Dionne and why she had moved from Atlanta. Only then would he understand why being in the midst of a scandal bothered her so much. "Let's sit down. You're right. It is time I tell you."

When he started to sit beside her on the sofa she quickly said, "No. Please sit over there." She indicated the chair across from the sofa. She wasn't certain of her control and needed space from Tag. She couldn't handle things if he were to sit beside her, touch her, breathe on her.

He stared at her for a few moments before doing as she asked. As soon as he was settled he met her gaze and waited for her to speak.

She curled up on the sofa, tucking her feet under her. "Before I came to New York I worked at a hospital in Atlanta and dated this doctor for almost a year before finding out he was also dating a nurse who worked the midnight shift. She didn't know about me like I didn't know about her but some of the other doctors knew and were taking bets as to when I would find out. Eventually I did and it was the talk of the hospital. It seemed everywhere I went there were whispers, looks of pity, even laughter. The embarrassment was humiliating. When I came here I promised myself that I would never get involved in any situation where I was the center of attention again. But it seems, once again, that I am."

Tag didn't say anything but stared at her, and Renee knew he was trying to formulate in his mind just what to say. "I regret what your ex-boyfriend did to you, Renee, but I'm not him," he said in a quiet voice. "I am not involved with anyone but you."

She sighed slowly. "That's not why people are talking and you know it."

"Okay, then, let's discuss why people are talking."

"No," she said softly, knotting her hands together in her lap. "We already have, numerous times, and you won't accept how it makes me feel."

He leaned forward and held her gaze. "Then maybe we need to discuss why the talk makes you feel that way in the first place," he said calmly. "Why you can't get beyond the color of my skin and the amount of money in my bank account." He continued speaking in a calm voice. "And before you answer, I want you to know how I feel about you, Renee. I love you. I think I fell in love with you that first day in your office. I want a future with you. A very happy future."

With his admission of love, tears Renee couldn't hold back any longer began flowing down her cheeks. Fighting for composure, she spoke straight from her heart. "And I love you, too, Tag. I didn't want to fall in love with you but I did that very same day as well. But that's just it. We can't have the happy future you want. All I can see is a future filled with the strain of proving our love to the world, constantly defending it, working harder than most couples just to preserve it. Then what if we want children? What will they have to go through?"

Tag got to his feet and crossed to the sofa. He reached out and took Renee's hand and gently pulled her up. "So what if our challenges will be greater than most? Our love will be there to sustain us. And as far as children are concerned, they'll grow up proud of what they are and who they are.

Times have changed, Renee. And they are still changing. There will always be people who are bitterly opposed to interracial marriages, but then you'll find there's an even larger number of people who see such unions as an indicator of what life will be like in an even more diverse twenty-first century."

"Dammit, Tag, I can't bank on an unknown future. I can only go by what's in the real world, now."

Both fury and pain flashed in Tag's eyes. "So you're saying that you can't accept me or my love because it will be a problem for others to accept it? Are you saying that you're willing to give up what we can have together because of how others think and feel? What about how we feel, Renee? Is that not equally important?"

"Yes, it's important, but can't you understand that I'm trying to protect you, as well? I heard whispers at the ball of how your grandfather would be against anything developing between us, and I refuse to be the cause of any rift between you and your family."

His face hardened. "I told you that how my family might feel about us didn't matter to me, so don't go there, Renee. Don't look for excuses."

He released her and took a step back. "I don't know what else I can say. I love you. I want to marry you. I want a future with you," he said quietly, feeling the strain of heartbreak and disappointment. "That is what you have to believe and what you have to accept. My wanting those things means nothing unless you want them as well. All I'm asking is for us to put our love to the test and tell anyone who can find any reason for us not to be together to go straight to hell and stay there."

"Tag, I don't think—"

"No," he said, cutting her off, struggling to contain his

anger. "The bottom line is whether you're strong enough to step out on faith and love. A week from today is my brother's wedding at The Tides as well as my grandparents' anniversary celebration. I want you to go there with me, not to seek any type of approval from my family but as two individuals who are very much in love and who have committed their lives to each other, and who are ready to make an announcement regarding their future together."

Renee shook her head sadly as tears once again filled her eyes. In a voice filled with frustration, she said, "I can't do that, Tag. I'm sorry, but I can't."

And before he could say anything else, she rushed to her bedroom and slammed the door.

Chapter 12

Renee whirled around. Her face was streaked with tears, her eyes swollen and tormented. "What do you mean you think I'm making a mistake?"

Debbie Massey met her best friend's glare as she handed her a wet washcloth. "Renee, you know me well enough to know I don't sugarcoat anything. You asked for my honest opinion so I gave it to you."

Debbie, who'd been out of the country on assignment, had shown up at Renee's place over an hour ago and found Renee still torn up over her dealings with Tag the night before. With a bossiness that Renee doubted she would ever get used to, Debbie had quickly taken charge and rushed Renee off to the bathroom, made her wash her face while she'd told Debbie everything.

"Didn't you hear anything I said regarding all the problems

Tag and I would be facing as an interracial couple? How can you say I'm making a mistake?"

"The same way you did when I broke things off with Alan last year. I didn't follow my heart and I've regretted it every day since."

Renee nodded. Alan Harris, a colleague of Debbie's, was fifteen years her senior. Concerned about what others would say about her dating a much older man, Debbie had ended their relationship after a brief affair. That had been over a year ago and this was the first time Renee had heard Debbie admit that maybe she'd made a mistake in letting Alan go.

Before she could ask questions, Debbie continued. "At some point in your life you have to do what makes *you* happy and not worry about how others may feel about it. You've admitted you're in love with Teagan Elliott and he has admitted that he's in love with you. He's a man—a wealthy one, I might add— who wants to marry you and make you happy. If only the rest of us could be so lucky."

Renee dropped into a chair at the kitchen table, struggling to control the tears that threatened to fall again. "But you weren't around to hear what everyone was saying once they saw those pictures of us."

Debbie frowned. "And it's a good thing I wasn't. People need to get their own lives and not worry about what's going on in other people's lives. It's time you stopped caring about what people are saying and thinking. No matter what, you won't be able to change their opinion about anything, so why bother? They are either accepting or they aren't."

Debbie then tossed the braids out of her face and peered at Renee over her glasses. "But none of what I'm telling you means a thing if you don't love Tag Elliott as much as you claim you do."

"I do love him," Renee said fiercely. "I love him with all my heart."

"Then act like it. There was a time you used to fight for what you wanted, what you believed in. I remember that day in college when Professor Downey gave you a B and you felt that you deserved an A. Where I would have taken the B and been giddy about it— being that it was a physics class—you didn't give the man a day's rest until he recalculated your scores to discover he'd made a mistake. You got your A and proved your point. Maybe it's time for you to prove another point, Renee. You, and only you, can decide your destiny."

Renee sipped her coffee as she thought about Debbie's words. She then asked, "Have you decided on your destiny, Debbie?"

Her friend smiled. "I think I have. It just so happens that Alan was in London while I was there. The moment I saw him I knew I still loved him. We were able to spend some time together and I've decided that I'm not going to let what others think stand in the way of my happiness. Maybe you ought to be making the same decision."

"Hey, you okay?"

Tag glanced up from his coffee cup and met Gannon's concerned gaze. It was Saturday morning and they had come into the office to take a conference call from Senator Denton's office. There would be a press conference from the senator's home at noon where he would admit that *Pulse*'s allegations were true.

The special edition of *Pulse* had flown off the magazine stands and already there had been another printing, so there was indeed a reason to celebrate. Both their father and grandfather—who'd returned to town that morning—had called to congratulate them on a job well done. The only sad note was that Gannon had to advise Peter that he would no longer be associated with the company. After all the man's years of dedicated service the decision had been hard, but necessary.

"Yes, I'm all right," Tag replied, running a hand down his face. Next week was his brother's wedding and the last thing he wanted Gannon to worry about was him. "Are you nervous about the wedding next week?" he decided to ask.

Gannon chuckled. "No, just anxious. I can hardly wait."

Tag nodded. "And have you decided where you're going on your honeymoon yet?"

"Yes, but I'm keeping it as a surprise to Erika. I'm taking her to Paris."

"That's going to be some surprise."

Gannon calmly sipped his coffee and after a few moments of silence he said over the rim of his mug, "I didn't ask how things went with you and Renee last night but I get the feeling they didn't go as you wanted. Let me give you a word of advice, kiddo. No matter what, don't let her go without a fight. If you love her as much as I think you do, you'll be making a big mistake if you give up on her."

Tag dragged a hand through his hair. "It's not me giving up on her, Gannon. It's Renee giving up on me. She knows that I love her. It will be up to her to decide if my love is worth all the challenges we might face in the future." He let out a long breath and added, "And it's my most fervent hope that she does."

By Wednesday, Renee was still trying to get her life back in order. So far, work had gone smoothly. Instead of whispering about her and Tag, everyone focused on the scandal involving Senator Denton and the press conference he'd held that weekend where he'd admitted all of *Pulse*'s allegations.

She sighed as she caught the elevator to the tenth floor to visit with one of her patients. For the past five days she had replayed in her mind, over and over, her conversation with Debbie, and it didn't help matters that she was missing Tag like crazy. She thought of him all the time and missed the good times they had shared together.

She let out a long breath. Nobody could make her see the errors of her ways more thoroughly than Debbie and she appreciated her friend for doing that. Since their talk, she'd been thinking of how a future with Tag would be versus one without him, and each time the thought of a life without him was too heart wrenching to imagine. She refused to let what others thought make her lose the best thing that had ever happened to her. She loved Tag and he loved her and together they would be able to handle anything. She smiled to herself, thinking that later tonight she planned to pay him a visit and let him know just how she felt.

Renee had stepped off the elevator and was about to round the corner when she heard the sound of Diane's voice. "Yes, she's been hiding out in her office, totally embarrassed. I would be embarrassed, too, if I had thrown myself at Teagan Elliott of all people. Maybe now she's learned to stay in her place. The nerve of her thinking she could cross over to the other side, and not just with anyone but with a member of one of the wealthiest families in New York. Can you imagine anyone being that stupid?"

Anger consumed Renee and she squared her shoulders and continued walking, remembering her last conversation with Tag and some of the advice he'd given her. Diane's back was to Renee, and the other nurse with whom Diane had been conversing saw Renee over Diane's shoulders. The nurse quickly made an excuse and hurried off, leaving Diane alone.

"Diane?"

The woman whirled around, surprised to find Renee standing there. She raised a brow. "Yes?"

"Do me a favor."

Diane relaxed and had the audacity to smile. "Sure, Renee, what do you need?"

"For you to go straight to hell and stay there."

Renee moved past the woman and then thought of something else, and turned around and added, "And the only stupid thing I've done was not accept Tag's marriage proposal."

Satisfied with the shocked look on Diane's face, Renee turned and resumed walking with her head held high. She couldn't go around telling everyone to go to hell like Tag had suggested, but she felt good about telling Diane to.

Tag rose from the sofa to turn off the television. It didn't matter that the Knicks were on a winning streak, even the basketball game wasn't holding his interest. The only thing consuming his mind were thoughts of Renee.

Renee.

More than once he had wondered if there was anything else he could have said to make her accept the love he was offering. He needed her in his life like he needed to breathe, and the pain of her willingness to give up and walk away was killing him.

He glanced around when the doorbell sounded, thinking it was probably Liam dropping by. As much as he loved his brother, Tag wasn't in the mood for company.

Opening the door he said, "Liam, I don't think—"

The words died on his lips when he saw it wasn't Liam like he'd assumed, but it was Renee.

"Hi," she said, smiling tentatively at him. "May I come in?"

A part of Tag was so glad to see her that he wanted to reach out and pull her into his arms but he knew he couldn't. He wasn't sure why she'd come but he did know there were still unresolved issues between them and until they worked them out, they were still at odds with each other.

"Sure, you can come in," he said, taking a step back to let her inside. He closed the door behind her. "May I take your coat?"

"Yes, thanks."

He watched her slide the leather coat from her body to reveal a beautiful turquoise sweater and a pair of black slacks. Both looked good on her. "Can I get you something to drink?" he asked, taking the coat she handed him.

"No, I'm fine."

He nodded and walked over to the coat closet to hang up her coat. He could feel the tension in the air and could tell that her nerves were jumping just as high as his. "It's good seeing you, Renee," he said when he walked back over to her.

"Thanks, and it's good seeing you, too. I was wondering if we could talk."

He nodded. "Sure, let's sit in the living room."

He waited until she sat down on the sofa and then, remembering her request the last time they'd talked, he took the chair opposite her.

Renee crossed her legs, feeling Tag's penetrating stare. Over the past five days she had done a lot of soul-searching and had made a lot of decisions, and she wanted to share them with him.

"Are you sure I can't get you anything to drink?"

"No, I'm fine." Then a few moments later she said, "No, that's a lie and I'm not fine." She stood and slowly began pacing the room. Tag said nothing as he watched her and she knew he was giving her time to collect her thoughts.

"I don't know where to begin," she finally said, coming to a stop not far from where he sat and meeting his concentrated gaze.

"I know one place you can start," he said calmly, soothingly and in a low voice. "You can start off by assuring me that you meant what you said Friday night. The part about being in love with me."

His words were spoken with such tenderness that Renee's lips began trembling. How could she not love such a man as this? And that was only one of the things she intended to reassure him about. "Yes, I meant what I said, Tag. I do love you and I will always love you… which leads me to the reason I'm here."

She took a step back, needing to say what she had to say without being tempted to lean down and kiss him like she wanted to do. That would come later if he still wanted her. "I thought about everything you said that night and I've made some decisions."

"You have?"

"Yes."

"And what decisions have you made?" he quietly probed.

She met his gaze. "If you still want me, if you still love me, then I'm willing to do whatever it takes to make a future work with you, Tag. I'm no longer worried or concerned about what others might say. All I care about is what my heart is saying, and right now it's telling me that you're the best thing to ever happen to me and that you are the one person I need in my life. Now and forever."

She reclaimed the step she'd taken earlier to stand in front of him. She reached out, grabbed his hands and gently pulled him from his chair. "I know things won't always be easy. I know there will be those not happy with us being together, but as long as we have each other, then it won't matter. Our love will be strong enough to handle anything. I truly believe that now. I want to marry you, Tag. I want to have a future with you. I want to have your babies. I want it all."

Tag smiled, let out a relieved sigh and pulled Renee into his arms. "Thank you for reaching that decision. And yes, I still want you and I love you. I will always love you, Renee. And I want to marry you, have a future with you, have babies with you to grow and nurture in our love. I—"

Renee smiled and instead of letting him speak, she stood on tiptoe and touched her mouth to his. Tag, needing the kiss as much as she did, began hungrily devouring her mouth the moment they connected. He reached out, gathered her closer and molded her body to his, desperately needing the feel of her in his arms, close to his heart.

She slid a hand to his shoulder, holding on, fighting for control of the emotions he was stirring to life inside of her. Renee groaned as his tongue relentlessly mated with hers, claiming, absorbing everything about him.

And when the kiss grew more heated and demanding, he lifted her into his arms and whispered, "I want to make love to you."

The kiss had aroused her, too, and thoughts of being naked in bed with him, joining her body with his and sealing their love once and for all had her whispering back, "I want to make love to you, too."

Tag headed for the bedroom and within minutes her wish came true. They were naked in bed, and Tag was staring at her with love shining in the depths of his eyes. When he reached into the drawer to get a condom, she stopped him. "There's no need unless you want to do that. I've been on the pill for a couple of years to regulate my periods."

He met her gaze and tossed the packet back in the drawer. "I've never made love to a woman without using a condom," he decided to admit to her. "But I'm aching to do so with you. And just so you know, I'm safe. Because it's one of EPH's policies, I take physicals on a regular basis."

Returning to the bed, he whispered, "I love you with all my heart," just moments before leaning down, moving his body in place over hers and taking her lips in a slow, sensuous exchange, deliberately stimulating her senses as he slowly entered her, merging their bodies into one, flesh to flesh.

Tag's presence back inside her body evoked such pleasure in Renee that she lifted her hips and wrapped her legs around his waist, not wanting him to go anyplace but here, locked to her. Desire as powerful as anything she could imagine began consuming her, filling her mind with all kinds of sensations, and of their own accord, her eyes drifted close.

"Open your eyes, sweetheart," Tag urged in a low, raspy voice. "Look at me and tell me what you see."

Renee complied with his request and looked up at him, taking in his handsome face, the majestic blue of his eyes and the long lashes covering them. Her inner muscles quaked just from looking at him.

She reached up and skimmed a fingertip along his lips, taking in the mouth that could drive her out of her mind. "What I see when I look at you," she whispered, "is a man who is my soul mate, my fantasy come true, the only man I love and want to spend the rest of my life with, the future father of my babies."

Tag's breath caught with Renee's words. She was so beautiful, captivating…and she was his. "I love you so much," he murmured, before capturing her mouth. He began moving the lower part of his body, feeling the hardened tips of her breasts against his chest.

He established a rhythm and began moving inside her to a beat only the two of them could hear. And then it happened. He threw his head back as a release of gigantic proportions tore out of him. He screamed her name as he relinquished his entire being to passion of the richest and most intense kind. And to the woman he loved.

As if the feel of him coming apart, exploding inside of her, was what she wanted, she followed him over the edge. "I don't believe this," she sighed at the peak of her pleasure. She cried out his name and bucked upward, tightening her legs around him.

"Believe it, baby," he whispered. "This is just the beginning of the rest of our lives together. Forever."

As more sensations tore into Renee's body, the only thing she could do was meet his gaze and agree. "Yes. Forever."

Epilogue

"Renee, I'm glad you came," Karen Elliott said, smiling, grasping Renee's hand in hers.

Renee returned the woman's smile. "I'm glad I came, too." She glanced around. It seemed Gannon and Erika's wedding, although it had been done on a small scale, still had numerous invited guests. Everything had been beautiful; especially the bride, and tears had touched Renee's eyes when she'd seen the depth of love shining in Gannon's gaze for Erika.

She glanced up at Tag. They had decided to marry next year on Valentine's Day since that day was so special to them. It was almost a year away but it would be worth the wait. They had decided to announce their intentions to only his parents and grandparents tonight since it was Gannon and Erika's day. But when the couple returned from their honeymoon,

Tag and Renee planned to make an official announcement to everyone.

"Where have Dad and Granddad run off to?" Tag inquired of his mother. He had remained at Renee's side throughout the entire wedding, always touching her in some way, making it known, just in case anyone had any doubt, that she was special to him.

Karen glanced around. "Probably in the library. Why?"

"I need to speak with them and I want you and Grandmother included in the conversation."

Karen's smile widened. "All right, let me go get Maeve and we'll meet you there in a few minutes."

When Karen walked off, the smile Tag gave Renee was reassuring, absolute. "You okay?" he asked, meeting her gaze, detecting some nervousness there.

She smiled back at him. "Yes, how can I not be? I'm in love with a wonderfully amazing man and what's so truly magnificent is that he loves me, too."

"Always," Tag whispered, taking her hand and lifting it to his lips. "Let's go congratulate Gannon and Erika in case we don't get a chance to do so later."

Renee nodded. What Tag wasn't saying and what she knew nonetheless, was that after telling his grandparents and parents about their plans, if anyone seemed the least bit not pleased, he intended to leave. He had meant what he'd said about not tolerating anything but total acceptance from his grandfather regarding their future marriage.

A part of Renee wasn't sure they would get it. She had seen the look in Patrick Elliott's eyes the moment Tag had walked into the room with her. Tag's grandmother had displayed a genuine open friendliness when introductions had been made moments before the start of the wedding. But

Patrick Elliott had been standoffish. Tag had gotten the same vibes and had placed a protective hand around her waist, reiterating silently that he didn't need, nor was he seeking, his grandfather's approval.

Tag and Renee walked into the library sometime later. A Victorian-style chandelier hung from the ceiling, illuminating the elegance of the stylish room. Tag had told her when they'd pulled into the estate from the private road that the entire house had been lovingly decorated by his grandmother.

"I understand you wanted to speak with us, Tag," Patrick Elliott said in a deep, gruff voice. Renee studied him. Tall, distinguished-looking, with a medium build, he actually looked at least ten years younger than the age Tag had claimed his grandfather to be. His hair was completely gray and his eyes were the same shade of blue as Tag's. And the one thing she noted was that there wasn't a hint of a smile on his face.

"Yes, I have an announcement to make," Tag said, holding Renee's hand and closing the door behind them. His parents were sitting on a gray sofa and looked at them expectantly. Tag's grandmother was sitting in a chair within a few feet of where Patrick stood with one elbow resting on the mantel of a massive fireplace.

"And just what is this announcement?" Patrick asked.

Tag met Renee's eyes and smiled. "I just wanted all of you to know that I love Renee very much and I've asked her to marry me, and she has agreed to do so next year on Valentine's Day."

Tag's parents, as well as his grandmother, immediately hugged the couple and offered words of congratulations. However, a quick glance at Patrick indicated he hadn't moved an inch and there was a stunned, frozen look etched on his features. "Marriage?" he finally asked, his deep voice drowning out everyone else's. "Are the two of you sure that is what you want to do?"

Tag's hand tightened around Renee's waist. "Yes. Marriage is precisely what we want and what we plan to do," he said, meeting his grandfather's gaze.

It was quite obvious that Patrick wasn't ecstatic with the news, and it was just as apparent that Tag wasn't letting his grandfather's lack of joy influence him in any way.

"I'll be telling the rest of the family when Gannon and Erika return from their honeymoon, but I wanted the four of you to know now."

It was Tag's grandmother, who knew her husband better than anyone, who decided the best thing to do was to make sure Patrick gave his blessing. She went to her husband. "Aye, 'tis a night to celebrate. On our anniversary day one of our grandsons got married and another announced his engagement to a very beautiful young woman. 'Tis a bit special, don't you think, Patrick?"

Patrick met his wife's gaze and everyone knew the woman that he loved more than anything was daring him to contradict her. He only hesitated for a brief moment before lifting her hand to his lips and saying. "Yes, darling, it is special."

Leaving his wife's side, he went to stand before the couple. "I wish the two of you the best," he said, shaking Tag's hand and then pulling Renee to him in a hug.

"Welcome to the family, Renee," he said in a voice that was still somewhat gruff. "And after this wedding takes place I fully expect you and Tag to start working on some great-grandchildren for me and Maeve to enjoy while we still can."

He took a step back. "Now we need to return to the wedding reception, which will be followed by Maeve's and my anniversary party." Without saying anything else, he walked out of the room.

Later than night Renee lay in Tag's arms, their limbs tangled, their bodies naked, after having just made love. She sighed with pleasure as well as contentment. Gannon and Erika's wedding had been beautiful and the anniversary party that followed for Tag's grandparents had been nothing short of exquisite.

"Are you sure you want us to wait until next February?" Tag asked, leaning over and nibbling at her ear. "That's a long time from now."

Renee smiled as she tilted her head back. "It's less than a year, but I'll find a way to keep you busy until then…not like you don't already have enough to do at work. At least by our wedding the feud between the different magazines will be over and behind everyone."

Tag nodded, looking forward to that day. "How about a big wedding at The Tides?"

Renee grinned. The suggestion definitely appealed to her. She had fallen in love with his grandparents' home. "I think that's a wonderful idea," she said, leaning up and touching her lips to his. "And of course we'll let your mother plan everything."

Tag chuckled. "Of course."

Renee's smile faded somewhat when she said, "Your grandfather hasn't accepted the idea of our marriage one hundred percent, Tag."

Tag met her gaze. "No, but that's his problem and not ours," he said fiercely. "However, I have a feeling that by the day of our wedding he will have come around. And if not, then oh, well. Nothing, and I mean nothing, is going to stop me from making you an Elliott a year from now."

With a smile, Renee leaned up and kissed him. "I like your determination."

"You do?" he asked. "And what else do you like?"

She reached down and her fingers found him hard, large and ready again. "Um, I definitely like the way you go about taking care of business," she said, shifting her body to let him know what she wanted and needed.

He leaned down and kissed her, and responding to him was so natural she took everything he was offering and more. And when he straddled her body and slowly eased inside of her, her mind went blank except for one thought. Yes, she definitely liked the way he was taking care of business.

* * * * *

REQUEST YOUR FREE BOOKS!

2 FREE NOVELS PLUS 2 FREE GIFTS!

Silhouette

Desire ®

Passionate, Powerful, Provocative!

SDESI0R

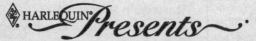

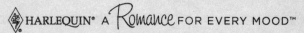

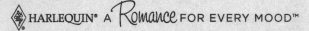
HARLEQUIN® A Romance FOR EVERY MOOD™

SUSPENSE & PARANORMAL

Heartstopping stories of intrigue and mystery—
where true love always triumphs.

Harlequin Intrigue®
Breathtaking romantic suspense. Crime
stories that will keep you on the edge of
your seat.

Silhouette® Romantic Suspense
Heart-racing sensuality and the promise
of a sweeping romance set against the
backdrop of suspense.

Harlequin® Nocturne™
Dark and sensual paranormal
romance reads that stretch the
boundaries of conflict and desire,
life and death.

Look for these and many other Harlequin and Silhouette
romance books wherever books are sold, including most
bookstores, supermarkets, drugstores and discount stores.

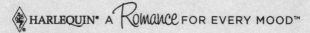

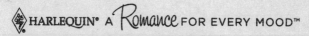